"You really mean that, don't you?"

"What? That women are trained from childhood to deceive? Yes, I meant it. Why? Do you expect all men to remain so fooled by you that they never realize what you're doing?"

Margaret barely kept her mouth from dropping open in astonishment. Her irritation flared to life again. "No. I'm simply surprised that you are so foolish. I had taken you for a brighter man than that."

Now it was Andrew's turn to look amazed. Obviously he had not expected her to answer back to him, Margaret thought. She might be mousy and plain and less than courageous, but she wasn't about to just stand there and let him slander her sex. She braced herself for his explosion.

But he said only, "Indeed?" and gave her a long assessing look. He never would have admitted it, but he was far less interested in their argument than in the way her eyes sparkled in anger. All he could really think about was how much he wanted to take her in his arms, how much he wanted to kiss her.

Dear Reader,

Kristin James is back, and Harlequin has her! Pick up *The Yankee* for a read you'll long remember. The town of Huxley, Texas, can't stop talking about the marriage of Andrew Stone—a Yankee, for heaven's sake!—to local girl Margaret Carlisle. It's the scandal of the year, but how much more scandalized will the good people of Huxley be when they discover that this unlikely pair, whose marriage began as a matter of business, have actually fallen in love?

Erin Yorke has long been another favorite with readers, and this month she offers *An American Beauty*. When a well-born British law student is asked to tutor an American girl living in London, the results are unpredictable. Theirs is a clash of cultures that leads to a passionate trial by fire and a life sentence—in each other's arms.

Next month, look for Lynda Trent and Louisa Rawlings, and in coming months expect books from Caryn Cameron and all your other favorites. History with a romantic twist—you'll find it in each and every Harlequin Historical.

Yours,
Leslie J. Wainger
Senior Editor and Editorial Coordinator

The Yankee

Kristin James

Harlequin Books

TORONTO • NEW YORK • LONDON
AMSTERDAM • PARIS • SYDNEY • HAMBURG
STOCKHOLM • ATHENS • TOKYO • MILAN

Harlequin Historicals first edition November 1990
Harlequin Historicals second edition January 1991

ISBN 0-373-28657-0

THE YANKEE

Printed in the U.S.A.

Books by Kristin James

Harlequin Historical

Satan's Angel #1
The Gentleman #43
The Yankee #57

KRISTIN JAMES,

a former attorney, is married to a family counselor,
and they have a young daughter. Her family and her
writing keep her busy, but when she does have free
time, she loves to read. In addition to her historical
romances, she has written several contemporaries.

Chapter One

Everyone called him "the Yankee." He lived on a ranch outside of Huxley and he rarely came into town. When he did, it was only on business, and he came and left in as short a time as possible. There were many townspeople who had never seen him at all, only heard about him, and just a few had seen him up close. He was dark, it was said, and tall, and walked with a pronounced limp. He usually rode in with a group of his men, and it was rumored that among them were gunslingers, hired to protect the Yankee from the presumably large number of people who wished to kill him.

Exactly who those people were, aside from Tom Murdock, who had a long-standing feud with him, or why they were after the Yankee, no one knew. But they did know that he never smiled and he never spoke to anyone. (Of course, none of the people of Huxley would have spoken to him, except in the course of business, but they resented the fact that they weren't given the chance to deliver the snub. A decent man, they reasoned, would have tried to fit into the local society, however little chance he had of being accepted.)

He was hated and feared. He was the local bogeyman, used to terrorize children into obedience: "If you don't go to sleep, the Yankee'll come in the night and carry you off.''

Margaret Carlisle was one of the people of Huxley, Texas, who had never seen the Yankee up close, but she had been in the general store once when he rode by on his way to the saloon and she had hurried to the window with Ida Mae McGee to peer out at him. So she recognized him when he pulled up in front of the house and dismounted, tying his horse's reins to the hitching post.

It was cleaning day and Margaret was scrubbing the parlor's windows when she looked out and saw him. She dropped her rag back into the bucket of soap suds and wiped her wet hands down the front of her apron, leaning closer to the window to get a better look. It *was* the Yankee; she just knew it. But what in the world would Andrew Stone be doing in front of their house, looking for all the world as if he were about to pay a call?

Of all the houses in town, she would have thought that theirs would be among the last he would visit. Margaret lived with her younger brother and sister and their widowed aunt, Charity Winstock, and her daughter in a small house on the south side of Huxley. Margaret's mother had died of a fever not long after she bore the last child, Zach, and their father had left them with Aunt Charity when he rode off to the War in 1862. When he had been killed in the Wilderness battle, they had continued to live there. Theirs was an entirely female household except for Zach, who was only thirteen, so there was no man among them who might have had business dealings with the Yankee. And it was well known that he had no social dealings with *anyone*.

Margaret realized that she was clearly visible from where she stood in front of the parlor window, with her nose pressed up against the glass, and she jumped back. She blushed to think that the Yankee might have glanced up at the house and seen her spying on him avidly. She whirled and ran into the hallway, where she found her sister halfheartedly scrubbing the floor.

"Annie! Wipe it up, quick! The Yankee's coming up the walk!"

"Who?" Annie looked up, frowning. "Have you lost your mind?"

"No, it's he. I swear, it's he." Margaret ran back into the parlor and grabbed a cloth, then returned and dropped to her knees to help wipe the floor dry.

"What could he want here?" Annie asked.

"I don't know. Dry faster! Aunt Charity will be humiliated if he walks in and finds the floor all wet."

"Well, he shouldn't come on cleaning day, then," Annie retorted reasonably.

Margaret cast her a warning look. "Annie... don't be obstinate."

Annie shrugged. "Well, I don't see what you're getting excited for. You'd think the man had never seen anyone in the middle of cleaning house before. Why should we care, anyway? Nobody even knows him—or likes him. He's a Yankee, for goodness' sake."

Margaret grimaced. "Because I don't want anyone—"

The knocker on the front door crashed down, interrupting her words. Margaret jumped to her feet, tossing the rags out of sight in the sitting room, and went to answer the door. Annie picked up the bucket of water and wet cloths and fled toward the back of the house.

Margaret wet her lips and drew a deep breath. She was shy around strangers, especially men, and she couldn't even imagine talking to someone with the Yankee's reputation. She opened the door with what she hoped was an air of calm dignity. "Yes?"

The man on the porch before her took off his hat politely. He was dressed in a black suit and white shirt, unrelieved by an ornament of any sort, unless the narrow black string tie at his collar could be termed decoration. From the severity of his dress, he could have been mistaken for a preacher or an undertaker. But the expensive black tooled-leather boots on his feet marked him as a man who spent most of his time on horseback, as did the suntanned color of his skin.

And he could only be the Yankee. The hat he held was the black felt hat of a Union cavalry officer.

His eyes were blue, so vivid it was startling, and they were made even more noticeable by the long black lashes that ringed them. "I am Andrew Stone. I would like to see Mrs. Winstock, please." His voice laid to rest any doubts as to his identity. It was clipped and brusque, with none of the slow, soft tones of Southern men.

He was here on purpose. Margaret blinked, trying to pull her thoughts together, to shake off the confusing, stunning effect of those glacial blue eyes. "Yes, yes, of course. Won't you come in?"

She stepped back, allowing him to enter, and closed the door after him. She hesitated, then led him into the parlor. It was more formal than the sitting room and they rarely used it, but surely that was the correct place to put a visitor as wealthy and unfamiliar as Andrew Stone— Aunt Charity would have her hide if it wasn't.

Margaret was very aware of his looming presence behind her as she walked into the parlor. Her dress was a faded old calico one that she wore only when cleaning, and it was not only ugly but also a little short and a trifle tight across the bosom. Her hair was covered by a kerchief to keep it clean. Andrew Stone might well think she was a maid, given the way she looked.

Margaret turned to him, gesturing toward one of the chairs in the fussy, ornate room. She folded her hands together to hide her nervousness. "Please have a seat. If you'll excuse me, I'll tell Mrs. Winstock that you're here." She hoped her voice didn't tremble.

She walked away, forcing herself not to hurry until she was out of his sight. Then she almost ran to the kitchen. There she found her aunt and Annie. Aunt Charity, already informed of the Yankee's visit by Annie, had taken off her apron and was busy tucking a stray piece of hair into her bun. She was a large, formidable-looking woman, and the severe black widow's dress she wore accentuated her intimidating manner.

"I—I left him in the parlor," Margaret said a little hesitantly.

Aunt Charity considered it for a moment, then nodded shortly. "The right choice, Margaret."

That wasn't a statement her aunt made often to anyone, even her own daughter. When they had first come to her aunt's house six years ago, it had seemed to Margaret that she could do nothing right. Aunt Charity seemed to find fault with everything she and her siblings did, from the way they dressed to the way they talked or ate or even sang.

Behind Aunt Charity's bulk, Annie made a bug-eyed face of astonishment, but Margaret was by now well-used to hiding her laughter and not a trace of her amusement showed on her face.

Aunt Charity strode through the door and down the hall to the parlor. Margaret and Annie followed her to the kitchen door and stood listening. They heard their aunt's clear voice and Stone's deeper rumble, but then Aunt Charity drew the sliding door closed, cutting off everything but the indistinguishable murmur of voices.

"Darn!" Annie exclaimed.

"Don't swear," Margaret replied automatically as she stepped back into the kitchen. She glanced at herself in the small mirror above the washstand. She looked as bad as she had thought; there was even a smudge of dirt along one cheek. Grimacing, she poured a little water from the pitcher into the bowl and washed and dried her face. Then she whisked the kerchief off her head.

It wasn't much of an improvement, she knew. Her hair was such a pale blond it was almost white, and pulling it back into a tight bun, as she wore it, only accentuated the pale, faded quality of her looks. There was nothing wrong with her features, she knew; they were regular and even. Her nose and ears were dainty and her eyes were large. But there was little color in her face and even less vivacity, and, given the pale brown color of her eyebrows and eyelashes, she seemed to fade into the background. Even her eyes, which were green, tended to look more a muddy brown over a foot or two away.

Margaret had long ago realized that she was what was termed "mousy looking," particularly when compared to her vibrant Cousin Emma, Charity's daughter. And, unfortunately, living in the same house with Emma throughout the time in which they had grown from girls into women, she had been compared to Emma often.

Margaret had been fifteen when she had come to live at her aunt's, and she did not recall how she had looked then, her cornsilk hair in long, thick plaits, her skin warmed by the sun and cheeks pinkened with excitement or laughter. Then her face had been alive with the warmth and generosity, the kindness and happiness that was her nature. But she had not often looked at herself in mirrors at that age, and she did not see how she had changed over the years, the life and spontaneity squeezed out of her by her aunt's rigid, controlling hand, her spirit dampened by constant comparison to her cousin's more spectacular looks.

Margaret sighed. "I looked like a ragamuffin when I answered the door."

"So?" her sister responded reasonably. "What does it matter?"

Margaret shrugged. "I don't know. It's just humiliating to have a man like that see me this way. Oh, Annie, if you could have seen his eyes! He could stare right through a person. He probably thinks we're poor white trash, the way I looked."

"Well, we're poor enough, that's for sure."

Margaret frowned at her. "But we aren't trash. The Carlisles have as good a name as anyone around."

"A good name doesn't bring in much that's useful, though, like money or food or horses."

"Horses!" Margaret had to smile. That's where her sister's mind was, as usual. When they had lived with Daddy out on the farm, they'd had a couple of horses and some other livestock. Annie had always loved taking care of the animals, especially the horses, and she had learned to ride when she was so little she looked ridiculous perched up on the large horse's back. But it had been seven years since she had had a horse to ride. When they had moved from the farm to Aunt Charity's house, their father had sold the horse that he hadn't taken with him and left the money with Charity to pay for their care. Annie had missed the animals and the exercise terribly. She was something of a tomboy, and their quiet, sedate life in town chafed her.

Annie sighed and there was a mature sadness in her eyes that Margaret had never seen there before. "I'm sorry. I know it's impossible. It's just—I still miss it. Don't you ever think about what it was like at home? Running and jumping, with nobody to tell you to act like a lady. Brushing the horses. Feeding the animals. Climbing up into the oak tree to see the road...."

"Having your own house to take care of," Margaret joined in wistfully. "With no one to correct everything you do or find fault with you. Having room to breathe." She thought of the frame house where they'd grown up. It hadn't been a great deal bigger than this one, but every window had looked out on the fields or the empty, rolling land. She felt cramped here, where everywhere she looked there were other houses.

"Yeah," Annie agreed wistfully. "I wish we could have stayed on the farm."

"It wouldn't have been proper. Us two girls with only a little boy to protect us."

"We didn't need protection. You and I can shoot as well as anybody in this county, I bet. You couldn't have had a better teacher than Daddy."

"That's true. But that's not the kind of protection I mean. We had to have an older relative, preferably a woman. You know that."

"It's still stupid. We'd a been a lot happier there. Maybe you *were* only fifteen, but you'd been running that house ever since I can remember." Margaret was seven years older than Annie, for their mother had miscarried once and had another child that died in infancy between the two sisters, and she was nine years older than their brother. She had assumed the role of mother hen to the others from the time their mother died, looking after both them and the house while their father worked in the fields.

"I know." Margaret was unaware of the sadness in her face and voice. She was a natural caretaker, a loving and giving person, and she was also quite competent at running a household. It had been hard to have to fall into a subservient role at her aunt's house, but Aunt Charity had made it clear from the beginning that she would brook no interference with her authority. Margaret had bowed her head and struggled to do as her aunt wished, not only because her gentle nature hated to argue and fight, but also because she knew that there was nowhere else that they could go, especially after her father died. The only way she could provide for her younger brother and sister was to live with Aunt Charity. Defiance would earn her her aunt's wrath and might even mean that Charity would take Annie and Zach away from Margaret.

Annie, of course, was a natural fighter, and Zach, too, could be as stubborn as a mule, which often got them into trouble with their aunt. Margaret, therefore, had striven even harder to do what she was told and to be as inconspicuous as possible in the hopes that it would balance her siblings' behavior in Mrs. Winstock's eyes.

Annie saw the sorrow on her sister's face and it tore at her heart. When she was younger, she had gotten angry with Margaret for not standing up to their aunt, but in the past few months, she had begun to realize why her sister had acted as she did, that the "mealy-mouthed" acquiescence Annie hated in Margaret was something she did for her brother's and sister's sakes more than for her own. "You could have left here a long time ago if it weren't for me and Zach."

"What?" Margaret looked at her in surprise. "What are you talking about?"

"Zach and me—we're a millstone hanging around your neck. You could have married and gotten out of this house years ago, but you didn't because you thought you had to stay here and protect us."

"Oh, pooh! As if there was anybody I wanted to marry! Or who wanted to marry me. The men who come calling do so for Emma, not me."

"Not all of them. I always thought Jim Mason was sweet on you."

"Not enough to ask me to marry him." Margaret shrugged. "Besides, I wouldn't have married him."

"Why? Because he wouldn't have taken Zach and me in the bargain?"

Margaret looked at her sister for a long, thoughtful moment. "Maybe that was part of it. But I didn't really want to marry him, either. I didn't love him. I've never fallen in love with anybody. I think I have the personality to be an old maid."

"Ha! There's nobody in the world who'd be a better wife and mother than you. Surely you want those things."

Margaret had to struggle to keep the tears from coming to her eyes. "Of course I'd love to have children and a home of my own. But I have you and Zach, and you all are family enough for me."

"I think you're lying, Margaret Ellen Carlisle. And you aren't happy. I could help, you know. I'm old enough now." She went over to her sister and took her hands, frowning with the intensity of her feelings. "I can look after Zach and me—if you were to find someone you wanted to marry. We could stay here with Aunt Charity and do well enough, even if she is an old battle-ax."

"Annie!" Margaret glanced around a little nervously, almost as if their aunt might suddenly pop out of the wall.

"Well, it's true, and you know it."

"I'm not leaving. No one's asked me to marry him, and there's no one I want to marry. Anyway, I'm certainly not going to desert the two of you."

"I don't want you to sacrifice yourself for us."

"I'm not sacrificing anything! You and Zach are the most important people in the world to me. Don't you know that? I've looked after the two of you all my life, and I certainly don't intend to stop now. There's no man who means more to me than you all do. Any man who loved me would want you to be with us, too." That pleasant solution to their problems had been something she'd dreamed about often, imagining some handsome, wonderful man who would come along and sweep her off her feet, carrying both her and the children far away from Aunt Charity.

"Really?"

"Yes, really."

Her sister smiled. "I'm glad. I didn't actually want you to go away."

"I don't want to, either. And I won't." Margaret reached over and hugged her sister.

The back door opened and Zach walked in. He looked at them curiously. "What are you all doing?"

His voice slid up into a squeak near the end of his question and he grimaced. His voice was changing and he hated its unpredictability. He had also been growing like a weed, and Margaret noticed with an inward sigh, that his trousers were too short again. She'd let out all his pants as much as she could; there simply were no hems left. That meant they would have to buy new cloth to make him some more trousers. Aunt Charity would be displeased. Margaret could imagine the way her aunt would purse her mouth and look at Zach, as though his youthful growth were something he had done on purpose simply to upset her.

"Just talking," Annie replied.

"I thought you were supposed to be working." It was obvious from the grimy state of his clothes and hands that Zach had been hard at work in the yard. He turned toward Margaret. "Annie never does anything. How come she always gets away with—"

"Hold on. Don't go off like a firecracker. Annie was working. We all were. But Aunt Charity has a visitor."

"So?"

"Andrew Stone," Annie explained importantly.

"Who?"

"The Yankee, stupid."

"Annie! You know better than to call your brother names."

"I'm sorry."

Annie and Zach were close enough in age and still young enough that they were almost constantly engaged in a struggle for supremacy.

"The Yankee!" Zach repeated, his eyebrows shooting up. He hardly noticed Annie's insult, so accustomed was he to trading such with his sister. "What would he want here?"

Margaret shrugged. "I don't know. That's what Annie and I were talking about."

"Well, gee..." He stuck his hands in his pockets and rocked back and forth on his heels, thinking. "Maybe he wants to buy the farm!"

The land they had inherited from their father had lain unused ever since he left for the War. They were, of course, unable to farm it themselves, but they had had little luck selling it, either. It was the one asset they possessed, but it had brought them no money.

Reluctantly Margaret shook her head. "I don't think so. After all, his land is nowhere near ours. I can't see why he'd want it."

"Good." Annie stuck out her chin pugnaciously. "I don't want to sell it. I want to keep it."

"Why? You going to run it by yourself?" Zach asked her sarcastically.

Annie started to reply hotly, but before she could get out the words, they heard the sound of the living room door sliding open. They jumped to their feet, and Zach bolted out the back door as the girls grabbed up cloths and began to scrub the floor.

Aunt Charity stalked into the kitchen. "Margaret."

Margaret jumped to her feet. "Yes, ma'am?"

"You are to come into the parlor. He wishes to see you. I told him it was quite unnecessary, but he wants to talk to you, anyway."

"The Yankee?" Margaret asked, astonished. "But why would he—"

Her aunt turned up her hands in a gesture denoting total lack of understanding. "Remember, after all, he is a Yankee. Who knows what they think?"

Privately Margaret suspected that Yankees were probably not so different from anyone else, but she wouldn't have dreamed of mentioning the thought to her aunt. Charity Winstock was a staunch Confederate. It was her belief that if the Southern army had consisted of people like herself, it would have won the War. Margaret was inclined to agree with her. Certainly she had never known anyone who had been able to defeat her aunt.

"Now, missy, remember to stand up straight and keep your opinions to yourself. No one wants to hear what a young girl thinks."

"Yes, ma'am." It was an admonishment Margaret had heard many times over.

"Don't disgrace me in front of *him*." Obviously Aunt Charity considered it a worse thing to be disgraced in front of an enemy than in front of friends. "Now, before we go in, so you won't be standing there gaping like a fish, I'm going to tell you what he wants. Colonel Stone has asked me for your hand in marriage."

The blood drained out of Margaret's face, leaving her pale as paper. Behind her at the table, Annie jumped to her feet. Margaret was unable to say anything, but Annie expressed emotions for both of them. "What?" she shrieked. "You can't be serious!"

Aunt Charity turned and fixed her gimlet eye on Annie. "Sit down, miss. No one asked for you to chime in."

"But you—you aren't going to say yes, are you, Aunt Charity?" Margaret asked breathlessly. Surely her aunt, staunch Yankee hater that she was, would never consider being tied by marriage to a former Union colonel! Why, he was despised and scorned by everyone around!

"Of course not! And I told him so in no uncertain terms. I would never permit my sister's children to marry so far beneath them. Heaven knows, I'd far rather that all of you continue to be a burden on me for the remainder of my life than to see you marry a Yankee!" She spat the word out as if it tasted foul in her mouth. "However, he insisted, rude man that he is, on speaking with you himself. I told him that you did as I bid you, but he wouldn't budge."

The memory of the man's obstinance sat poorly with Aunt Charity. Her eyes flashed and her mouth tightened. It amused Margaret to think of anyone thwarting her aunt and she almost smiled, but she remembered in time to keep her mouth straight.

Aunt Charity swept out the door and down the hall and Margaret followed, keeping her spine straight and her hands folded demurely together, as her aunt insisted. They walked into the parlor. The Yankee was standing by the window and he turned at their entrance. Margaret felt once again the cold power of his blue eyes and she dropped her own eyes, unable to face that kind of strength.

"Here is my niece, as you see." Aunt Charity glowered at Andrew Stone. She turned toward Margaret. "Sit down, Margaret. Don't stand there like a post."

Margaret's cheeks flushed with embarrassment and she plopped down quickly in one of the uncomfortable straight-backed chairs. She carefully kept her spine away from the chair back and perfectly straight, as she had been trained to do for years.

"If you please, I would like to speak to the girl alone, Mrs. Winstock," the man said. His voice was a low, deep rumble, and there was a warm quality to it that didn't show in his face. Margaret raised her head, surprised.

"Colonel Stone!" Aunt Charity looked shocked down to her toes. "Leave a young girl alone in a room with a man? Certainly not!"

Stone's smile was without humor. "Especially when that man is a former Union officer, who are universally known as defilers of young ladies, isn't that right?"

It was all Margaret could do to suppress a smile. That was precisely Aunt Charity's opinion, but on his lips it sounded ludicrous.

Aunt Charity did not reply to his barb, simply narrowed her eyes and sat down defiantly on the only comfortable chair in the room. Colonel Stone gave her a long look, then turned toward Margaret. "Miss Carlisle?"

"Yes?" He still looked hard and cold, but after the way he'd set down her aunt, Margaret couldn't help but like the man a little. She'd often yearned to be able to say something similar to the woman, but she'd never had the courage.

"I came here today to ask for your hand in marriage. Now, before you give me an answer, I would like you to hear me out."

"Of course, Colonel Stone." No doubt that would make her aunt seethe, but Margaret couldn't resist the small defiance.

"Good. And I no longer go by my military title, Miss Carlisle. It's been four years since I was in the army. Now I am plain Mr. Stone."

"All right. Mr. Stone."

"Thank you. You seem to be a reasonable young woman."

"I hope that I am."

"I am in need of a wife. I have a daughter, aged eleven, who badly needs a mother's care and training. Of course, I wish her to have the example of a genteel woman, one of good name and character. Also, my household, I'm afraid, needs a woman's touch. Perhaps even more of a consideration is my daughter's future place in the local 'society.' Being my daughter, what would you estimate that place to be?"

Margaret blinked and tried to search for a tactful way to express what she thought.

"Truthfully, Miss Carlisle."

She glanced at her aunt, but there was no help there. She turned back to the colonel and said softly, "Truthfully, sir—none."

"Exactly. I am an outcast. Therefore my daughter is one, also, and always will be...unless I do something about it. Since I cannot change the fact that I am from the North and fought on the side of the Union and since I have no desire to move from Texas, then I must do what else I can to change her position here. The only way I can see to do that is to marry a woman of good standing in the community, a woman whose parents were settlers in the area and who knows everyone for miles around, who is respected and admired, who has a firm place in what passes for society in Huxley."

"I see." She did. Her family was prominent in Huxley despite the fact that they were now in financial straits. Her father and mother had been one of the three families that originally settled there, and her father had always taken a lead in community affairs. Aunt Charity, disagreeable as she was, was a leader in everything social. Perhaps if Stone's daughter had a stepmother like Margaret, over the course of the years she would be gradually accepted by the people of Huxley. "Still..." Margaret frowned. "That doesn't explain why you are going about it this way. There are several such women in town. I would think you would want to court one, to find someone and—well, you know."

She broke off, a little amazed at her audacity, but Stone finished for her, "Fall in love? Marry for love?" If it were possible, his eyes grew more forbidding.

"Well, yes."

"No." His words were clipped. "I have no interest in falling in love. I married once before for love, and as you have no doubt heard, it was a disaster. Love is the last thing I'm seeking. I don't want a woman who turns men's veins to fire. I want only a biddable, acceptable wife, one who will raise my daughter and run my house. That is all."

And that woman was she. Curiously, Margaret felt a stab of disappointment. He couldn't have said more clearly that she was a woman whose looks did not threaten his heart, that he did not care that she was no beauty. She was biddable—everyone knew that. She was the meek little mouse, Margaret, who did precisely as her aunt told her. Her looks were "acceptable." She was not ugly. Her features were even and attractive, and it did not matter that with her pale blond hair and pale white skin, she looked bleached out. Mr. Stone didn't care for beauty.

"I am looking for a reasonable woman, one who will accept my bargain for what it is."

"And what is that?" She was a trifle surprised at how sharply her words came out.

"A large home over which to rule, ample spending money, security, the good things of life for herself—and her family. I am a wealthy man and I have influence with the state government. Do you want a fancy carriage, beautiful clothes—you will have them. A fine horse to ride? A good home for your brother and sister? I would, of course, gladly accept them into my house. And I'm sure Laura, my daughter, would welcome having playmates."

Margaret gazed at him while her mind raced. She thought of Annie's face at the sight of a stableful of horses from which to choose.

"You could provide beautiful clothes and parties when your sister is old enough for her coming out," he went on, laying out further enticements.

All the things Margaret herself hadn't had. Annie wouldn't have to take a second seat to Charity's daughter, Emma, wearing hand-me-down gowns that didn't look good on her or sitting beside Emma to provide a foil for her vibrant prettiness, as Margaret had done. Annie could have beautiful new clothes, lavish parties, whatever she wanted.

"And I understand your brother is a smart young fellow. Perhaps he'd like to go to college. Or, if not, there would be a place for him at the ranch. Maybe land of his own."

Margaret swallowed, imagining Zach going off to college, pursuing whatever career he wanted to, instead of hiring out as a hand on some farm or ranch or toiling as a clerk in the bank in town.

"Having a home of your own." Stone, watching her face carefully, played his last and highest card.

Her own house, with no Aunt Charity to kowtow to. No more punishments for Annie because Aunt Charity found her tongue too fresh. No more scrimping and saving and having to be grateful for the home that their aunt had given them. No more living at someone else's mercy. Temptation shimmered before Margaret like a mirage.

"That's why I thought of you," Stone continued. "You fit the requirements I had for a wife, and I thought that you would be able to appreciate the benefits you would have as Mrs. Andrew Stone."

Aunt Charity stuck in fiercely, "No niece of mine would ever stoop to that level, I can assure you, *Colonel*."

"Well?" Andrew Stone directed a look of cool inquiry at Margaret. "Could you bring yourself to marry me, Miss Carlisle?"

Margaret glanced from the Yankee to her aunt, who sat with chin confidently raised and face smug. She would fly into a conniption fit if Margaret did something like marry the Yankee. Margaret looked back toward the colonel, as remote and uncaring about her answer as if he had no part in this drama.

Her voice came out tremulous and small, but her shoulders were set squarely and she looked straight into the man's face. "Yes. I accept your proposal."

Chapter Two

"Margaret, you can't! You just can't marry him!" Annie spread her arms out wide, her face a mixture of pain and horror.

It was a statement Margaret had heard over and over since the front door had closed behind the Yankee a half hour before. First, her aunt had treated her to a severe tongue-lashing on the subject of what she thought of Margaret's decision and the impossibility of it coming about. She wailed about Margaret's insanity, her disloyalty, her treachery, her stupidity and her greed.

Margaret had said nothing, simply stood with her hands clasped and her face pale, her eyes fixed on the floor. Annie, hearing her aunt's harangue, had come rushing in to save her, Zach following closely on her heels, but when Aunt Charity had told them what Margaret planned to do, the two young people had stopped and simply gaped at her in disbelief.

Annie had looked at Margaret and asked, "That's not true, is it, Maggie?"

Margaret had swallowed and admitted that it was true. She had glanced at her sister and brother, tears sparkling in her eyes, then had hurried from the parlor and up the stairs to her room. Thank goodness Cousin Emma was away visiting a friend on a farm for a few days or she would no doubt have added her protests to everyone else's!

But Annie had followed her and burst into the room they shared to continue her pleas. Margaret looked at her sister, then away, and gripped her hands together tightly, willing herself not to cave in, not to burst into tears and agree not to do the thing that appalled everyone so much.

"Oh, hush, Annie," came Zach's newly deeper voice, and he shoved past his sister into the room, closing the door behind him. "Can't you see you're tearing her apart?"

"Hush yourself! I'm not going to let her do this. It's crazy. She can't really want to. She doesn't even know the man!"

"Don't be stupid," her brother replied scornfully. "Don't you realize why she agreed to marry him? It's for us, dunderhead!"

"Zachary..." Margaret began warningly.

Annie stared at him. "For us? How?"

"It's obvious—at least to anybody but a hothead like you. If you didn't go off half-cocked all the time, if you'd thought about it, you'd have realized. Margaret's marrying Stone because we haven't got a cent to our names and we have to live on our aunt's kindness, which is in rather short supply most of the time."

"Don't you dare say she's marrying him for the money," Annie retorted furiously, knotting her hand into a fist. "I'll knock you to Kingdom Come if you—"

"Just try it," he retorted. "Of course she's not doing it because *she* wants the money. Whenever does Maggie do something for herself? She's doing it so you and I can live in comfort, in style even. She's doing it so we can move out of here and live in a nice house, with everything we want. Isn't that right, Maggie?"

Understanding dawned on Annie's hot young face, and she turned toward her sister. "Is that true? Is it?"

"Partially." Margaret smoothed her hands down her dress and swallowed hard. She had to bring herself under control so that she could make them understand. "I do want you to have a nice place to live and money to do what you want." She raised her head and looked into her sister's eyes. "He's got horses, Annie, lots and lots of horses. You'll be able to ride anytime you want."

Zach snorted. "That ought to make you change your mind."

His younger sister glared at him. "I'm not that selfish! Maggie, I'd love to have horses to ride, but not enough for you to—to—sacrifice yourself!"

"It's not only the horses. It's having plenty of food to eat whenever you want or being able to buy cloth or a new hat or a fan without always thinking about what a burden we're being. I bet you all will each have a room of your own, nice big ones, probably. I've heard the colonel's— Mr. Stone's—house is quite large. Annie, I know you don't think about this now, but in a couple of years, you'll be wanting to wear pretty dresses and go to parties, have dances. And you'll be able to! You won't have to go around in hand-me-downs or have your hands red from scrubbing. You can have hats and ribbons and yards and yards of new material." Margaret's face glowed. "You'll be so pretty, and you'll have a wonderful time. You'll be able to marry any boy you want to."

"As if anybody would have her," Zach commented.

Margaret fixed him with a look. "I'll have none of that from you, young man. You keep a civil tongue in your head. Annie's not the only one who'll benefit by this, you know. You won't have to spend all your time chopping wood and weeding in the garden. You'll be able to ride, too, and to study. Why, Mr. Stone said he'd send you away to college if you wanted when you're older, and if you don't, you can work on the ranch. You'll be his brother-in-law. He'll see that you're—''

"I don't want anything from him!" Zach slammed his fist into his hand. "Damn! I wish to God I wasn't just a kid! I oughta be the one taking care of you, not the other way around. I can't stand by and watch you *sell* yourself for Annie and me just so we'll have a lot of comforts. I don't want to go to college. I don't want none of it!''

"Well, I want it for you." Tears welled in Margaret's big green eyes. "And I'm *not* selling myself, any more than hundreds of other women do when they get married. I'm twenty-two years old and I'm on the shelf. I have a right to have a home and family, like any other woman, and if the only way I can do that is by marrying a man I don't love, then I'll do it. It isn't the first time I've thought about it, believe me. There were a few times that a man courted me, even once or twice that one asked me to marry him, and I considered it."

"But you didn't do it," Annie put in. "Probably 'cause they couldn't or wouldn't take in Zach and me, too."

Margaret shrugged. "Perhaps. Besides, I couldn't bring myself to pretend to a man that I loved him when I didn't. I hated the thought of living a lie, of knowing that he cared for me when I had married him to take care of my family and to get away from here. But it's different with Andrew Stone. He doesn't pretend to love me and he doesn't ask me to pretend, either. It's more—more of a business arrangement, actually. I won't have to live a lie. I won't have to feel guilty every time I look at him. He needs a mother for his daughter and a wife for his household, and I need a home where all of us can live."

Her brother and sister looked at her, nonplussed. Margaret seemed bent on doing this thing, and she was terribly calm. She hardly seemed like a woman throwing herself on the pyre in sacrifice so that her family could have a good life.

Seeing her advantage, Margaret pressed on, "It wouldn't be just for you two, you know. I wouldn't mind not having to clean and cook all the time. I'd like to have pretty dresses myself. And I would love—I would dearly *love* to get away from Aunt Charity."

Annie couldn't stifle a giggle at that remark, and even the serious Zach had to smile. "That's the truth."

"There have been times," Margaret said softly, "when I have sworn that I would do anything rather than have to live the rest of my life under her thumb." She looked pleadingly at her brother and sister, and there was a stark agony in her eyes that neither of them had ever seen before. "I want a home of my own. I want a family. I want to have babies of my own to care for. I want to have things that belong to me. I'm so tired of living on somebody else's charity!"

"I'll go out and find a job," Zach said fiercely. "I mean something all day, not just chopping wood and hauling water for people after school. I'll quit school and I'll work at the stables. Mr. Landry needs a helper. Maybe with that and what I make chopping wood, we'd have enough money to live on our own."

"Yeah," Annie put in excitedly, "and you and I could take in sewing or something."

Margaret chuckled. "You haven't sewn a straight seam in your life."

"Then I'll work in the stables, too!"

"Mr. Landry wouldn't hire a girl to do that, and you know it," Zach reminded her.

"Besides, where would we live?" Margaret pointed out gently. "In Mrs. Hampton's boarding house? We'd have to get two rooms, and we'd still not be on our own, in our house."

"We could live at the farm!"

"And Zach would walk into town every morning and back every night? He'd spend his whole life walking and working. No, really, this is the only way. I told you, I want to get married and have a family. It's what I've always wanted to do. It's what any woman wants."

Annie grimaced. "Not me. I'd take a horse over a grubby-faced kid anyday."

Margaret smiled. "You'll change that opinion when you're older."

"But you could marry someone besides *him*." Zach scowled. "He's a Yankee. And, besides, I've heard things about him..."

"Yes," Annie put in. "Remember, Mrs. Murdock was married to him once and she divorced him. He must have been pretty awful for her to do that."

Margaret frowned and dropped her gaze. She, like everyone else in Huxley, knew that Damaris Mason, whose father owned the mercantile store, had married Andrew Stone before the War, when he had been stationed in Texas with the U.S. Army. He had been from faraway Pennsylvania, and he and Damaris had moved back there when the War began. Sometime during the War, Damaris had divorced Stone and when the War had ended, had moved back to her parents' home. It was scandalous to be divorced, particularly for a woman, and even though the townspeople had closed ranks around one of their own against the Yankee and had accepted Damaris back into their society, her name would always carry with it a whiff of scandal. Margaret, like Annie, knew that a woman would not take on such a burden except under the greatest provocation. Her husband must have committed adultery or deserted her. Those were almost the only things that would make a court grant a divorce. Even in a place as foreign to her as Pennsylvania, surely such laws would be the same.

Well, she thought, she wasn't worried about the colonel deserting her, not when he would be leaving his ranch and daughter, too, and adultery didn't bother her much, either, considering the fact that she didn't even care for him. In reality, she would probably be glad if he went to the women at the saloon and left her alone. That part of marriage, the bed part, was the only thing that made her reluctant to go through with what she had decided.

"I've heard that he was mean and cruel to her, that he beat her and did horrible things."

"Those are just rumors, Annie. You and I don't have any idea what happened."

Annie shrugged. "There must have been something."

Margaret was inclined to think so, too. After all, she had heard of more than one husband who sneaked down to the saloon to visit the women there, and their wives certainly didn't divorce them. And Mrs. Pritchett's no-good husband had left her years ago and she'd never tried to get a divorce from him. She had just been relieved that he was gone.

"Well, he was a Yankee. Her mother said that's why she did it. Because he was going to be fighting against her family and friends and country," Margaret pointed out. It was that reason above all else, Margaret thought, that had made Damaris's divorce acceptable to the townspeople— that and the fact that she had soon married Tom Murdock, the wealthiest man in the county, except for Andrew Stone himself.

"I don't know," Annie said reluctantly. "I think he must be cruel. I mean, think about how he's kept Mrs. Murdock away from her daughter. I hear that he won't even let her see the girl."

Margaret's stomach knotted inside her. The court had given the child to her father, which everyone agreed was just what you'd expect from a Yankee court, but it had been cruel of Colonel Stone to take his daughter from her mother. Especially since he had been away in the War at the time and no doubt had left the child with servants or relatives. Margaret didn't know Damaris Murdock well—the woman was older than her and married—but from what she had seen of her, Damaris had struck her as rather vain. But, then, what woman of Damaris's startling beauty would not be vain? And vanity was no reason to withhold a daughter from her mother. The father, by doing so, was being unkind not only to his former wife but to his own child, as well. She thought of the hard set of Stone's face—how aptly he was named!—and the cold, penetrating eyes. Was that the sort of man with whom she wanted to spend the rest of her life?

"It's all rumors," Margaret murmured, almost to herself. "Just rumors. Everyone hates him because he's a Yankee."

Zach gave her an odd look and Annie said, "That's reason enough, isn't it?"

Margaret looked at her thoughtfully. "I'm not sure. I'd never really thought about it until today. But when I was sitting there looking at him, it occurred to me that it's silly to dislike a man just because of where he comes from. He's like us, after all. He looks the same, speaks the same language, is concerned about the same things—his daughter, his house, his land."

"Except that he fought against us." Zach's eyes, green like his sister's but of a pale hue, flashed. "He was on the other side."

"No doubt he thought he was as right as any of our men did." Margaret paused. "You know, before the War, he was down here in the army protecting us."

"That doesn't make him a good person."

"Well, I don't think that his being a Yankee necessarily makes him bad, either. Do you? Honestly?"

Zach's brow wrinkled. He'd never heard anyone, especially his quiet sister, express such startling views.

"I mean, didn't Daddy always teach us that you shouldn't judge a man by how he looked or talked? Remember when you were little, Zach, and that man came by, looking for work and he talked so funny? He scared us because of the way he talked. You started crying and ran to Daddy. And afterwards Daddy told us that he wasn't anybody to be afraid of. The man talked like that because he was from a different country. You understood that. We all understood. I don't think any of us would be scared of a man now just because he spoke with a German accent, do you?"

"It's not the same. I'm grown now."

"Then it's even sillier to be scared of the Yankee, isn't it?"

"I'm not scared of him!"

"No? It seems to me that that's the way everybody acts. As if they are scared of him."

For a moment both her brother and sister were silent, looking at her. Finally, Zach began tentatively, "Maggie, you aren't—you don't have a liking for this fella, do you?"

Margaret's eyebrows vaulted upward. "No! My heavens, I don't know him." She thought it better not to mention that she herself had in some ways been rather frightened by his look and manner. "It just seems unfair, the way everyone treats him."

Zach's face was set stubbornly, giving nothing away, but Annie said slowly, "I can see what you're talking about. Maybe you're right that it isn't fair. I think Daddy would agree with you." Annie had adored their father, and usually based her opinions on what her father's had been. "Maybe what people say about Colonel Stone isn't true. But that doesn't mean I want you to marry him. I mean, maybe he isn't fair or kind, either. What if the things they say *are* true!"

"That's right," Zach agreed. "You know, Mr. Murdock hates him. I heard once that Mr. Murdock says Stone stole some of his land."

"Mr. Murdock is also married to Damaris Mason. He's bound to dislike Andrew Stone. Besides, that's just rumor, too."

"Well, this isn't—I've seen him ride into town, and there are always a bunch of hands with him. A couple of them are real mean-lookin' fellas. They wear their holsters tied down to their legs. That's a sure sign of a gunfighter, you know."

"No, I didn't know," Margaret snapped. "I'm afraid I'm not as conversant as you with gunfighters and outlaws." She drew a shaky breath and her eyes brimmed with tears. "Why are you fighting me on this? Don't you understand that I'm doing it for all our good? Because it seemed the best way out of here for us? I knew Aunt Charity would do everything she could to stop me, but I never figured I would have to fight you, too—"

Margaret broke off, her voice too choked with tears to continue. She turned away, wrapping her arms around herself. Annie and Zach glanced at each other guiltily; they were instantly contrite.

"Ah, gee, Maggie, we didn't mean to fight you," Zach said, going to stand beside her. He reached toward her, then dropped his arms and just stood awkwardly.

"That's right." Annie looped an arm around her sister's shoulders and leaned her head against hers. "We're clumsy, sis. You know that. We aren't good at being sweet with people like you are. We weren't trying to go against you."

Margaret tried to smile, but her mouth was quivering too much.

"It's because we love you," Annie went on. "We don't want you to be unhappy. We don't want you doing something you'll hate simply to take care of us. That's all."

Margaret patted her hand and this time her smile was more genuine. "I love you, too, and I know I'll *be* happy if we can be together and away from here. Giving you two a good life will make me happy. Please, promise me that you won't try to keep me from doing it?"

Annie hesitated, then sighed. "All right. I won't try to stop you."

Margaret looked at her brother. He nodded. "Me, too. I won't fight you."

"Thank you." Margaret reached out and took Zach's hand, too, and squeezed it. "I know this is going to be the best thing. It's going to work out. It just has to."

Andrew Stone came to call on Margaret two days later. Her aunt was out of the house, and Margaret was on the back porch, churning the butter, when Annie slipped out the door, her eyes wide, and told her that the colonel was there.

Margaret had been splashing the paddle with vigor, driven by the energy of her clashing, racing thoughts. Ever since her talk with Zach and Annie, she had been torn, wondering if she had really done the right thing in accepting Andrew Stone's offer of marriage. What if Zach was right and she was selling herself for the temptations of wealth and comfort? What if the Yankee was the monster everyone said he was? What if he beat her, hurt her or her family? She had assumed that she could live with his remoteness and coldness. After all, she had managed to put up with her aunt for years, and surely he couldn't be any worse than that. But what if she were wrong?

Now, at the announcement that the man she had been brooding over was waiting for her in the parlor, Margaret let the butter paddle fall to the bottom of the churn with a thud. "He's here?" she repeated, nervously wiping her hands on her apron.

Annie looked at her strangely. "Yes. In the parlor. Go on, I'll finish the butter."

"All right." Margaret glanced around vaguely as though she would find some answers here before she faced the man, untying the strings of her apron as she did so. She turned and went inside, pulling off the apron and wadding it up into a ball that she threw onto the kitchen table. She glanced in the mirror and attempted to smooth back her hair. The exertion of churning had made her face a trifle flushed, and the stray hairs around her face were damp and straggling.

She walked down the hall to the parlor, hoping that she didn't look as heated and flustered on the outside as she felt inside. She hesitated on the threshold of the parlor. "Colonel—I mean, Mr. Stone?"

He was standing looking out the window and he turned. He was a little surprised. He had remembered her as being rather washed out, but there was color in this woman's face, and the wispy hair curling around her face softened the severity of her pulled-back hair. She looked prettier, less emotionless, more flesh-and-blood.

"Miss Carlisle." He limped toward her and took her hand to bow over it. "I took the liberty of calling on you. I hoped that as your fiancé, I would have the right."

"Of course." Margaret felt breathless. She didn't know what to say to him. She wished someone was here with them—Annie, Cousin Emma, even Aunt Charity!

When he released her hand, her skin tingled where he had touched it. She folded her fingers into her palm, pressing her fingernails into the flesh, trying to still the funny sensations running through her. She walked over to one of the chairs, making a gesture toward the couch. "Please, sit down, won't you?"

He sat where she had motioned and for a long moment, they were silent, simply looking at each other. Margaret glanced away first, blushing. She didn't know what to say and it was disconcerting sitting beneath his cold, penetrating stare. What did he expect of her? Of this meeting? She hadn't even thought about the fact that he might come calling on her before they were married. It had seemed like too much of a business arrangement for that. Now, sitting here looking at him, it occurred to her that if she married him, there would be many moments like this, that she would be alone with him often. Why hadn't she thought of that the other day when she'd agreed to marry him, she wondered. How could she manage to live with someone around whom she felt so uncomfortable?

She cleared her throat. "It's been unseasonably warm the last few days, hasn't it?"

Stone cocked an eyebrow. "Reduced already to talking about the weather?"

"I—I'm afraid I don't know what to talk about." Margaret's face grew paler, the warm flush of minutes before draining away, and she looked down at her hands. "It's—this is an unusual situation for me. I'm sorry. You surprised me. I hadn't expected . . ."

"That I would come calling? I thought it would be too odd an engagement and marriage if I did not. It's customary."

"Yes, of course."

"Also, I thought we should discuss some things."

"Of course, if you wish. What things?"

"Well, the date of our wedding, for one."

"Oh. How silly of me."

"I was thinking of a month from now. Would that suit you?"

"Yes, if you wish." Her voice was even fainter. A month! Somehow, she had thought it would not be so soon, so close.

"Do I frighten you, Miss Carlisle?" There was no resentment or anger in his tone, only a faint curiosity.

"No, of course not," she lied.

He smiled a little. "I suspect that you are being somewhat less than truthful. It's all right. You can be honest with me. In fact, it is one thing which I insist on."

"I try to always be truthful."

"Except when it's more expedient not to be?" There was a bitter twist to his mouth.

"No!" Indignation lent Margaret courage and she looked him straight in the face, her eyes flashing. "I was merely trying not to be rude!"

"Then I take it that what you think of me would not be especially flattering."

She'd worked herself into a corner with that one, Margaret thought. Well, he'd said he wanted the truth. "Frankly, Mr. Stone, I don't know you well enough to have formed much of any impression of you, but what I have seen is, yes, a little frightening. . . ." Her voice trailed off at the end, her momentary courage draining away in the face of his flat gaze.

He didn't look at all affronted. In fact, his face didn't move a muscle. He merely said, "Thank you for your honesty. I would presume you are scared of me. I seem to be the demon they use to frighten children into obedience around here." He shrugged. "Perhaps you would do well to be somewhat frightened of me. As I've told you, I will not brook dishonesty—nor unfaithfulness. This is an arrangement, not a love affair, granted, but I will not abide a wife who is not loyal, no matter how little she cares for me. Nor will I permit any besmirching of my family's name. It is an old and honorable one."

"Sir!" Margaret jumped to her feet. Her cheeks flushed with color and her eyes were bright with fury. "You have gone too far. You tell me what *you* will permit and not permit. Well, I will tell you what I will not stand for—I will not sit here and listen to you impugn *my* honor or *my* family name. The Carlisles have lived here since long before you, and, unlike your name, mine is respected here. My father was one of the original settlers, and he was a good, worthy man. There has never been a hint of scandal to his name, and I swear that I will never do anything to stain it. In fact, agreeing to marry you is the closest I have ever come to putting a blot on his memory. *If* I married you, I would be a loyal and honest wife because that is how I was raised. That is what I believe in. Not because of your threats." She paused, almost panting in her fury, her arms and legs trembling. Afterward, she would be amazed at her temerity, but at the moment she was too swept up in righteous indignation to even notice what she was doing.

The Yankee looked at her for a moment, then, amazingly, a smile broke across his face. He looked suddenly younger, and Margaret realized with a start how very handsome he was.

"Well, well, you have thorns, I see. I had not realized."

Margaret started to retort that that was not the only thing that he had not realized about her, but she was out of her fit of anger now and the courage suddenly drained out of her body. She was rarely hasty in her temper—and what a person for her to display it to! "I—I am sorry," she said shakily. "I am not usually so forward, but—"

"I made you angry. I seem to have a talent for doing that to people." He shrugged. "Don't apologize. You are right to defend your name and your honor. I'm glad to see it. Besides, I am not such an ogre that I would punish you for speaking your mind. I don't beat women or mistreat children—and no matter what the good people of Huxley say, I have never been in the habit of dining on babies for breakfast."

Margaret had to smile, though a bit shyly, at his statement. "I had heard to the contrary on that matter."

Andrew Stone felt a curious twist in his stomach. She was prettier than he had thought, as well as possessed of a sense of humor and the fire of anger. Perhaps this marriage would not be as uncomplicated a thing as he had thought. Then again, perhaps it would not be as dull, either.

Margaret sat back down. His reaction to her anger was reassuring. He hadn't squashed her for her impertinence, as many men would have. As her aunt would have. For the first time, a faint hope stirred in her chest like a curling ribbon of smoke—perhaps this man would turn out to be like her father, a kind and loving man. Perhaps someday they would look at each other the way her parents had, their eyes glowing with love and tenderness.

No. She pushed the thought away. She mustn't let herself get carried away. It was a foolish girl's dream to think that a marriage that began like hers would ever develop into the kind of deep and abiding love her parents had known. Why, her parents had loved each other practically since they were children.

"I didn't come here to insult you," Stone went on to say. "I came because I thought there would be things we would need to settle, questions you might have."

His statement ended on an interrogatory note, and Margaret racked her brain to think of a question that might reestablish them on a better footing.

"Well . . . I would like to know more about your daughter."

"Laura?" His face warmed a little and Margaret knew she had made a good choice. "She is eleven and quite bright. She has my coloring. She is . . . a quiet child."

"I should like to meet her."

"Of course. I'm sure she would like to meet you, too. I haven't told her yet, but she will be pleased, I'm sure, to have a mother."

It was all Margaret could do to hold back a retort that Laura already had a mother. However, she felt quite sure that *that* answer would not be received by the colonel with a smile. She wondered why he hadn't yet told the child? Had he been afraid that Margaret might back out? Or was it that the little girl would be angry? Margaret could well imagine her disliking another woman taking her mother's place, taking over the house. If she was a spoiled child, Margaret was afraid that she might have real trouble with her. Laura wouldn't like the idea of her father sharing his time with someone else or of a stranger now being in charge of her.

"What is she interested in?" Margaret asked, hoping for a description of a sunny, affable child.

"Interested in?" He looked a little blank. "Well, oh, the usual things, I guess. Mmm, she has quite a few dolls. She reads a good deal." He paused. "As I said, she's a very quiet child. She doesn't talk easily, especially to strangers. I hope that you won't take that the wrong way. She may seem a bit aloof, but it takes her time to warm up to a person."

Margaret's heart sank. He was warning her that the child wouldn't talk to her at first. No doubt she would be sullen and resentful. Margaret would have to win her trust and respect. That would be difficult to do when the child's father didn't even respect Margaret. He had doubted her veracity and faithfulness, and there could be no clearer sign that he had little respect for her. The reason, she supposed, was because she had agreed to become his wife on such a cold, businesslike basis. He must think, as even Zach had said, that she was selling herself to him. She guessed, if she was entirely honest with herself, that she would have to admit that she was. But she was not doing it for the money the Yankee had; she was marrying him in order to get the things she wanted—her own home, freedom from her aunt, a good life for her brother and sister. Perhaps she had been only trying to excuse herself by calling it a fair bargain—however cold and devoid of love it was. Perhaps it was devoid of honor, too. She wondered if her father would have been ashamed of her.

Yet what else could she do? She had to take care of Annie and Zach! A woman had few options.

"I am sure that your daughter and I will get along," Margaret told him staunchly, hoping that she wasn't lying.

"I am a patient person. I can wait for her to get to know me." What would she do if the girl hated her? If she never accepted her? Stone would no doubt be furious.

"Good. I assume that you will be able to take care of the wedding arrangements." Margaret nodded, though her throat closed up a little at the thought. "Have the expenses billed to me."

"Expenses?"

"Yes. Material for dresses, whatever." He made an impatient gesture with his hand. "I'm afraid I don't know what is necessary. Of course, you will need some spending money, too." He reached into his jacket and withdrew a money clip.

Red flooded Margaret's face and she stood up jerkily. "No! No, please don't." He was actually going to pay her, hand her a wad of money as if she were merchandise he had purchased at the store. "I couldn't."

Stone frowned. "Don't be silly. Take it." He rose and extended his hand, filled with money, but Margaret stepped back as if she'd been stung.

"No." Tears filled her eyes. "I don't need it. I can't take it."

His frown deepened. "Why not? We're engaged to be married. Surely you can't consider it improper for a man to provide for his wife."

"I'm not your wife yet."

"Are you planning to back out of the arrangement?"

"No."

"Then what is the difference between accepting money from me now and a month from now? You need the money. There will be quite a few expenses connected with the wedding, I should think."

Margaret said nothing. She couldn't bring herself to argue with him, yet neither could she take it. She couldn't even explain why. She just shook her head and retreated a step.

Her future husband sighed. "Doubtless I have trodden on sensitive Rebel toes, although I fail to understand how." He thrust the money back into his pocket. They faced each other awkwardly. Margaret found she couldn't meet his eyes, and she ducked her head.

To her astonishment, he crossed the room and took her hand in his. She glanced up, her eyes wide. His expression softened. Large, luminous and fringed by thick pale lashes, Margaret's eyes were her best feature. Though they looked hazel at a distance, up close he could see that they were a dark green, made even clearer by the moisture of tears welling in her eyes. Again he felt that funny tightening in his chest.

"I am sorry for offending you," he told her softly, and raised her hand to his lips. He brushed his mouth against her fingertips.

His fingers were slim and strong around hers, his lips warm and soft. Shivers forked through Margaret like lightning.

"I had better take my leave before I do any further damage. May I call on you next week?"

She nodded numbly. Her tongue felt locked to the roof of her mouth.

Stone stood looking down at her for a moment. She had eyes a man could die for. He found that he wanted to bend down and press his lips against hers. It would probably scare her to death. Instead, he simply gave her fingers another squeeze and released them. Then he turned and walked out of the room.

When he had gone, Margaret sank down into her chair. Her cheeks were flushed and her corset felt much too tight.

She thought about crying. She thought about the touch of his lips upon her flesh. The fingers of her left hand curled around her right one and she squeezed the spot he had kissed. For a long time, she simply sat and stared.

Chapter Three

For the next few days, Margaret's aunt tried to wear Margaret down with silence. Aunt Charity didn't speak to her niece, and when she looked at Margaret, her face was icy with contempt. The very air was frigid. Zach and Annie stood firmly beside Margaret, of course, despite whatever doubts they had about their sister's plans. But Margaret knew that their support was not wholehearted and it couldn't begin to counter the weight of Aunt Charity's disapproval.

The tactic had worked well before, but this time Margaret was determined not to knuckle under. The very strain of living around her aunt made her more and more determined to seize this opportunity to escape the woman's domination. She felt the iciness, as she always did; the fearsome glances pierced her, stirring up guilt and anxiety. But she walled herself off from them, recounting like a litany in her head, "Living with *him* couldn't possibly be worse than this."

Still, she felt horribly alone and weak in her daily struggle. Then, much to her amazement, she received reinforcement from an unexpected source. Emma, Aunt Charity's daughter, who had been away visiting the past few days, returned to the house, and when she heard that the Yankee had proposed and Margaret had accepted, she smiled and said, "Good for you!"

Margaret stared, dumbfounded. The last person in the house she would have expected to support her was Cousin Emma. When the Carlisles had first moved here, Emma had been jealous of them. Margaret, Annie and Zach, on the other hand, had thought Emma a spoiled brat, selfish, vain and insistent on getting her own way. Over the years the four of them had eased into a more comfortable relationship, but they were not close. Margaret couldn't help but envy the other girl's good looks and ease with people; she always felt like a clumsy wallflower beside Emma. Emma was sometimes careless and flighty; she was often selfish and vain.

"You don't think it's terrible?" Margaret asked in astonishment.

"No—though I'm sure Mother does. She knows that she'll be losing three servants." Emma had followed Margaret up to her bedroom after supper to pry out of her what had happened that had caused such a freeze in the house, and she was sitting on the bed Annie and Margaret shared, her legs crossed in front of her in a most unladylike fashion. Now she threw her forearm up against her head dramatically. "Gad! That means I may have to do some work!"

Margaret smiled at her cousin's histrionics. Emma had a certain charm of personality that was hard to resist. "But he's a Yankee."

Emma shrugged. "What difference does it make which side he fought on? It's been over four years. Anyway, I think the whole subject of 'the War' is stupid. War is just something men do to occupy themselves." She grinned, casting a sideways glance at Margaret. Emma often spoke about men in a careless, even contemptuous way. Margaret thought that it was because she had found it easy to manipulate so many of them with her beauty. "I find it much more important that Colonel Stone is handsome as the devil."

"Handsome? Do you think so?"

"Of course! Don't tell me you didn't notice! No girl jumps into marriage without looking at a man."

"Well..." Margaret summoned up the colonel in her mind, seeing again the sharp angles of his face, the chiseled lips, the tanned skin and the startling blueness of his eyes against it. "I guess he is handsome. I mean, his features are quite regular and—"

Emma snorted indelicately. "Don't be so prissy! Admit you noticed that he is tall and has shoulders this wide and a face that sets your heart aflutter. And those eyes!"

"I—I don't know. His eyes were cold and his face so hard—he—I thought he was a little scary."

"But of course." Emma gave a shiver. "That's what makes it so delicious."

Margaret recalled the turmoil in her stomach during the man's visit. Had it all been fear, or was Emma right? Had there been something else? She glanced at Emma doubtfully.

Emma laughed. "Poor Cousin Margaret. Don't tell me you really did it so Annie and Zach could live well?"

"No. Of course not. I wanted to leave this house, too. That is, I mean—" She stopped in confusion, realizing that what she had been about to say was decidedly uncomplimentary to Emma's mother.

"Don't worry. I won't tattle on you."

"No. Of course not." That was one thing you had to say about Emma: she had never been one to tell her mother what everyone else said and did. "I didn't think you would. But what I meant to say was that I didn't want to be a burden on Aunt Charity any longer."

"Don't be so mealymouthed. You'll have to learn to stand up for yourself if you're going to marry this Yankee. Say what you mean, that you can't wait to get away from my mother." She shrugged. "I have to love her, I suppose—she is my mother. But I'm not blind. She's never been fair or nice to you. Heavens, *I'm* her beloved daughter, and there are lots of times I'd give anything to get away from her."

Margaret stared, surprised. She had never thought that Emma, the spoiled daughter of the household, might want to leave it, too. "But you must have had many opportunities. I mean, several men have asked you to marry them."

"None that I wanted to marry." For an instant, the normal vivacity dropped from Emma's face and her eyes were serious, even shadowed. Then she shrugged and the brightness returned to her features. "I don't find it so hard to live with Mother. I've done it all my life. However obnoxious she may be, I know she loves me. I'm in an enviable position, you know. Able to flirt and dance all I want with whom I want, with plenty of men to flatter me and no husband to tell me what I can or can't do. I'm not about to give that up."

"Do you—do you think it's wicked of me to marry him without love?"

"Wicked? No. It's eminently practical, that's what it is. How else can a woman get anywhere in life except by marrying well?" She lifted her hand as though to stop Margaret's response. "Oh, I know—that's not why you did it. It's for Annie and Zach. I know you well enough to realize that. But I also know love isn't always all it's made out to be." She flashed Margaret her dazzling smile.

"Now, let's get onto the important things. When are you getting married?"

"In a month, he said."

"'He said'!" Emma rolled her eyes. "You're beginning it all wrong, my dear. You have to set the pattern right from the first. *You* make the plans."

"I don't think so. Not with him." Margaret shook her head.

"Of course, with him. He's just a man."

"I can't imagine him letting anyone, especially a woman, tell him what to do."

"Well, you have to do it the proper way of course. You have to twist it around so that he thinks that he came up with the idea. But it's quite simple. You'll see. By the time ya'll are married, you'll be leading him around by the nose." She drew her features into a mischievous face, cutting her eyes at her cousin. "Or should I say, by another prominent part of his anatomy?"

"Emma!" Margaret blushed up to her hairline.

Emma laughed throatily and flung herself back on the bed. "Oh, this will be fun! *I* am going to help you wind this man around your little finger."

Margaret, her hands pressed against her hot cheeks, thought of Andrew Stone and shook her head, unable to suppress a giggle. "No. Not this man. He's different. You'll see."

"Ha! He's a man, just like any other man, and I know how they think—and with what." She sat up again, flipping a fat curl back over her shoulder. "Believe me, your whole life will be much easier once you have him eating out of the palm of your hand."

"But I'm not like you. I'm not pretty, and I can't flirt."

"Obviously he isn't impressed with those things or it would have been me he asked to marry, wouldn't it?"

"He chose me because he thought I would be practical—and probably tractable and quiet, too. And because he knew that I would be more likely to accept his proposal because of Annie and Zach and our living on your mother's charity."

"Nonsense, there are plenty of women around who would have been happy to marry him. I am positive—beyond anything—that there is more about you that attracts him, even if he doesn't realize it yet. No man would ask a woman to marry him if he didn't want to find her in his bed."

Margaret blushed again. "Emma! I've never heard you talk this way."

Emma shrugged. "This is no time for playing the game of sweet little blushing maiden. Just because you and I aren't married doesn't mean we have to be stupid." Her grin flashed again. "We're just supposed to act that way."

Margaret had to smile back. She had never before liked her cousin half as much as she did right now. It occurred to her that Emma's selfishness was a healthy quality to have around her mother. Aunt Charity would have worn to dust anyone less confident and self-interested than Emma. Nor was it any wonder that Emma was vain. She had every right to be. She was a lovely young woman, with thick black hair and huge, melting brown eyes. The only woman in the whole county who was any prettier was Damaris Murdock, and everyone knew that *she* was beyond compare.

"Now," Emma said, rubbing her hands together and plotting, "what shall we do to entrance that devilish-looking man?"

"I can't imagine."

"First of all, we'll do something new to your hair. Mama can't fuss about your not working now, not when you're going to be married in a few weeks. We'll have all the time we want to try out new hairstyles."

Margaret's hand flew to her plain bun, hesitated, then dropped away. "Do you really think . . ."

"Yes, I 'really think.'" Emma mocked her gently. "You wait and see. And you'll need new clothes. Lots of new clothes."

"But I have clothes."

"Something that's not brown or beige or gray. Something that's not practical. Party dresses. Afternoon tea dresses."

"But Aunt Charity will never allow me to spend so much money. She doesn't even want me to get married!"

Emma frowned. "She will be a problem, of course. I have a couple of dresses that we could take up for you." Margaret was both shorter and less buxom than her cousin. "But most of my clothes aren't the right colors for you. You need pastels. Rose pinks and royal blues will never do." She thought for a moment, then perked up. "I know! Some of my old dresses. They're smaller anyway, and when I was only sixteen or seventeen, Mama made me wear all those insipid pinks and blues. They looked atrocious on me, but they'll be just the thing for your coloring. And there's your mother's trunk upstairs."

"Yes. But they're so old. They'll be out of date."

"We'll simply have to work on them. You're a whiz with a needle, and I'm adequate. Even Annie could rip up a few seams or do a hem or two." She went on, happily plotting, never allowing one of Margaret's objections to stand.

Margaret found that her cousin's plans worked. The next morning, they hauled out the two old trunks and went through the clothes, taking out whatever they could use. Then, by much ripping, sewing and adding trinkets, lace and ribbons raided from Emma's trunks and drawers, they began to transform the dresses. Margaret was astounded at her cousin's accurate eye for how a dress could be changed. Childish ribbons cut off here, a neckline lowered there, an extra flounce of lace added around the bottom of a skirt, a skirt altered from a full one to a bustle-effect, pieces of different dresses put together to form a new whole—soon the dresses looked quite different.

Margaret neglected her chores shamefully. Annie and Zach took up some of them, but others were simply left undone. To Margaret's surprise she found that nothing happened. She realized then that with her aunt not speaking to her, she wouldn't have to endure any lectures.

It wasn't long before Aunt Charity realized the same thing and abandoned the silent treatment. She then launched into a series of harangues about her niece's ingratitude, heartlessness and general lack of redeeming qualities.

Margaret grimly endured two such hours, but the next time her aunt brought up the subject, Emma was in the room, and she lifted her limpid eyes and said, "Why, Mama! What is that Yankee going to think of us if your own niece goes to marry him in rags? He'll say you couldn't even take care of your kin." Emma sighed lugubriously. "I'd be so ashamed, Mama...havin' a Yankee think we're poor as white trash."

Aunt Charity stopped in midtirade, and she looked at her daughter sharply. "He won't think that because I won't allow her to marry him!"

Emma shrugged. "Now, as to that, I don't know, ma'am. But I do know how I'd feel watching Cousin Margaret walk down the aisle of the First Baptist Church in that old gray linen thing of hers, the one with the patches on the skirt." She let her voice float up inquiringly at the end.

Margaret could see from her aunt's face that she was much taken aback by the thought of such a scene, and Margaret had to stifle a giggle. She'd always known that her cousin had a way of managing Aunt Charity, but she'd never seen it so clearly in action as now.

"She's not marrying him," Aunt Charity reiterated firmly, but Margaret noticed that the woman left the room and did not again come in to thunder about the time that Margaret was wasting making over the dresses.

"Next," Emma promised, "we'll get money from her to buy material for the wedding dress."

Margaret thought of the money the Yankee had offered her and she wondered whether she had been honorable or merely foolish.

Andrew Stone came the following Tuesday afternoon to call on her, as he had said he would. A man rode with him, a still, faintly sinister-looking sort, who dismounted and stayed with the horses in front, leaning casually against the hitching post but constantly watching the street. Margaret, peering out her bedroom window as she waited for Stone to arrive, shivered slightly as she looked at the man. Zach was right; certainly this man looked the part of a gunman. Why would Stone need the services of a hired gun?

She shoved the thought to the back of her mind and went down the stairs to meet her intended. Emma and Margaret had carefully selected the dress she wore today for her fiancé's call: a pink gown of her mother's, slashed and draped to reveal a white underskirt frothing with ruffles. The gown was cinched in tightly where it met the fitted bodice, reducing her waist to nothingness. The worn decoration at the neck had been torn out to form a low neckline and filled in with another spill of ruffles to hide the tops of her breasts. The skirt was pulled back to a small bustle in the rear, so that the material was stretched across her flat abdomen.

During their spare moments during the past days, Emma and Margaret had worked on hairstyles, and now, instead of wearing her pale hair pulled back tightly and screwed into a practical bun, Margaret's hair was brushed to a sheen and wound in three long, soft curls that fell over her shoulder and down onto the soft white skin of her chest.

Margaret was nervous and excited, and it showed in the color in her cheeks. Emma had bade her rub her lips together hard, so that her mouth was a deep rose. She took a deep breath and opened the door.

"Good afternoon, Mr. Stone." Margaret's voice trembled slightly with nervousness.

Andrew stared at her, slightly stunned, and he took her hand almost as if in a daze. This was surely not the creature he had asked to marry him little more than a week before, not even the more engaging woman of the flashing eyes and surprising spirit that he had called upon two days later. That woman had been small and pale, almost drab, with only her fine, large eyes to commend her. But this woman—this woman was lovely. Her hair was the color of moonlight, and its soft curls begged to be crushed in a man's hands. She was fragile, almost ethereal, her waist so small his hands could span it, yet there was no delicacy, only womanliness, in the soft swell of her breasts. His eyes touched the ruffles that lay across her breasts and the drape of skirt across her stomach.

Suddenly, hungrily, he wanted to put his hands on her, to explore the curves and planes of the body that only last week he had barely noticed. He found now that he was eager to lay his claim to her. He wanted to look down into the luminous green pools of her eyes and pull her up to him to kiss. The very salaciousness of his thoughts surprised and shook him.

Andrew Stone had thought himself long ago invulnerable to the wiles of women. Last week he had known himself immune to this woman, but now he wasn't so sure. Now there was fire spreading through his loins.

"Miss Carlisle." There was a faint tremor in his voice, though Margaret was too shaken by the look of sheer animal hunger in his eyes to notice what he said.

Stone raised her hand to his lips, as he had last week, but this time his eyes stayed on her face as he kissed her fingers and his lips pressed harder into her flesh. He turned her hand over and kissed her palm. Margaret felt his breath on her palm. It was hot.

She drew in a shaky breath and stepped back.

"You are beautiful."

Emma, who had followed her cousin down the stairs, a little bit behind her, surveyed the couple. The Yankee looked as if he might fall upon Margaret at any moment. Now was the time for her to enter. That would keep the colonel unsatisfied and wanting more. "Well," she said, going down the last step into the entry way. "I am Emma Winstock, Margaret's cousin."

She swept forward, and Margaret glanced at her, her stomach knotting at her cousin's presence. They needed a chaperone, of course, and her aunt certainly didn't seem likely to perform the service, but she felt the familiar twist of jealousy and inadequacy with Emma there. Andrew would look at Emma and forget her.

But, curiously, he hardly glanced at Emma. "How do you do? Andrew Stone." His gaze returned to Margaret.

The three of them went into the parlor and sat down, stiffly exchanging a few pleasantries. Emma was the only one who paid attention to anything that was said. The other two spoke in off-hand, disjointed phrases that often made only partial sense. Emma smiled to herself, thoroughly enjoying the situation. The last thing she had ever expected to see was the Yankee, as hard and remote a man as she had ever seen, gazing at Margaret with a bewitched expression. His eyes stayed on Margaret's lips, only sliding down now and then to her breasts, hugged by the form-fitting bodice.

When Emma judged that enough time had passed in this manner, she began to hint that the time for the colonel's visit was over. After some minutes, he realized what she was saying. He rose to take his leave, at which point Emma tactfully excused herself from the room.

Andrew took Margaret's hand as they walked reluctantly toward the hallway. Emma had slid the parlor door shut behind her as she left and for the time being, they were enclosed together in a private world. Stone's fingers slid between Margaret's to clasp her hand. Margaret felt each fraction of an inch of his skin as it brushed across hers, hard and rasping. His thumb rubbed over the back of her hand, tracing the tendons and bones.

He stopped and turned to look down at her, a heated, slumberous look in his eyes that made Margaret's heart start to slam in her chest. His gaze went to her mouth. Her breath was suddenly rough and spasmodic. She waited. His face loomed closer.

Margaret closed her eyes. She felt his breath against her cheek, then his lips touched hers. They were warm and soft and as light as a butterfly's wings. Margaret knotted her hands in her skirts. His hands came up to curl around her arms, just below the puffed sleeves of her dress. His skin was rough compared to the soft flesh of her arms, and she could feel the latent strength of his hands.

He kissed her again, his lips lingering this time, and his hands slid slowly down her arms and up again. Her skin tingled wherever he touched it, and she found herself going up on tiptoe, her mouth pressing back into his. She heard his inhaled breath of surprise and the kiss deepened. His lips rocked gently against hers, opening them slightly. His tongue touched her lower lip. Margaret's eyes flew open and her feet went back down flat. She stared back up at him, her eyes rounded, her lips forming a soft O of surprise.

His eyes were a fierce blue, as though lit by a flame from within. Margaret could not look away. She felt weak and melting inside, as though this man could move and twist her any way he chose.

His eyelids came down, shuttering the intense gleam, and when he opened them again, the fires inside were banked. He raised a hand and wrapped it around one thick curl of her hair. He slid his hand down the curl, feeling it twist back into shape around him. Then he released it and stepped away.

"Good afternoon," he said, and though the words were formal and ordinary, the huskiness of his voice betrayed the feelings churning in him.

"Goodbye, Mr. Stone."

His eyebrow went up sardonically. "Don't you think you should call your fiancé by his first name?"

"All right." Margaret still felt a trifle breathless from their kiss. "Andrew."

"My friends even call me Drew."

Margaret blushed. Somehow a nickname seemed entirely too familiar a thing to call this almost stranger.

"And what would you have me call you? Miss Carlisle?"

She shook her head. "My name is Margaret. I—I would be honored if you would call me by it."

"Then, goodbye, Margaret."

"Andrew." His name seemed rather daring on her lips.

He turned and left the room, striding quickly to the front door and out. Margaret's hand went up to her mouth. Lightly she touched her lips with her fingertips, remembering the feel of his lips there. She thought of his hand on her hair. Suddenly she turned and ran into the kitchen to the mirror above the washbasin. Zach, loading wood into the bin, glanced at her, surprised, but she didn't even see him. She gazed at her reflection, somehow expecting to see some result of Andrew's kiss, but there was none. She looked the same except for the heightened color in her cheeks and the sparkle in her eyes. No man had kissed her before this, even lightly. She smiled a small, secret, feminine smile and dropped her gaze, as though to hide the thoughts in her head even from her reflection.

She wondered when he would return.

In fact, Andrew was back sooner than she would have dreamed. He came to call again only two days later. But this time, unfortunately, her aunt was there and it was she who met Andrew at the door, blocking his way inside. Margaret, who was in the kitchen paring potatoes for supper, heard the rumble of a male voice in the hallway and the raised voice of her aunt. Margaret dropped both potato and knife and ran into the hallway. She saw that there was a confrontation between Andrew and her aunt, as she had feared, and she hurried forward.

"Aunt Charity! What are you doing?"

Her aunt turned and shot her a disdainful glance. "I am denying admittance to my house to this—" she looked at

Andrew Stone, and her lips curled in contempt "—this carpetbagger!"

"He is my fiancé," Margaret said, and her hands curled into her apron. Fear clutched her heart as it always did when she fought with her aunt. She would lose, as she always lost, and somehow she couldn't bear the thought of looking so weak in front of Andrew.

"That doesn't change the fact that this is my house, and I can deny admittance to anyone I want to. You may be willing to disgrace your name by marrying this man, this enemy to your own people, but—"

"Enemy! He is no longer our enemy, Aunt. The War was over four years ago."

Charity Winstock whirled to face her niece, and the man she detested stepped quietly into the house and closed the door behind him. "It doesn't matter when the War was over! This man conquered your homeland. He killed your father and uncle."

"Aunt Charity, I'm sure it was not Mr. Stone's bullet that killed my father," Margaret replied reasonably. She didn't add, though she would have liked to, that her uncle, Charity's husband, had not fallen in battle, but had died a year after the War of a lung ailment.

"You are too soft," Mrs. Winstock said bitterly. "It is your sort who will forget all that we have suffered and make peace with *them*."

"I have not forgotten Father's death." Margaret raised her chin. "I never will. But neither will I spend my whole life in bitterness, blaming every man who wore a blue uniform for his death."

Andrew Stone watched Margaret, an odd look on his face. It had been a long time since he had seen anyone come to his defense. Even though Margaret had agreed to marry him, he had not expected her to give up the resentment the townspeople shared against him because he was a Yankee. Certainly, he hadn't dreamed that his fiancé would stand up for him against her formidable aunt.

"You're a traitor," Aunt Charity told Margaret flatly. "Selling yourself to the conqueror, just like a common who—"

"Stop it!" Andrew Stone's voice thundered through the small hallway, silencing even Aunt Charity. His icy gaze sliced through the older woman. "You will not missay my fiancée, not in front of me nor anyone else. You will not hurt her or revile her in any way. I don't give a damn what you think about me. But you will not bring pain to that girl, or I will ruin you. Is that clear?"

Charity stared at him, her eyes wide. No one, man or woman, had ever dared to speak to her that way, and she was stunned. She knew, too, that this man would do what he said. Not only that, he had the power to. He was the wealthiest man around and he was friends with several men in the military government that ruled Texas. "Yes," she said finally, and Margaret had never heard her voice sound so weak.

Stone turned toward Margaret. "Margaret? Come with me onto the porch. That way I shan't defile this woman's house."

He strode out the front door, and Margaret followed him, slipping around her aunt, who was still standing, stunned, in the middle of the hallway. Margaret closed the door behind her and looked up at Andrew shyly. "Thank you for what you said to my aunt. For protecting me."

He looked at her oddly. "You are to be my wife. Did you think I would not protect you?"

"I don't know. I guess—I guess I hadn't really thought about it." For the past few years, ever since her father had left her in their aunt's care, she had been defenseless, with no one to rescue or help her, just Zach and Annie dependent on her to take care of them. It was a novel idea to think of being wrapped in the protection of this man's strength—and warming, too, as if his arm were actually curled around her, shielding her from harm. Tears gathered in her eyes. "Thank you."

Andrew wanted to go to her and wrap his arms around her, to cradle her against his chest; the desire to hold and comfort her was almost overpowering. But he remembered that they were standing on the front porch in full view of anyone who happened to be passing by, not to mention his man Whitman, standing with the horses. To even touch Margaret in public would be to damage her reputation. So he stayed where he was and shoved his hands into his pockets to keep them from reaching out for her. "It is I who should thank you."

"Why?"

"For coming to my defense that way. I guess, for believing what you do—that I am not a monster and a murderer because I fought in the U.S. Army."

"My father went to fight for his home, his land. It was something he believed in. He knew that it could mean his death and he was willing to face that. He chose it. He taught us that that was the way life was. He used to say 'You dance to the music and you have to pay the piper.' He didn't believe in bitterness or regrets. He also believed in treating people fairly and not judging them by external things. And that's the way he raised us to be."

"He sounds like a good man. I wish I could have met him."

"He was." Margaret blinked away her tears. "He'd have been the last person to hold it against you that you fought for the North."

He smiled. "That I'm a Yankee?" He stressed the word teasingly, and it sounded funny in his flat, clipped accent.

Margaret had to smile. "You can't say it right."

For a moment they stood, simply grinning at each other, feeling a little silly, yet liking the feeling, too. Finally Andrew reached inside his suit jacket and drew out a small box. "I'm sorry. I almost forgot why I came here today." He extended the box to her. "I brought your ring. The engagement ring."

"Oh." Margaret hadn't even thought about a ring.

She took the box and opened it. Inside lay a gold ring with a simple setting of a single large opal. "It's lovely." She reached in and pulled out the ring, holding it up so that the sunlight picked out its hidden colors. She wondered if this was the ring he had given to his first wife, if Damaris had once worn it on her elegant hand. Somehow the thought made her throat feel tight and blocked. She wanted to ask him, but she didn't dare.

What was she thinking didn't occur to Andrew. The expensive, elegant ring Damaris had chosen was still in her possession. He would not have touched it again. This ring was one that had belonged to his grandmother, and he had chosen to give it to Margaret for an engagement ring because it seemed to suit her, with its pale, almost secret beauty.

Andrew took the ring from her hand and slid it onto her finger. It fit well; she was a dainty woman, as his grandmother had been.

"Thank you. It's a beautiful ring." Margaret smiled at him. It felt strangely heavy on her finger. She wished she knew whether Damaris had worn it, too.

There was silence for a moment. Margaret felt foolishly tongue-tied. "Well," Stone said finally, "shall I call on you again, or will it create too many problems?"

"Yes. Please call. I—I'll see what I can do with my aunt. I'm sorry. I apologize for the way she acted toward you."

He shrugged. "I've heard far worse, believe me. But I have no wish to make your position in her house any more uncomfortable."

"I will be fine. Don't be concerned about me."

He took a step back. It wasn't what he wanted to do. "Then I will see you next week?"

Margaret nodded. "Yes. Goodbye."

He turned and went down the steps and along the path to his horse, feeling her gaze on him as he walked. He was suddenly very conscious of the irregularity of his walk, the slight hesitation every time he set his right leg down. It had happened so long ago that usually he didn't even think of it, but now he saw it as if it were new. He limped. When Margaret Carlisle looked at him, she saw a damaged man. He doubted that she had any idea how badly damaged he was, more inside than out. She wouldn't know what she was getting into. She was too young and naive.

That was one of the reasons he had picked her.

Andrew nodded to Whitman and swung up onto his horse. He glanced up at the house. Margaret still stood on the porch, and she raised her hand in a discreet wave. He tugged at the brim of his hat in the salute that stood for greetings and farewells here, then wheeled his horse and trotted off, with the hired gun right behind him. He wondered what she thought of the fact that he had hired Whitman to ride protection for his ranch. Did she think he was a coward? Or that he used a gunslinger to force his will on others? He made himself not glance back at the porch to see if Margaret was still watching. It didn't matter whether she watched him or not. Damn it, it didn't matter!

Nor did it matter what she thought of him—or that she must be a good twelve years younger than he was. None of that mattered. He had known it all along. It had been part of his calculations. He'd wanted someone younger because she would be easier to control. He had counted on being able to intimidate her into obedience and faithfulness. Andrew had looked at Margaret Carlisle and seen a mousy little thing, always in the shadow of her formidable aunt and pretty cousin. That was the kind of woman he had wanted. Much as he needed a mother for Laura, he wasn't about to go through the hell he'd endured last time with Damaris. There would be no marriage for love, no tender attempts to awaken his wife's sensuality, no gentle consideration.

He had concluded that there would be a bargain instead, and that he would marry a woman who would be content with that. He had studied the local candidates, and Margaret Carlisle had seemed the perfect woman to be his wife. She would obviously bend to his will; she would not fight him or try to seduce him into giving her what she wanted. He did not love her, so she could not break his heart. She was not pretty enough that the men would flock to her, tempting her to be unfaithful. And she would be young enough and scared enough of him that she wouldn't even think of betraying him.

He had been sure he had made the right choice, but the last two times he had seen her, it had shaken him. Her defense of him against her aunt had warmed and surprised him. And she was much prettier than he remembered, not pale and mousy. He found himself wanting her more than was necessary for the purpose of breeding children or satisfying his male lusts. He wanted to help and protect her, to shield her from that harridan of an aunt.

That wasn't wise. It wasn't wise at all. Desire was one thing; a man couldn't help that. But he would be damned if he fell into the trap of tenderness and love again. He knew too well the deceit of women and what love could do to a man.

He would simply have to be more careful in the future. He would have to make sure that Margaret understood how things were to be: he would have to guard against the unexpected pleasure he had found today in looking at her. It was a bargain, nothing more, and he would remember that.

Chapter Four

It was Emma, in her own unusual way, that brought Aunt Charity around on the subject of Margaret's marriage to Andrew Stone. At the supper table that evening after Stone's visit, Emma piped up, "I must say, Mama, that was awfully brave of you to toss the Yankee out on his ear like that this afternoon."

Margaret stopped eating with a forkful of food halfway to her mouth and shot a dismayed look at her cousin. She had thought that Emma was on her side!

Aunt Charity preened a little at the compliment, but said only, "Where did you hear that?"

"Why, in town, of course." That was a lie, Margaret knew. Emma hadn't even been into town this afternoon. Annie had told her that she and Emma had heard the whole argument this afternoon by crouching by the banister upstairs. "Everybody's talking about it. They were saying how you can't control your own niece, and she's marrying the Yankee and all. They said how brave you were, defying Colonel Stone like that, no matter how powerful a man he is. Why, do you know, Mr. Jackson said he'd heard tell that any enemy of the colonel's was apt to be taken up by the military governor for questioning—

and sometimes never heard from again. They say that he's a close friend of—"

"What twaddle!" Aunt Charity blustered, her heavy jowls quivering, but she couldn't conceal the flash of fear that Margaret had seen in her eyes.

Margaret eyed her cousin thoughtfully.

"That's what I said," Emma agreed blithely. "I told them you never backed down from anything. And, of course, we all know how important it is that Cousin Margaret not marry that Yankee. Why, we'd be ruined in society for the rest of our lives." Emma forked a bit of mashed potatoes into her mouth and chewed, her brown eyes rounded and innocent.

"Ruined?" Whatever fear had been in her aunt's face fled before the fury that Emma's remarks had raised in her breast. "I, Charity Winstock? Ruined in society? I'll have you know, miss, that I am the backbone of society in Huxley."

"Yes, ma'am, I know you always have been. But with your own niece married to someone like the Yankee, well, it's positively disgraceful. I heard Lucinda Maxwell say that she didn't think she'd ever be able to speak to you again. I fear that we will be ostracized, Mama."

Aunt Charity's eyebrows rushed together. "Ostracized! I'd like to see them try! As if Lucinda Maxwell were anyone of importance. Why, if I cut that woman dead on the street tomorrow, no one would speak to her for weeks."

"But not even you could save our name if it becomes attached to the Yankee's."

Aunt Charity's face flushed bright red, and for a moment she was too furious to speak. Her daughter went on calmly picking at the food on her plate, downing this tidbit and that as if she hadn't just precipitated a storm at the dining table. Margaret, staring at her, realized how neatly her cousin had trapped Aunt Charity.

"Our name is too good to be besmirched by anything, including marrying some no-account from Pennsylvania!" Charity declared, her eyes sparking fire. "I'll tell you this, if I chose to accept him, everyone in this town would acknowledge that Yankee."

"Really?" Emma's face was awestruck now as she looked at her mother. "Could you do that?"

"Of course. If I gave a party and invited the man, everybody would come running to it. You can bank on it."

"You mean, if you were to accept him, so would the rest of Huxley?"

"Of course."

"And if everybody accepts him, it wouldn't be a stain on our family name if Cousin Margaret married him, would it?"

"No." There was a hesitation in Aunt Charity's voice, as though a suspicion had slipped into her mind that she was being maneuvered.

"I should have realized you'd do that."

"Do what?"

"Accept the Yankee as Margaret's husband, of course. It's very clever of you. I mean, it would effectively take the wind out of everyone's sails, wouldn't it? You could steal the march on Lucinda Maxwell, too. Why, that woman is just waiting to take advantage of this situation. She wants to steal your position in this town away from you."

Aunt Charity's eyes narrowed. "Lucinda always was a sneaky thing, ever since she was a little girl. That sounds like a trick she would pull."

Cousin Emma nodded. "You're right, Mama. But when you invite the Yankee over, and everyone comes to your party, Mrs. Maxwell will see that your position is as strong as ever, and she'll know she hasn't a prayer of stealing it away from you. After all, she won't be able to gossip about how you couldn't control your niece and how no respectable woman would be related to Andrew Stone, even by marriage. You will have already made him respectable! It's such wonderful reasoning.''

Charity Winstock blinked. Then she straightened, gave a gracious nod to her daughter, and said, ''Thank you, Emma, dear.'' Her gaze went to Margaret and turned decidedly more chilly. ''Well, young lady, despite your disrespect, it looks as though you are going to get what you wanted. I am giving you permission to marry Colonel Stone.''

Margaret had to swallow and wait for a moment to keep from laughing. ''Yes, ma'am. Thank you.''

She glanced across the table at Emma, whose eyes were dancing. She remembered another time when Emma had looked at her in that triumphant, even smug, way. It had been when Emma had convinced her mother that some misdeed or other of Margaret's should keep her from attending a dinner at Mr. and Mrs. Quinn's house. Margaret had felt equal parts dislike for Emma, for trying to spoil her evening, and amusement, because what Emma hadn't known was that Margaret always dreaded going there since the Quinns' son pestered her so. Now, looking at her cousin, Margaret wasn't so sure that Emma hadn't known how much she disliked the Quinns. Guiltily she wondered if there had been other times when she had taken at face value what Emma said or did without even noticing the subtle way she had maneuvered Aunt Charity. Could it be that Emma had been a better friend to her than she had ever suspected?

The next day, Charity Winstock sent a small, monogrammed notecard by messenger out to the Stone ranch.

In it, she asked the colonel to call on her the following day. When he did so, he found only Mrs. Winstock at home, her daughter, nieces and nephew having been sent on errands. Intrigued and wary, Stone followed her into the parlor and listened as she graciously gave him permission to call on and marry her niece, then proceeded to set the wedding date back two more weeks in order that the requisite social functions could be accomplished.

Stone didn't trust her, and he didn't understand why she had so suddenly and easily capitulated. He could not imagine anything Margaret might have said to her yesterday having that much force. But he went along with her plans, agreeing to the engagement party and the changed wedding date and the other parties that she assured him would come about now that she was endorsing the marriage. After all, acceptance of him and his daughter by the local society was one of the things he had hoped to accomplish by marrying into the Carlisles.

Unlike her niece, Charity Winstock had no hesitation whatsoever in accepting money from Stone to defray the costs of the engagement party and the wedding. He thought, with a twisted little smile, of how surprised he had been by Margaret's refusal to take the money. But naturally the minx had been playing a part, making herself look noble and virtuous, knowing that her aunt would later move in to take the money.

He had to give Margaret credit; the girl was more clever than he had thought. He wondered if the way she had stood up for him the other day had been part of an act, as well. She had seemed so real and convincing. But then, acting was something that women—especially Southern ones—had been trained in so well that it was second nature to them. He had learned that with Damaris. He remembered her once telling him scornfully about the ruses and ploys she had used to lead him along the path to marriage. Damaris had played him like a trout, reeling him in and letting him out, until he was so desperate to have her that he would have done anything.

Well, he had been a boy then, hot-blooded and naive. Now he understood. He was older, cooler, wiser. He could afford to go along with Margaret and her aunt just to see where it would lead, knowing that their pretenses did not fool him, that he could call a halt to whatever they were planning at any time.

So Andrew and Aunt Charity parted, if not amicably, at least without argument. Afterward, Aunt Charity admitted that for a man—and a Yankee, to boot—Andrew Stone had been fairly reasonable.

Now that Charity Winstock was managing the wedding, things began to happen. Margaret was amazed to see that her aunt had no hesitation about spending money. She hired the local seamstress, Mrs. Evans, to make the elaborate wedding gown, as well as the pale pink silk gown Margaret would wear to the engagement party. Margaret and her family sewed the bridesmaids' dresses, as well as the trousseau. Materials for all the dresses had to be purchased, as well as the accessories, and since Annie was hardly a seamstress, most of the sewing fell to Margaret and Emma. There was also the engagement party to prepare for, with all the cleaning, cooking and general sprucing up that was required. As if that weren't enough to occupy Margaret's time, there was suddenly a veritable flood of social activity.

Once Aunt Charity had put her seal of approval on the marriage, almost everyone Margaret knew came to call, eager for news about the Carlisles' astonishing alliance with the Yankee. There were several invitations to teas and parties in honor of the occasion. Margaret, always a wallflower, was amazed and appalled to find herself the center of attention. She was almost never alone anymore. Even when there wasn't a party or a formal caller, there was someone or another at their house every afternoon to help with the sewing or addressing invitations.

Margaret soon came to dread these afternoon get-togethers, even though she knew that they were necessary in order to get all the work done. And it was kind of the other women and girls to help. But she also knew that the others were driven more by curiosity and a desire to gossip than by any generous impulse. She hated their constant prying and questions, the sly sideways glances as they spoke of her fiancé. Of course, everyone wanted to know how they had met and fallen in love and what the Yankee was really like. They wanted to admire her ring, then speculate upon the wealth that would now be hers. And always, always, they wanted to talk about Andrew Stone.

Margaret was rather inept at dealing with their questions and comments. No matter what she answered, it seemed that there was some sort of trap waiting for her. If she was proud of the ring, she was flaunting her future wealth; if she was offhanded about it, she didn't appreciate her good fortune. When they offered veiled—and not-so-veiled—criticisms of her future husband, she could not retort angrily or bluntly, for she had to remain in the women's good graces for Andrew's daughter's sake. But neither could she let what they said go unchallenged; after all, she would soon be the man's wife and she was too loyal a person not to stand up for her husband.

Fortunately, Emma was usually there, and she was much more adept at fielding questions and blunting nasty comments. She would answer for Margaret in a silly way, making everyone laugh, or she would turn the question back upon the person who had asked it. She would draw attention away from Margaret and onto herself—so skillfully that most of the women didn't even notice and Margaret was left wondering whether Emma did it to help her or simply because she couldn't stand not being the center of attention.

However, one afternoon Emma was out of the house with her mother, returning calls, when, much to Margaret's dismay, the Chauncey sisters, two of the silliest young women in Huxley, chose to come over and help their "dear and good friends," Emma and Margaret. Emma had been known to socialize with the two; Huxley was too small a town not to. But she was hardly a good friend of the Chaunceys and Margaret had spoken to them but a few times.

The two sisters sewed hems in the delicate cotton nightgowns and undergarments that would go in Margaret's trousseau, and all the while they giggled and chattered. Margaret, standing on a stool with Mrs. Evans, the seamstress, crawling about her feet, pinning a hem in her new evening gown, was virtually a prisoner to their conversation. She couldn't even claim a headache and flee the room.

Camilla, the older sister, told Margaret what a wonderful catch she'd made—financially, at least. Veronica, bobbing her head eagerly, agreed, "Oh, my, yes, they say his house is enormous, and he owns more land than Mr. Murdock, even."

"He'll probably give you a huge allowance for food and clothes and such. I mean, a young bride and all. They say men in such a position are very generous."

Margaret gave them a cool stare that would have stopped anyone less obtuse than the Chaunceys. "I'm sure I don't know the details of Mr. Stone's assets."

"You should find out, then," Camilla assured her. "A woman mustn't go into these things blindly. Make sure you'll be adequately provided for. After all, you're risking your social position to marry him—and who knows what else."

"That's right." Veronica's eyes rounded with a kind of horrified glee and her voice sank to a stage whisper. "I've heard terrible things about him. About, you know, what he made his first wife do."

Margaret tried to maintain her cold, quelling look, but a chill ran through her at the words. "I don't listen to gossip about my future husband."

"Don't be silly. *Everybody* listens to gossip. Especially about someone they're going to marry. Why, then's when you need to know it the most. After all, whatever he did to his first wife, he's likely to do to you, too."

"It had to be something terrible or she wouldn't have gotten—" Veronica's voice dropped again "—divorced."

Margaret knew she ought to make them stop talking about Andrew Stone's first marriage and the subsequent divorce. It wasn't the sort of thing a wife would let someone say. But her curiosity was too much; she couldn't bring herself to cut their revelations short.

"I heard that was why she did it," Veronica went on, leaning forward confidentially. "Because of what he made her do—in bed, you know."

"Unnatural things," Camilla chimed in.

Margaret's heart began to pound harder and she felt slightly sick. "What things?"

Camilla shrugged, looking disappointed. "I don't know. Beth Ann told me about it. She said that Damaris Murdock herself had told Beth Ann's mother. But Beth Ann's mother said that it wasn't fit for young ladies' ears, so she wouldn't tell her what it was."

"It's just gossip," Margaret said faintly, struggling to keep up an air of unconcern.

"Well, it would scare me."

"Me, too. Think of marrying a man who demanded things like that of you!"

Things like what? Margaret wondered confoundedly. It wasn't the first time that one of her visitors had dropped a hint that the Yankee indulged in depraved acts.

"They say he's insatiable." There was an avid light in Camilla's eyes.

"A devil."

Margaret's stomach knotted. What if they were speaking the truth? What if he did demand horrid things of a wife? What if he were cruel and debasing? If only she knew what they were hinting at. She wasn't completely ignorant of what the marital act consisted of. After all, she'd grown up on a farm. But she knew nothing about lying in bed with a man. Such things were kept secret from unmarried girls. Married women talked about the subject in hushed tones, stopping whenever a girl was close by, so that Margaret had never heard anything except fragments of conversation that added up to almost no knowledge at all. Even the intricacies of pregnancy were a closely-guarded secret among married women.

What would be abnormal? Would he hurt her? Would it frighten her? Or would it be degrading and humiliating rather than painful? She thought of the funny breathless feeling she got when Stone had kissed her hand—part fear and part excitement—and she wondered how that fit in with the rest of it. Once she had heard one of Emma's friends say that a husband had the right to see one naked, and the thought of that was enough to make her blush right down to her toes. But surely that wasn't true. After all, whatever happened, it happened at night and beneath the covers of the bed. Everyone wore nightclothes to bed. So what was there to be seen?

But the thought of unknown things was somehow scarier than knowing. It left you wondering and with such a vague, vast dread. Margaret wished she could have asked somebody about the subject, but Emma wouldn't know any more than she did, and she couldn't imagine approaching her aunt about something like that! Aunt Charity would probably breathe fire at her niece even wondering about such things!

Margaret's worries were not alleviated by the call her fiancé made to her the next day. He was cold and remote, with none of the cordiality that he had shown the last time or two he had called. He brought his daughter, who was a quiet little thing. She shot Margaret a resentful glance when her father introduced them, then kept obstinately silent the rest of the time. Margaret sighed inwardly; the daughter was going to be difficult to deal with.

Margaret glanced at Andrew, sitting stiff and straight in his chair, about as friendly as a stone wall. She could easily imagine him as an army officer, leading his men fearlessly into battle, maintaining strict order among the troops. It was more difficult to imagine him as a husband, sitting cozily by the fire with her in the evenings or at the breakfast table. He seemed so stern, so unapproachable.

He gazed back at her, unsmiling; his fierce blue eyes were unsettling. She remembered the smile that had softened his face and wondered how rarely she would see it during their marriage. She wondered if she were condemning herself to a lifetime of fear and unhappiness. If only she knew what those things were that he would demand of her in the isolation of their bedroom!

She looked away quickly, hoping that he could not read her thoughts. She could feel the heat of embarrassment rising in her throat. Quickly she said to his daughter, "Well, Laura, how old are you?"

"Eleven," the girl replied sullenly, not looking at her.

Margaret wondered who dressed the girl. She looked so drab and plain in that brown dress, like a little sparrow. Where were the ruffles and bows and pretty pastel colors that a little girl should wear?

"Do you go to school?"

The girl shook her head and Andrew answered for her, "She has lessons at home with her governess."

"I see." So there was already a woman who looked after the child. No doubt she would resent Margaret's intrusion into their lives, too. "I look forward to meeting her," she finished lamely. What else was there to say?

A silence fell upon the room. Aunt Charity decided to fill in the gap. It took only one of her long-winded forays into her family's past before Andrew Stone stood up and took his leave of them.

Margaret bid him a formal farewell, then ran up the stairs to lie down on her bed and indulge in a good cry. She wasn't looking forward at all to her engagement party the following night. With Andrew Stone acting so cool and distant, it would be obvious to everyone that he did not love her, that they were marrying purely as a matter of mutual gain. No doubt there would be many who called her a traitor and an opportunist. People would be rude or cold toward her fiancé, and he would respond with a hard look. It would be an awful mess.

Still, the next night, when she was dressed in her new gown and Emma had pulled her hair up onto the crown of her head and secured it with combs, letting it fall down from that spot in a cascade of artful curls, Margaret couldn't help but be excited and hopeful. Emma went back to her room to dress, and Margaret stood gazing at her reflection in the mirror. She had never seen herself look so pretty. The dress was beautiful and rich—she couldn't believe Aunt Charity's generosity in providing it for her—and the pale pink shade complemented her delicate coloring. There was pink in her cheeks and her skin glowed with her excitement. Even her pale hair was pretty, she thought, in the feminine way Emma had done it. She had never realized before how much it had detracted from her appearance to have her hair skinned back tightly from her face and knotted into a bun.

Perhaps Andrew Stone would not be as cool tonight. Perhaps he would look at her and see something better than a logical person to marry. Maybe he would dance with her and whisper something sweet in her ear.

Margaret closed her eyes for a moment, swaying gently.

Annie burst into the room, disturbing her reverie. "Maggie, are you—" She stopped short and emitted a most unladylike whistle of amazement. "Whooee! Aren't you something! You're beautiful!"

Margaret chuckled, her cheeks turning pinker with pleasure. "I wouldn't go that far." She swung back to the mirror. "But I do look better, don't I?"

"You look grand! Emma'll be a wallflower next to you."

Margaret laughed at the absurdity of Annie's statement. Emma would never be a wallflower. But it was nice to hear that she was pretty, even if the statement did come from her little sister.

"I bet the Yankee's eyes'll pop when he sees you," Annie went on. "He's going to realize what a lucky man he is."

"Thank you." Margaret's cheeks were pink with gratification. "But I doubt that Colonel Stone will be quite that
enthusiastic."

"Then it's up to you to make him be," said a voice from
the doorway, and both girls looked over to see Emma
standing there. She was lovely, as always, in a pale blue
gown, but for once Margaret didn't feel bleached out by
comparison to her. Emma was pretty, but tonight so was
she.

Margaret smiled gaily, unaware of how much her smile
added to her beauty. As much as her drab dresses and plain
hairstyles, it had been her quiet, subdued personality that
had created her mousiness. Having stood up to—even won
out over—her aunt had greatly increased her confidence,
which in turn had opened the doorway to some of the spirit
she had possessed as a child. Even if she was a little
frightened of her future husband, she was also excited at
the prospect of getting married and having a home, a life,
of her own.

Emma swept into the room and walked around Margaret, inspecting her appearance. She straightened a ruffle in
Margaret's skirt and pulled a curl into place, then stepped
back and smiled. "You look perfect. Now, if all this still
doesn't enchant that solemn old Yankee, you'll just have
to use a little charm." She raised her fan and snapped it
open to flutter it under her eyes while she cast a flirtatious
glance at Margaret.

Margaret tried to follow her example, but she couldn't
capture the look. Her gaze was too direct, too honest. She
felt foolish doing it.

"No, that will never do," Emma said. "I know. Don't
try to flirt, just look at him with those big eyes, all solemn
and soulful, as if he were the only man in the world. I'm

positive you can do that. And smile at him. That smile of yours could melt hearts."

"My smile?" Margaret chuckled. "Don't be silly."

"Don't underestimate your resources, my girl. What you have is powerful. Sweet, loving femininity—it may not hit him like lightning, but it can grow up around him like ivy on a tree, and before he knows it, he's rooted to the spot."

"I don't think Mr. Stone is that easily fooled."

Emma shrugged. "It may take some effort. Anyway, where you're concerned, it's not artifice. You *are* sweet, loving and feminine. All he has to do is open his eyes and see it." She grinned. "Even a Yankee should be able to do that."

"You have to stop speaking of him that way."

"Why?" Annie asked. "That's what he is."

"Well, a person may be an idiot, too, but that doesn't mean it's polite to call him one. The way we all say *Yankee*, it's a—a pejorative word."

"My, my, my, such language," Emma drawled. Her eyes danced teasingly. "Well, all right, if you're so adamant on the subject, we shall stop referring to him as a you-know-what."

"Thank you." Margaret grinned. She really was getting bold now; she couldn't ever remember telling Emma what to do. She drew a breath and let it out slowly. "I suppose we ought to go downstairs now."

Emma shook her head vigorously. "Oh, no! The—I mean, Mr. Stone—hasn't arrived yet. You have to wait."

"But why?" Margaret looked puzzled.

Emma grimaced. "Because, silly...you want him to first see you sweeping down the staircase. That way he gets the full effect and you get his full attention."

"Oh, Cousin Emma...what does it matter? He's engaged to me, not courting me."

"I keep telling you, you're the one who has to turn it into a courtship. Believe me, you'll understand the difference when you see his face as you're walking down those stairs toward him. Be sure and keep your head up. Look at him, not down at your feet."

"What am I supposed to do until he comes, just hide up here and twiddle my thumbs?"

"Of course. You can't sit down or you'll wrinkle your dress." Emma crooked her finger and motioned for Annie and Margaret to follow her out into the hall. On tiptoe, they crept down the hall to the top of the staircase, standing where they could not be seen, but within earshot of the conversation in the entryway beneath them. Margaret gripped her fan tightly; her palms were beginning to sweat and dampen her dainty lace evening gloves.

Finally there was a knock at the door, and a maid, hired for the evening from Mrs. Cherry down the street, opened it. There was the rumble of a man's voice. Margaret and Emma glanced at each other significantly. Emma nodded, and Margaret moved to the top of the stairs. Below them they heard Aunt Charity greeting Mr. Stone. Emma motioned to Margaret, and she started down the stairs.

Chapter Five

Margaret walked slowly down the staircase, one hand on the rail, careful to keep her head up as Emma had commanded. She turned the corner of the landing.

Andrew stood at the foot of the stairs, talking with her aunt. He was more handsome than she had ever seen him. His suit was black, as always, but this one was made of silk, and the white shirt beneath it had a row of ruffles down the front and at the cuff. At the sound of her footsteps, he raised his head and she met the full force of his blue eyes. She saw surprise, then admiration chase across his features before he shut them down again. Even then, there was a different look in his eyes, something hot and fierce that hadn't been there before.

Seeing Margaret hit Andrew Stone like a blow to the gut. She had been prettier every time he saw her, but tonight! Her skin was creamy white, tinted with pink at the cheeks, as delicate and lovely as fine porcelain. She seemed to glow from within, and her fine, expressive eyes shone. Her hair shimmered. The rich satin dress cinched in her tiny waist, and above the low-cut neckline rose the swelling tops of her breasts, full and soft. Andrew's hands ached to cup them. He wanted to bury his mouth in the succulent flesh. He wanted to taste her and smell her and touch her. He wondered how he was going to wait three more weeks to have her in his bed.

His reaction irritated him. Damn it! He'd thought that he'd gotten past being led around by his— Andrew drew a deep breath. He had gotten past it. Maybe he felt desire for Margaret, but he wouldn't let it rule him. He would rule it instead. He wasn't about to be a fish wiggling on the end of her hook. He had learned the first time. He had worshiped a woman once, been ready to do anything for her, give her anything. He had been so hot to possess Damaris that he hadn't been able to think straight, hadn't seen the flaws in her character, hadn't even realized that she didn't love him in return. She had sliced him to ribbons.

He had learned his lesson well. No other woman would ever control him like that, no matter how pretty or enticing she might be. He was armed against that sort of maneuvering, and he would make sure that Margaret learned that quickly. He wouldn't stand for any of her feminine tricks.

Margaret, having seen the flash of desire in her fiancé's face, was surprised to see his features harden into a scowl. By the time she reached the bottom of the stairs, he was staring at her as coldly as if she were an enemy. She almost took a step back from the flat, unfriendly glare.

He nodded and took her hand in greeting. "Miss Carlisle."

"Mr. Stone." Margaret turned to her aunt. "Aunt Charity."

Aunt Charity looked her over and nodded shortly. "You look quite suitable, Margaret."

"Thank you."

She had hoped for a compliment from Andrew, some sign that he found her attractive, but he said nothing. The excitement began to drain out of her. Perhaps she had only been fooling herself when she thought she looked prettier. Maybe she had imagined that first startled look of admiration on Andrew's face.

Aunt Charity launched into a long lecture on the mechanics of receiving their guests, on what Margaret should do and say and how she should act. Margaret only half listened, having heard it many times before. She clasped her hands in front of her and gazed down at the floor, letting her mind wander. Unfortunately, at the moment she couldn't find any pleasant thoughts to wander to.

The older woman's monologue irritated Andrew even more. Margaret, so bright and lovely as she came down the stairs, was obviously wilting under the weight of her aunt's words, and he felt a cold, fierce anger at seeing her droop. He cut harshly into the woman's speech. "Mrs. Winstock, really, I believe that is enough. Miss Carlisle is an adult and well aware of the manner in which she should act. I see no reason for you to lecture her as if she were a child."

Charity looked at him, her mouth thinning. "She is my niece and ward, sir, and I have the responsibility for rearing her correctly. It is a reflection on my family's name if she—"

"She is about to become *my* wife. That means that henceforth you will treat her with respect. She is no longer a Carlisle, but a Stone."

Margaret felt a surge of gratitude at Andrew's defense of her. Perhaps he did have some feeling for her, after all. She sneaked a glance at his face. It was as hard and set as before. He wasn't defending her, she realized in disappointment. It was only his name that he cared about; now she belonged to him and would carry his name, and he would not allow someone else to mistreat whoever carried his name. Margaret swallowed against the lump suddenly in her throat.

It was silly, she knew. What did it matter why he defended her? What was important was that she wouldn't have to fear anyone—except him, of course.

But, somehow, that wasn't satisfying.

The guests began to arrive, and Emma, Annie and Zach came down to join the party. Margaret smiled at people and shook hands until her arms and her cheeks ached. Her throat grew dry and raspy, and she longed for a cup of the cool punch that the guests were drinking, but she could not leave the receiving line. Finally, after several minutes had passed without a new arrival, Aunt Charity decided that they could break their line and join the party.

Margaret started toward the punch bowl, but along the way she was intercepted by her Aunt Ida, who grasped her arm with the strength of an eagle's talons and loudly demanded to know why Margaret had seen fit to marry a Yankee. Blushing, Margaret tried to divert their aunt to another subject, but there was no distracting her.

"Why, I wouldn't have let that fellow in my parlor," Aunt Ida declaimed, shaking an accusatory finger in Margaret's face.

"Aunt Ida, please, couldn't we discuss this another time?"

"Eh?" The old woman cupped her hand around her ear.

"I said, could we talk about this another time?"

"Why?" Ida glanced around the room. "It's no secret you're marrying him."

Margaret quailed inside at the several interested stares that were now turned in their direction. "No, of course not." She had to talk loudly or the old lady would make her repeat it. "But it's a private matter, a family matter."

"Whole town knows about it. Don't see how it can be private. Now, why're you marrying a traitor?"

"Aunt Ida, he's hardly a traitor. I mean, he's not even from Texas. He fought for *his* country."

"Yeah, and against yours. Doesn't that mean anything to you, young lady?"

"Aunt Ida, please..."

"What?" Aunt Ida banged the tip of her cane against the floor in irritation. "What'd you say? Speak up!"

A hand touched Margaret on the arm and she glanced up. She was surprised to see that it was Andrew Stone. Her cheeks flamed with embarrassment. She didn't know what to say.

He, on the other hand, appeared completely unperturbed. He held out a small crystal punch glass to Margaret. "I brought you a drink, my dear."

"Thank you." Margaret seized the cup gratefully and took a sip. "It's very kind of you."

"I thought you must be thirsty."

Margaret nodded and drank again. Her gaze crept over to her old aunt, who was standing there glaring at Andrew Stone. She wanted to sink into the floor with humiliation. Why did Aunt Ida have to choose tonight to make a scene?

Andrew followed her gaze to the old woman and he returned Aunt Ida's glare with cool deliberation. "If you will excuse us..." He sketched a bow and, placing Margaret's hand on his arm, led her away from Aunt Ida.

Margaret sagged with relief and her fingers dug into his arm, holding on. He glanced at her. "Are you all right?"

"Yes. Of course. I would like to sit down, however, if that's possible." She glanced around a little hopelessly. Her aunt's house was not a large one, and tonight it was crammed with people. The furniture in the adjoining sit-

ting and dining rooms had been cleared out and the doors
between the rooms opened so that people could dance.
Guests stood at the edges of the two rooms, in the entryway and in the parlor across the hall. There were chairs in
the parlor, but all of them were taken at the moment. Andrew left for a moment, then returned with one of the
dining room chairs, which had been stuck away in the
kitchen, and set it down for her.

"Thank you," Margaret murmured and sat down, sip-
ping her punch. Her thirst was quenched now and she was
off her aching feet. But she still felt acutely uncomfortable. It was awkward to try to converse with Andrew, what
with him standing and her sitting, and, besides, she could
think of nothing to say. She cringed inside at the thought
of what he had heard her aunt say.

She didn't notice that a number of appreciative glances
were being sent her way by several young men standing in
the hallway. But Andrew Stone did. He wasn't surprised
when one of the men came over and asked Margaret for a
dance. She looked up at him, astonished, and stammered
out that she could not. The second time it occurred, she
was not quite as amazed and she managed a more digni-
fied refusal.

Stone glanced down at her. He didn't like the thought of
her dancing with any of the men. He didn't even like them
looking at her. Still, it was unfair to expect a young girl to
stay off the dance floor. He leaned down. "Are you sure
you wouldn't like to dance?"

Margaret smiled, her eyes lighting up. "If you'd like to."

For an instant an intense, despairing desire to take
Margaret in his arms and dance with her pierced Andrew.
He thought of his hand on her waist, her body only inches
from his, her face smiling up at him. He had come to terms
with his damaged leg over the years; he hardly noticed it

anymore. He no longer had to use a cane except on the few occasions when a blue norther blew in and set up an ache in his knee. It kept him from doing very little that other men could. But he could no longer move gracefully.

He shook his head regretfully. "No, I didn't mean with me." He glanced down at his leg. "I'm afraid I an unable to oblige you."

Margaret's eyes widened as she realized her mistake. She had seen the regret in his eyes and knew that she must have hurt him with her thoughtless words. "Oh, I'm so sorry. I didn't mean—that is, I didn't think . . ." She trailed off miserably.

He shook his head, dismissing it. "It's all right. It doesn't matter. But you don't have to be chained to your chair simply because I can no longer do a Virginia Reel. Why don't you dance the next time someone asks you?"

"No, I don't mind. Truly."

"There's nothing improper about it and I shan't be angry. You have my blessing."

She glanced across the hall at the dancers, then shook her head. "That's all right. It's not something I do much, anyway."

He smiled. "I find that hard to believe."

She looked at him, puzzled, then her face cleared. "Oh. You mean because Jody Means and Whit Morrell asked me to dance? That's just because I'm the honoree of the party. You know. Because it's for us and our engagement. Usually I dance very little."

"I can't believe that it's because of lack of invitations. Texas men aren't that stupid."

Had that been a compliment? Margaret wondered. There was no sign of a smile on his face. Yet what else could he have meant except that many men ought to be interested in dancing with her?

She didn't know what to reply, so she murmured, "I really don't care to dance, thank you."

But not long after that, Zach came over to talk to her, predictably bored with the party, and Margaret rose to dance with him. There couldn't be anything wrong with dancing with one's brother, could there? She enjoyed dancing with Zach, freed from the awkwardness she usually felt dancing with a strange man. For years, Zach had been roped into being their dance partner when Emma and Margaret and even Annie wanted to learn to dance, and as a consequence he had turned into an excellent dancer. With all the times they had practiced, they danced together well, executing complicated turns with precision.

To Andrew Stone, watching them, it seemed as though they were the epitome of youth, grace and carefree happiness. Somehow the picture made him hurt inside, as though a rough hand had squeezed his vitals. He could remember dancing with Damaris; he had gazed down at her, enthralled with her beauty, head-over-heels in love, pulsing with a desire that was barely held in check. It had shaken him to the core to hold her in his arms, so close and yet unable to crush her to him and kiss her as he wanted. He had seethed with frustrated desire, so hungry to wed and bed her that he was blind to anything else. There had been those who had tried to warn him, but he hadn't listened. Thank God he was no longer that foolish. And yet—there was a bittersweet ache in him at having lost that capacity to trust and be happy.

Sternly he pushed unbidden thoughts away. Any ability he had to love a woman had died long ago. It was as much use dreaming of such foolishness as it was to wish he had full use of his leg again.

It was irritating enough that he felt so much desire for Margaret; he hadn't expected his eyes to be drawn to her wherever she went or to have a fire start burning low in his belly when he looked at her. But desire was something he could control; it wasn't like love, which seized a man and tore out his insides until there was nothing left but a shell.

When Margaret and Zach finished dancing, another man asked her, and, after an uncertain glance toward Andrew, Margaret accepted. Andrew watched them take the floor, watched the other man draw her into his arms and, even though he had told Margaret that he didn't mind, a dark anger surged through him. He was amazed to find that he was still capable of jealousy. He didn't like the feeling and he liked even less the idea that she was able to inspire it. His eyes narrowed as he watched the couple dance. They looked more suited to each other, certainly, than he and Margaret did. The man was about her age; he was no thirty-six-year-old with touches of gray in his hair and lines of experience on his face. No doubt he was a local boy, the kind she'd grown up with. And when Margaret smiled at the man shyly, he returned it with open admiration. No doubt it was this kind of man, one of her own, whom she should be marrying.

Andrew realized that he was clenching his jaw and he forced himself to relax. It didn't matter that this girl might be better off with another man. The fact was that she was his; she had agreed to be his wife, and he could offer her the security and wealth that many men couldn't. He knew that in the long run, such things were more important than a nice face or a pleasant personality. Margaret was no different from other women. She might smile at a man or flirt with him, but it was Andrew's money and position that had caused her to say yes to his proposal.

On the dance floor, Margaret was in truth enjoying the dance far less than her fiancé imagined her to be. She wasn't sure whether she should have agreed to dance with someone other than her fiancé or a family member. She kept thinking about Andrew Stone and wondering what he was thinking. She wished that it was he who guided her through the waltz, not Billy Ray Campbell, whom she remembered best for pulling her pigtails in church when she was ten years old. At first, as they danced, they had smiled and exchanged a few pleasantries, but then Billy Ray had asked her why she was marrying the Yankee. She was beginning to get tired of the question. She tried to answer civilly, but it was difficult and she was glad when the dance was over.

She slipped away from her partner and started across the hallway toward Andrew, but Mrs. Lipscomb reached out and stopped her, drawing her into a conversation with her and her daughter, Milly.

"I think it's a shame," Mrs. Lipscomb told her dolefully. "I declare, it is, when a sweet young girl like you has to accept a marriage proposal from a man like that."

Margaret clasped her hands tightly in front of her and tried to keep a pleasant smile on her lips. "I wasn't forced to accept his proposal, ma'am."

"Of course not. I wouldn't suggest such a thing about you. What I meant was that circumstances should be such that you would have little choice but to marry him. If it weren't for the War and all we lost..." She shook her head sadly.

Margaret pressed her lips together to keep from blurting out a rude response. She would have liked to have told the woman that her marriage had nothing to do with circumstances, but, of course, that was untrue. And telling her to mind her own business would have been satisfying but not socially acceptable. "Indeed, ma'am," she began sweetly, "we did all lose a lot in the War. I lost that which was most dear to me when our father was killed. However, I can assure you that my marriage was nothing that was forced upon me or into which I enter reluctantly." *Well,* she thought, *that sounded prissy enough.*

"Of course, dear, I understand that you would never breathe a word of complaint. You are not the sort to begrudge your lot in life. But when I think of your poor dear mother—" she sniffed and sighed "—well, I guess it's better that she's gone, so she doesn't have to see you marrying a Yankee."

Margaret was flooded with anger. Her eyes flashed, and she said, "Indeed, ma'am, I could never be glad that my mother is dead, and I would give a great deal if she were able to be here and see me marry. My mother never had a mean bone in her body and she would have been happy that I was marrying a good man, the man I *wanted* to marry. She wasn't one to hold grudges or spites, and neither was my father. Daddy always judged a man by what he was, not where he came from. I think they would both have been very proud of me. Now, if you'll excuse me, I'd like to rejoin my fiancé."

Margaret stalked away from the woman toward Andrew, scowling. It was all she could do to hold on to even a shred of her patience and even temper.

Stone, seeing Margaret's stormy face, thought only that she hated to return to him after dancing with the other man. The thought didn't improve his temper, though he, too, tamped down his feelings. "I hope you enjoyed your dance."

"Yes," she replied shortly. She had to get out of here and take a breath or two, get rid of the pent-up irritation and anger clanging around inside her. "If you will excuse me, I'm afraid I'm feeling a trifle—indisposed. I think I will step outside for just a moment."

The first thought that flashed across Andrew's mind was that she was stealing away to meet her dance partner. He had no reason to think that, but his suspicion was too fast and innate for reason to hold any sway against it. "Certainly. I wouldn't mind taking a turn around the garden myself."

Margaret was surprised. She hadn't expected him to accompany her. How was she to talk herself into calmness with him right there beside her?

Stone saw the surprise and the faint look of dismay before she collected herself. He didn't like it.

He held out his arm and she took it, directing him through the hall and kitchen and out the rear door into the yard. "Aunt Charity would be horrified to learn that I'd taken you through the kitchen," she told him as he closed the door behind them and followed her down the steps into the yard. She could imagine her aunt and what she would say, and the humor of the situation pierced even her irritation and anger.

"Why?"

"Because it's an ordinary, everyday room. You know, mundane and practical."

"Well, I'm mundane and practical, too, so I should think it wouldn't matter."

Margaret smiled a little. "Yes, but you're a stranger. One shows only her best side to someone who doesn't know."

"It would seem wiser to show your best side to people you *do* know." They strolled along a path through the back yard.

"But that would be too difficult. One can't keep up a pretense all the time."

"I don't know. Some people are quite good at it."

"I'm afraid I've never been very good at dissembling."

Margaret was looking down at the uneven path and so did not see the cynical doubt that crossed Stone's face at her words. Obviously she didn't know that he was aware of her subterfuge with his money, pretending she wouldn't take it, then allowing her aunt to take it. "I never met a woman yet who wasn't raised on it."

She glanced up, surprised by the bitterness of his tone in a conversation that she had assumed were merely light chatter. There was a twist to his mouth that told her that he was not merely joking about the deceptive qualities of women, as man so often—and so irritatingly—did. "You really mean that, don't you?"

"What? That women are trained from childhood up to deceive? Yes, I meant it. Why? Do you expect all men to remain so fooled by you that they never realize what you're doing?"

Margaret barely kept her mouth from dropping open in astonishment. Her irritation flared to life again. "No. I'm simply surprised that you are so foolish. I had taken you for a brighter man than that."

Now it was Andrew's turn to look amazed. Obviously he had not expected her to ever answer back to him, Margaret thought. She set her jaw. She might be mousy and plain and less than courageous, but she wasn't about to just stand there and let him slander her sex. She braced herself for his explosion.

But he said only, "Indeed?" and gave her a long, assessing look. He would never have admitted it, but he was far less interested in their argument than in the way her eyes sparkled in anger and her cheeks glowed. All he could really think about was how much he wanted to take her in his arms, how much he wanted to kiss her.

"Yes, indeed," Margaret went on boldly when he said no more. "You are calling all women liars! Cheats! That includes me, your daughter, your mother—do you think that we are all deceivers? I can't imagine why you would even want to marry if that is your opinion of women!''

Stone's jaw hardened and he looked away from her. ''If a man realizes the subterfuge, then he can keep from being deceived.''

''And that is your idea of marriage?'' Margaret stared at him, appalled. ''That I will try to trick you, to lie to you and you will always be suspicious of me? Do you think that that is a way anyone can live?''

''No. I don't expect our marriage to be that way. I don't intend for it to be. That is why I am marrying you, with clear-cut benefits on each side and no emotion to muddy the waters. That is why I have made it clear from the start that I will not tolerate lies or unfaithfulness from you. I am giving you wealth, servants and a house to run however you see fit. I am giving your brother and sister a future. In return you will carry out your wifely duties and be a mother to my child. And you will *not* try to control me.''

''That's it? We live in the same house like two business partners? Or a servant and employer? You don't want any ties to develop between us? No affection or fondness?''

His head snapped around and he gazed straight into her face, his eyes savagely bright. His words came out short and hard, as if hurled from him. ''No! There will be no affection. I don't believe in love, so don't bother trying to scheme your way into my heart.''

Margaret paled. She felt as if she had been punched in the stomach. ''Oh. I see. I hadn't realized…'' She walked away from him and sank down onto one of the stone benches placed along the walkway.

Stone followed her and stood looming over her. ''Is that more than you had bargained for? Do you want to call it off?''

"I—I don't know." She wasn't sure if she could bear such a lonely, cold life. She hadn't expected a mad, passionate love. But she had at least thought that over the years some tenderness and caring would grow between her and her husband. It seemed too painful to live otherwise. "I had thought," she said softly, looking down at her hands, "that we would have more of a real marriage than that. I had thought we would ... have children, and ..."

His eyebrows rose and he took her chin in his hand, tilting her face upward. "Oh, don't worry about that." His voice was low and husky, almost a whisper. "We will have children."

Pink tinged her cheeks. "But you said—"

"I did not mean that I would not bed you," he replied crudely, and her blush deepened. "But that is desire, not love."

Margaret was embarrassed to talk of such a forbidden subject, but her curiosity was even greater. "You mean, this—this 'bedding' is done even though you feel no caring?"

His hand slid up her jaw, his fingers fanning out over her cheek in a soft caress. "A man who spends his nights pleasantly is more content." His eyes gazed straight into hers. His thumb slid across her lips. "Happier. More tender. But that is an entirely different thing from being blind with love." His thumb retraced its path. His eyes dropped to her mouth, watching the slow movement of his thumb across the soft, rosy flesh. "Will that make our arrangement acceptable to you? If I give you children?"

Margaret could scarcely breathe, let alone speak. His voice, his eyes, his touch filled her with warm, shivery sensations that were utterly foreign to her. Her heart was racing and her skin was suddenly, strangely hot. She was confused, scared, eager. "I—I don't know. I'm not sure."

His hands went to her arms and he lifted her to her feet. "You're trembling," he whispered wonderingly. Her virginal uncertainty sent desire stabbing through him. He bent closer, his lips only inches from hers. "It will be a pleasure to give you children."

Margaret could feel his breath against her mouth. She wanted him to kiss her again, as he had the other day. Every nerve in her body was alive and sizzling.

His hand slid from her jaw onto her throat and went slowly downward. His callused fingers brushed across her soft skin. Margaret's breath came faster in her throat and her heart was pumping so wildly she thought it might explode. Unconsciously, she leaned her head back, arching her throat against his hand. Her artless response nearly drove him wild. It was all he could do not to dig his fingers into her and kiss her bruisingly.

He bent and kissed her upper lip softly, then her lower. He could feel the breath rushing through her opened lips. He covered her lips, taking her breath into his mouth. Slowly his lips rocked on hers, pressing her lips farther apart. His hand slipped down her throat and over her chest, bared by the low neckline. His fingers brushed the swell of her breast, supremely soft and pillowy. Her flesh trembled beneath his touch. He curved his hand around her breast, encompassing it. He ached to yank down the top of her dress and expose the luscious orb, to take its weight in his palm.

The touch of his hand on her breast shocked Margaret; she had never even imagined a man doing that to her. But it also sent a spear of white-hot excitement shooting down through her abdomen. Andrew's mouth was intoxicating, thrilling. Her hands went up instinctively to his shoulders, but she didn't know quite what to do with them. They curled timidly against the fabric of his coat. Even that slight provocation seemed to enflame him. His lips dug into hers as if to crush them, and his tongue filled her mouth.

Margaret drew in her breath at this invasion, but his arms went around her, pressing her tightly into his body, and one hand clasped her neck, holding her captive to his predatory mouth. His breath was rasping and harsh in her ears. She could smell him and taste him—*feel* him all through her. Her loins melted like wax, and she made an odd little noise in her throat.

She had thought Andrew could kiss her no more deeply or fully, but then he did, groaning in a way that had nothing to do with pain. Margaret clutched his coat and pressed upward into his body, kissing him back unreservedly. Andrew turned his head to slant their lips a different way, and his hands slid down her back to her hips. The stiff wire construction of her bustle thwarted him; he wanted to rip it off. He wanted to rip everything off her body.

Margaret felt something stiff pushing against her abdomen through her clothes, and she knew that this had something to do with his wanting her, with what happened in bed between a man and a wife. She pressed her hips forward and felt the swelling response.

Andrew groaned and jerked away from her. He straightened his arms out, holding her away from him. "No." His voice was hoarse and almost unintelligible. "No. We can't—I mustn't."

Margaret opened her eyes and gazed at him. Her eyes were bright, velvety and rounded with awe. "Oh . . ." she breathed. She could do nothing but look at him, aching and unsatisfied, not even knowing what she wanted or what he had done to her. She only knew that her entire body was suddenly strange to her, a wild and fiery thing that wanted to rub against Andrew and feel his hands on her. She wished he would kiss her forever. Her lips felt bruised and heavy and she wet them tentatively.

That one gesture almost did him in. It took every ounce of control he possessed not to pull Margaret back into his arms and begin kissing her all over again. But he knew that this time he would not, could not, stop. And he must not disgrace them both by tumbling on the grass with her like a randy youth with a willing maidservant. He sucked in his breath and turned away. "Perhaps you had better go back to the house."

Margaret felt strange and confused; something ached in her, unfulfilled. Andrew had turned away from her. Why? Was he angry with her? She wished she could see his face. "I—I'm sorry. Have I done something wrong? Have I displeased you?"

His chuckle was harsh and raw. "No. No, far from it." He turned and looked at her. His face was flushed, his chest rising and falling rapidly, and his eyes glittered in a way that sent heat all through her. "You please me...a great deal."

Margaret broke into a smile. "I'm glad."

His teeth dug into his lower lip until they almost drew blood. "Please. Go inside."

"All right." A shadow touched her eyes, but she obeyed him, turning and starting back up the path. She paused and looked back. "But what about you?"

"I will stay here a moment to...how should I say it? To regain my calm. I will join you later."

Margaret nodded. She thought that there was a good deal of her calm that needed to be reclaimed, as well. She would have liked to know how one did that, but she suspected that her question would irritate him. She didn't understand Andrew Stone at all. One moment he was icy and distant, the next he was kissing her ardently.

She turned away and walked back to the house. She slipped in the back door. There was no one in the kitchen, and she tiptoed over to the washstand to peek in the mirror, wondering if what had happened in the yard was written all over her face. Not a hair was out of place; there were no marks on her, only a rosy softness to her lips. No visible sign, and yet . . . her face glowed in a way she had never seen before and her eyes were sparkling and alive. Her fingers crept up and touched her lips. She closed her eyes, tasting his crushing mouth, and that red-hot sensation coiled in her abdomen again.

The Chauncey sisters had called him depraved. Surely what he had just done to her was not what they were talking about. It had felt too wonderful, too exciting. Or maybe she was depraved, too. Margaret giggled and had to clamp her hand over her mouth. She felt so giddy and strange she didn't know how she could go back in and talk to anyone normally.

Maybe what they had done would eventually lead to the depravity, the awful and painful things the Yankee required of a wife. What were they? It must be that he would change into that cold, angry person who didn't believe in love. How could he not believe in love and kiss her the way he had? When his lips had dug into her, she had thought she would simply melt and slide all down him. Her only thought—if a vague, pulsing yearning could even be called thought—had been to please him, to hear him groan again, to feel his breath hot and panting on her skin.

Margaret put her hands up to her cheeks to cool the rush of heat that her thoughts had brought there. She wondered if she was going mad. The man she was going to marry scared her; she feared his anger; she feared the things that were rumored about him and what he had done. Yet at the same time, her blood was hot and racing and she was so eager to feel his kisses again that she could hardly wait to marry him.

The days went by with maddening slowness. Margaret spent them in continual debate with herself. One moment she was cold and shaky, dreading her new life, and the next, her stomach was knotted with eagerness. Her fiancé's visits didn't help. Most of the time Andrew was rigidly polite and distant, but every now and then, she would turn or raise her head suddenly and she would catch a look in his eyes that burned right through her. Then she would know that he still wanted her, that he was just waiting for the day when he would have the full right to put his hands on her, to take his pleasure.

Only four days before the wedding, Margaret went to a tea in her honor at the home of Agatha Conners. She was tired of the parties; even the lure of wearing her new, attractive dresses was wearing off. She dreaded the afternoon of stifling boredom. However, as soon as she stepped inside the house, she caught several sideways glances from the other women and she sensed the general air of anticipation. She looked at her cousin. There was a small frown on Emma's face, and Margaret knew that she sensed the change in the atmosphere, too. Then someone stepped aside, and another woman shifted, and, as if a curtain had parted, across the room Margaret saw Damaris Murdock.

For an instant her heart stopped, then began to pound furiously. She heard the hiss of Emma's indrawn breath. "That witch, Agatha Connors," Emma commented beneath her breath. "I should have known she'd do something underhanded like this. She's hated my family ever since her daughter lost that silly Richmond boy to me four years ago."

"What'll I do?"

Emma smiled at her with utter calm, even though her eyes were blazing. "Don't let on. That's the most important thing. Ignoring her will entirely ruin Agatha's plans. Just talk to me and smile."

Ignore Damaris Murdock? Her future husband's first wife? The most beautiful woman in three counties—probably in all Texas? It was like saying to ignore the wind.

Margaret went through the motions, trying to follow her cousin's advice. She smiled and she talked to everyone she met, and she didn't again look toward Damaris. Afterward, however, she had no idea what she or anyone else had said, and finally she gave in to the urge to sneak little glances at Mrs. Murdock. She had seen Damaris before, of course, at a party or in town, but in the past Margaret had never had such an acute interest in her.

Damaris was older than Margaret by several years, closer to Andrew Stone's age, but her beauty had not been diminished by the passage of years. Her hair was a rich auburn, and her eyes were a blue so deep, it was almost purple. Her complexion was milk white, soft and translucent. Even Emma looked drab compared to her striking beauty. Margaret's stomach knotted. How could a man who had once been married to a woman like that have any interest in herself? He was bound to compare her to Damaris, and she was bound to come up short. No wonder Andrew said he could have only a loveless marriage. He was surely still in love with Damaris.

Margaret wanted desperately to get away by herself and indulge in a bout of tears, but she had to struggle through the social amenities for the next two hours. The party, after all, was in her honor, even if the hostess had arranged it so that she would hate it. With Emma's help, she managed to avoid coming close to Damaris until finally, just as people were beginning to leave, Margaret found herself standing alone by a window and turned to see Damaris approaching her. Emma was nowhere around to rescue her, nor was there anyone else to engage in quick conversation.

She just stood, watching sickly as the woman approached, noting the generous curve of Damaris's breasts and the subtle sway of her hips. Damaris stopped in front of Margaret. "Miss Carlisle, I am so sorry if I have spoiled your afternoon." Her voice was soft, like velvet, and sweet.

Margaret shook her head, wishing she could somehow extricate herself from this. She couldn't bear looking at this woman, all the while thinking how Andrew Stone must have kissed and caressed her, how he must have whispered low, heated words of love to her—and her alone.

"It was wrong of me to nag dear Agatha into inviting me." Damaris smiled a little. "Now she will suffer Mrs. Winstock's wrath for years to come. But I wanted very much to meet you. I felt it was . . . my duty."

Margaret looked at her huge pansy eyes and her sweet mouth. She was beautiful in such a rare and perfect way, like a marvelous work of nature, that she seemed almost unreal.

"I know you think I'm terribly rude . . ."

"Oh, no," Margaret found herself reassuring her quickly. There was no other way to respond to this woman. Margaret wanted to dislike her, to find some flaw in her, but she was too lovely.

Damaris smiled kindly. "You are a sweet girl to say so. That is exactly why I knew I must talk to you. Warn you."

"Warn me?"

"Yes. About . . ." A shadow touched her perfect face. "Andrew. Andrew Stone."

Margaret's chest tightened. She wanted to run; she didn't want to hear this. Yet she stood rooted to the floor, unable to move.

"I'm sure you know that I was once married to him." Her voice dropped, and Damaris looked down and to the side. "I never speak of it—it is my shame." Her head came back up and she fixed her eyes earnestly on Margaret. "But when I heard that he had caught you in his snare, I knew I could not keep silent. I had to tell you." She laid her hand entreatingly on Margaret's arm. "You must not marry him. You are so young and innocent, just as I was. I can't bear to see that innocence soiled, then cast aside. He will use you, hurt you." Tears swam in her eyes. "As he did me. He is a cruel man, a man of huge and—and disgusting appetites."

Margaret swallowed. Her legs felt precariously shaky all of a sudden. "But what..."

"I cannot speak of it." Her hand came up to dab at her eyes with a dainty handkerchief. "No decent woman could. It is so unfair that a sweet young girl like you should have to suffer his indignities, his cruelties."

But what did he do? Margaret's mind screamed the question, though she did not dare to ask it. It was something too terrible to speak of, too horrible to contemplate. What happened after those dizzying, delicious kisses that turned it into something so awful?

"I am promised," Margaret protested weakly. "Our wedding is only days away."

Damaris turned soulful eyes upon her. "Once he almost killed me." One hand went unconsciously to her graceful white throat, and Margaret could imagine Andrew's long, sinewed hands around that throat, squeezing. She felt cold inside. "My back still bears the scars of other times, but none of them are as deep and lasting as the scars on my pride, my soul." Her eyes blazed as she leaned closer to Margaret. "He will humiliate you," she whispered. "He delights in it. He will force you to do unspeakable things, and then he will laugh when you cry."

"No. No. I can't believe it."

"You must." The huge, violet-colored eyes turned implacable. "For your own sake, you must. Do you think I would have come here and told you this otherwise? Exposed myself to the ridicule? To the shame of telling you? Don't you think I would far rather leave it buried in the past?"

It was a forceful argument, and so was her posture, her gestures, every inch of her being. To argue against it, Margaret had only a stubborn belief inside her that Andrew Stone could *not* be that kind of man. He could not kiss her and touch her like that, and then hurt her. Oh, please, he could not.

"I can't believe you. He isn't like that."

"You little fool!" Damaris's voice was laced with scorn. "He's deceived you, too. Do you think I don't know what he's like? What he does?"

"He wouldn't hurt me." Margaret's face took on what Aunt Charity called her mulish look.

"Oh, he will. Believe me, he will." Damaris clenched her hands around the fan she carried until suddenly it broke, startling them both. Margaret glanced at the pieces of the fan, then back up at Damaris. She was taken aback by the intensity of her gaze. "I only wish I had been able to save you from your own folly."

Damaris whirled and walked away. Margaret stood looking after her, wondering if she was, indeed, a fool.

Chapter Six

Margaret could not stop thinking about what Damaris Murdock had told her. She had frightening dreams from which she awoke sweating, her heart pounding, but she was unable to remember what she had dreamed.

She could not bring herself to accept Damaris's story. It was possible that she had lied. After all, Damaris had divorced Andrew Stone; she must have very bad feelings toward him. Besides, she was married to Tom Murdock, and everybody knew that there was bad blood between those two men, and had been for years. The dispute between them was so serious that last year one of Stone's men and Murdock's nephew Henry had gotten into a fight in the saloon, with the result that Stone's man had been killed and Henry Murdock had had to flee to the New Mexico territory to keep from being prosecuted. How could she trust what a Murdock said abut Andrew Stone?

He couldn't have done the things Damaris had alluded to—whatever they were. However distant he might seem at times, however harsh or cold his words, his touch was not rough. His kisses had been wild the night of the engagement party, but they had been exciting, not hurtful. His offer to take in her family and give Annie and Zach the opportunities of wealthy children was not the act of a cruel man, either.

But as soon as Margaret convinced herself that Andrew was innocent of Damaris's charges, doubts would begin to creep in. Damaris had no real reason to lie, Margaret told herself. How could it help her or her husband if Margaret backed out of marrying Andrew? She might very well dislike him, but was that enough to put herself in such an embarrassing light? Besides, the fact of her divorce from Stone spoke as much *for* her charges as against them. It would take something extremely serious to make a woman get a divorce; it exposed her to great scandal and shame. Damaris's reputation had never been the same, even though she was married to one of the wealthiest men in the county. It made one suspect that there must, indeed, have been something unspeakable that caused Damaris to do it. And why else would Murdock hate Stone so much unless he knew that Stone had debased and hurt the woman he loved?

Then Margaret would feel sick and scared and tell herself that she was a fool to go ahead with the marriage. But always, she would remember the feel of Andrew's arms around her, his lips sinking into hers, and she would go hot and weak all over. She would remember the rare times he had smiled or chuckled at something she had said. And she would be certain that he hadn't done anything vile. She couldn't believe he would hurt a woman.

When he came to call on her two days later, she watched him closely, trying to read what was in his face. She had heard people say that a person's eyes were the windows to his soul, but she could not see anything through Andrew's. Emma, there to chaperone as usual, talked brightly about one thing and another, but Margaret and Andrew said little. Emma cast a despairing glance at Margaret, and

Margaret knew that her cousin was wondering why she was sitting there like a lump, making no effort to entrance her future husband.

Finally Emma made a great show of searching for something, then laid aside the delicate embroidery upon which she had been working. "My goodness, I can't seem to find my yellow thread anywhere. Colonel, Margaret, if you will excuse me, I'll run upstairs and look for it. I can't imagine where it could have gotten to." She flashed a veiled glance at Margaret from beneath her lashes, and Margaret knew it would be some time before Emma returned.

Emma left the room. The silence stretched. Finally Stone rose. "I brought your bride's gift."

He stepped outside and came back in with a package, too large to be jewelry. It was a white box, tied inexpertly with pink ribbon. "Laura put on the ribbon," he explained.

Margaret smiled. "It's lovely. You must tell her." She opened the package. Inside, nestled on tissue paper, lay a sterling-silver dresser set. "It's beautiful." It was lovely, and a perfectly proper gift from a fiancé. She lifted each piece—the soft-bristled brush, the mirror, the comb, the filigreed silver stand and its glass perfume bottle—and ran her hands across the smooth silver, tracing the ornate, swooping initials engraved on each one. The central, largest letter was a curling *S*, flanked by a smaller *M* and *C*. Her new monogram, her new name. She had sewn it on several handkerchiefs and linens in the past weeks, but somehow it hadn't struck her as it did now. This would soon be her name. She would become a Stone, possessed by this man who appeared as hard as his name.

"Thank you," she told him, smiling up at him, but her smile was a trifle wobbly.

He saw it and frowned. "Is there something wrong? Have I made an error?"

"No. Oh, no." Margaret shook her head quickly. How could she explain that the silver felt hard and cold, that she was suddenly scared of losing her name, of being swallowed. "I-it must be the jitters." She fumbled with the dresser set, putting the pieces back into the box. "You know how brides are."

Andrew reached down and took her hands, stilling them. "Your hands are icy." He set the box aside and pulled her to her feet. She kept her head bent. She was afraid if she looked at him, he would read the fear on her face. What if she began to cry? He would think her a fool, when he had wanted her precisely because she wasn't foolish, but pragmatic and reasonable. "Look at me."

She made a little shake of her head, but he tilted her chin up with his finger and she had to meet his gaze. "What's the matter?"

Margaret wet her lips nervously. She couldn't imagine not answering him or lying. "I—I am a little frightened."

His frown deepened. "Of marriage or of me?"

She glanced away. "Both—a little—I think."

"What is unknown is always frightening," he said slowly, as though searching for the right words.

Margaret nodded. It was somehow less frightening when he held her hands, which was silly, of course, since he was the very thing she was afraid of.

"If you wish to call it off, I won't hold you to your word. But I would like to think that marriage to me will not be so awful."

"Oh, no! I didn't mean—" Margaret blushed. "That is—"

He shook his head and a smile touched his lips. "It's all right. I told you before, I'm not an ogre. I will do my best to hurt you as little as possible."

Margaret's eyes widened. What did he mean by that! Hurt her as little as possible? "Must you hurt me at all?"

"I'm afraid it's unavoidable. But after a time, it becomes—easier. Damnation!" He dropped her hands and swung away. "I have no way with words for a frightened virgin. Hasn't your aunt explained about your wedding night?"

Margaret shook her head. "No. I'm sorry. I didn't mean to irritate you. I will talk to my aunt, I promise. No doubt I am being silly."

"No. It's not silly." He looked at her and there was something bleak in his eyes. "I wish I could reassure you. I wish I could tell you that I would not touch you. But it wouldn't be the truth. I will come to your bed—I'm not stronger than any other man." He grimaced. "Weaker, I think sometimes. I have learned that some women do not share that pleasure, and I promise that I will be as considerate as I can." The fear was clear in her eyes, and it scored his soul. His voice roughened. "I will be gentle with you. I swear it. But more than that, I cannot promise. It would be only empty words."

Margaret nodded. At least he was honest. Perhaps he was right, and, whatever it was, she would become used to it. Not sharing pleasure was not exactly the same thing as pain, after all. Maybe Damaris Murdock had exaggerated. Maybe what he enjoyed was simply unappealing, not hurtful. And he had promised he would be gentle; somehow she was certain that, whatever else he was, Andrew Stone was a man of his word.

"Thank you." Her voice was little more than a whisper.

A look of frustration crossed Andrew's face and he cursed shortly. He glanced about, and Margaret thought that he would have liked to throw something. Instead, he only walked to the hat rack and jerked his hat from it. He hesitated, then turned. "Are you still willing to marry me?"

Here was her opportunity to get away without any trouble. No one would blame her for backing out on him. But, despite the anxieties and doubts darting around inside her, she knew that she didn't want to. "Yes." Her voice was low but firm. "Yes, I will marry you."

"I will see you, then, on the wedding day."

"Yes."

He turned and left the room. Margaret heard the front door close behind him and moments later, the sound of his horse's hooves pounding off down the street. She sank back into her chair. Her knees were suddenly too weak to hold her. Well, she'd done it. There would be no going back now.

Andrew dug his heels into his horse's sides and the roan stretched out into a run. It wasn't often that he was given his head like this, and the stallion took full advantage of it. They raced out of town and along the road, leaving Andrew's man Whitman far behind them. Andrew bent low over the horse's neck, moving with him, as though he could run the anger and frustration out of his system.

That was impossible, however, and soon he pulled back, slowing the horse to a trot and, finally, a walk. He couldn't outrun his demons. He knew that.

Damn it all! Margaret was going to be like Damaris when it came to sex. He had been foolish to hope otherwise, to think that her response to his kisses at the engagement party had meant that the fires of passion could burn within her. When he saw the fear in Margaret's eyes today, the reluctance on her face, it had stabbed him like a knife. It would be as it had been before, with him fighting his desire until he could not hold out against it, then breaking down and going to his wife's bed. She would not deny him or tease him as Damaris often had; Margaret was too frightened of him for that. But she would lie white and still beneath him, her face turned away, her nightgown rucked up to her waist, while he sweated and pumped and groaned on top of her until at last the shuddering release came. Then he would roll off her and return to his cold bed, spent but still unsatisfied, feeling like an animal for forcing himself on her when she so obviously hated it.

The stallion danced and rolled his eyes, blowing out air, and Andrew realized that he had unconsciously stiffened all over, jerking on the reins. He forced his muscles to relax and he unclenched his teeth. Was he crazy? Was it abnormal to want a wife who would enjoy the marital bed, too? Were other men content to share their lust with bought women and only couple briefly and respectfully with their wives?

He remembered how he had tried with Damaris, how gently and tenderly he had made love to her, doing everything he could think of to arouse her. He had held himself back until he thought he would burst as he stroked and kissed her, but none of it had ever brought her delight. She had remained rigid and cold and, when it was over, she had looked at him with eyes like glass. As time went by, she had refused him more and more often, complaining of illness or tiredness or picking a fight with him right before bedtime. She said that she could not sleep with him taking up so much of the bed and petulantly asked him to sleep in another room. Finally, one evening when he was caressing her, trying to arouse her, she had told him flatly that she hated his touch. He would never forget the look on her face as she twisted away from him and jumped out of the bed. Her face had been so filled with hatred and anger that she had actually looked ugly.

She had screamed at him, "My flesh crawls whenever you touch me! I hate it! All women do. It is only men who enjoy such low, disgusting things. It's base and vulgar. No lady would ever like being besmirched like that!"

After that, he had fought his passionate nature. He had told himself that his love for her was strong enough, pure enough, to do away with the physical side. But he had never been able to stay away. And he had always wound up feeling like a brute.

He hadn't wanted to believe that she spoke the truth when she said all women hated it. But he had thought of the cool formality between his own parents. He had seen how frequently other men turned to whores instead of their wives. His uncle, one of the most notorious skirt-chasers Andrew had ever known, had told him once that he slept with other women to spare his wife. He had looked into the eyes of the mistresses and whores he had used after the divorce and had seen their indifference, despite their pretence of passion.

Now Margaret had proved it to him all over again.

He was a harder man than the boy who had married Damaris. He would not allow this wife to play him for a fool as Damaris had. He would take her when he wanted, just as he would a mistress. He was, after all, paying her, if it was less directly. They had a bargain, and her body was part of it. He would be gentle, as he had promised her; he had no wish to cause her pain. But he would have her.

The night before the wedding, Aunt Charity drew Margaret into the sitting room for a quiet, private talk. Margaret realized that this must be the conversation that Andrew had told her she should have with her aunt. She was glad. She had thought several times since his visit about asking her aunt, but she hadn't been able to work up the courage.

She sat down demurely and waited for her aunt to speak, careful to let none of her eagerness show on her face. She knew that Aunt Charity would disapprove of any interest in such things. Aunt Charity said nothing for a long time, letting the moment stretch out until Margaret thought that she would scream.

Finally she began ponderously, "This is a difficult subject for me to speak of. It is for any well-bred lady. However, since your poor mother is dead and I am your closest female relative, it is my duty."

Margaret, feeling that some response was called for, nodded. "Thank you, ma'am."

The older woman sighed. "It is hard to see one's child grow up and take on the responsibilities of womanhood. Of marriage. And you know that I look upon you as my own child."

"Yes, ma'am." When was she going to get on with it?

"As it says in the wedding ceremony, a husband and wife become one. You will be—" Incredibly, Aunt Charity's fat, wrinkled cheeks turned pink. She was blushing. "You will be the sacred vessel for his seed," she intoned, staring at the wall. "And because of that, you will be blessed with children."

There was a long silence. Margaret looked at her aunt. Was that it? Was that her entire explanation? "But, Aunt Charity, what happens?" she blurted.

Her aunt turned shocked eyes on her. "Margaret, a little propriety, please! A lady does not need to know such things. A lady does not even *wish* to know such things."

"But Mr. Stone said that you would explain it to me."

"Mr. Stone!" Aunt Charity's eyes bulged. "You have been discussing this with a man!"

"Well, not discussing exactly. He asked if I was scared, and I said I was, and he said that you would explain it to me. And I still don't understand!"

"You don't need to understand. You will find out what happens on your wedding night, just as I did, and as every decent woman does. And you will endure it, as all ladies do, because it is your marital duty. It is something men enjoy, though only God in His Infinite Wisdom knows why. It is vulgar and crude, and no woman could enjoy it, unless, of course, she is—" Aunt Charity's voice dropped "—loose. Fortunately, men don't expect their wives to enjoy it. Why, they wouldn't even want them to, for no true lady could and no man wishes to have a slut for a wife."

Margaret felt sick and more scared than she had before. "But . . . does it hurt?"

"Of course. It is simply one of the many pains that women must endure. And your reward will be a child."

"I—I would like a child. But—how much does it hurt? Does it happen often?"

Her aunt fixed her with a stern look. "Really, Margaret, you ask the most immodest questions. A lady doesn't think of such things. A person would think you were raised in a barn, the way you talk."

Margaret blushed and fell silent. Why was it wrong to be curious about what would happen to her? It always seemed to be that way. When she first came to live here, practically everything she said and did had horrified her aunt. She had learned to keep her mouth shut, but she had never understood why.

"It happens," Aunt Charity continued, her mouth drawn up primly, "as often as your husband wishes. Some men, of course, are more gentlemanly than others." Her look implied that a Yankee could not be relied on to be gentlemanly about anything.

Margaret wanted to ask if what some men did hurt more than what others did, if there were desires, as Damaris had implied, that were even more crude and brutal than what was normally done. But she couldn't work up the courage. "Aunt Charity, I'm scared."

"Of course you are, dear." Her aunt leaned over and patted her hands, seemingly pleased with her admission. "We all were, once. But, remember, tomorrow night it will all be over, and after that it's never as bad."

"But I don't know what happens. I don't know what to do."

"Do? *Do?*" Her aunt withdrew her hand, her face once again astounded. "My girl, one doesn't 'do' anything. He does it all. All you have to do is submit."

Tears started in Margaret's eyes. It sounded so bleak and horrible. And Aunt Charity was talking about a normal marriage, when a man loved his wife! What happened when the marriage was loveless? When the man had evil, dark desires?

"There, now." Aunt Charity stood up. Apparently the talk was over. "I'm sure you will act as befits a Carlisle and a well-brought-up girl."

Margaret nodded, struggling to hold back her tears. Her aunt swept from the room, pleased with a duty done, and Margaret followed her more slowly. Like a doomed woman she went into the kitchen, where they had been taking turns all evening bathing in the big tin tub. Annie, rosy from her hot bath, helped her undress. When Margaret had worked the precious, sweet-smelling soap into a lather and had washed her hair, Annie sluiced fresh water from a pitcher over her head to rinse it clean. Margaret finished bathing quickly and hopped out to dry off. Often she liked to soak in the tub, daydreaming, but tonight her thoughts were not pleasant companions.

Annie helped her comb through her long hair and braid it into several plaits. Emma had assured her that letting her hair dry that way would give it body and curl. Margaret hoped so, for tomorrow, for one of the few times in her life, she would go out in public with her hair hanging loose around her shoulders. Of course, it would be nearly hidden by the veil, but afterward, Andrew would see it.

She went to bed and lay awake for hours, listening to Annie's gentle breathing beside her. Her heart ached, just hearing it. It would be the last time she would do so. From now on it would be a stranger lying beside her. She cried a little and she worried, turning restlessly in the bed. It was a long time before she fell asleep, and when she did so, her sleep was restless.

It was almost a relief when she awoke from a fitful doze and saw that the sky was lightening; it was almost dawn. Margaret slipped from the bed quietly, so as not to awaken Annie, and went to the window. She sat down on the windowsill, leaning back against the wall, and gazed out. It wasn't the first time she had sat so, watching the sun rise through the lacework of the trees. In fact, she had sat here often right after her father went to the War, missing him and her home and dreaming of the time when he would come back. It had been years ago, but for a moment she felt again the pang of loss that had haunted her then. The pain had healed long ago, but the wound was still there, down deep; there was still the loneliness, the feeling of being cast adrift, without her beloved father or the home that had been so dear to her.

Margaret shivered. The night air was cool upon her skin. Even though the autumn days were still almost as hot as summer, the nights were beginning to grow cool. The eastern sky had turned to shades of blue and purple, and gradually they began to melt into rose and gold as the sun grew stronger. Behind her in the room she heard Annie begin to stir.

She drew a deep breath. This was it. The day of her wedding. Her stomach twisted, sick with a combination of fear, excitement and lack of sleep. She wondered if she had done the right thing.

"Maggie?" Annie asked sleepily from the bed, sitting up and yawning. "What are you doing?"

Well, it was too late now to sit around wondering if she'd made a mistake. Forcing a smile onto her lips, Margaret turned, saying, "Waiting for you to awaken, sleepyhead. Better get up. We have lots of things to do."

At one o'clock that afternoon, Margaret began the walk down the aisle to the front of the little Methodist church, where Andrew Stone stood waiting for her. He was dressed as always in a black coat and trousers, but a froth of ruffles down the front of his shirt broke the severity of the suit. Margaret started toward him, her fingers digging into Zach's arm beside her. She felt oddly breathless, and the aisle looked a mile long. She hoped she would not disgrace herself by fainting.

Margaret had no idea what a picture of fragile beauty she presented as she walked toward Andrew in the dress of white satin and lace, the demure lace veil floating over the pale glory of her hair. But Andrew Stone, watching her, felt the full effect. She looked like a fairy princess, he thought, lovely and ethereal, as though she might vanish into the mists at any moment. Yet there was also something primitively stirring about the sight of her hair tumbling loose and free down her back, barely concealed by the lace; his hands itched to tear the veil from it and sink his hands into the pale gold mass.

She stopped beside him, and her brother stepped back— a little reluctantly, Andrew thought. He had already seen that Zach disliked and distrusted him. Andrew took Margaret's hand and slipped it through the crook of his arm. She glanced up at him through the gossamer veil. Her face was stark white, her eyes huge. Her hand was cold and trembling slightly. She was scared to death, he realized, and he wondered if it was of him or of the ceremony. He covered her hand with his, warming it, and she turned her face up toward him again shyly, almost smiling.

Margaret had passed into a state of numbness She concentrated only on standing upright despite the weakness in her knees. She scarcely heard what the minister said, and Andrew had to press her hand to remind her to speak when the minister paused for her response. Her voice was small as she recited her vows.

Then it was over. Andrew was lifting the veil from her face and spreading it back over her hair. He was bending down to touch his lips to hers. Margaret stood as if rooted to the spot. He turned, neatly maneuvering her around and tucking her hand inside his elbow. She went with him, grateful for the support of his arm. She saw the faces turned toward her, but they were all a jumble without meaning.

Stone whisked her outside and down the steps. Once they were out of sight of the audience, he curled his arm around her waist to give her more support, and at the street, he lifted her up bodily and set her on the seat of his surrey. By the time the others began to emerge from the church, he was already up beside her and clicking to the horses.

"Are you all right?" he asked, looking down at her with a frown.

"Yes. I'm sorry." Margaret tried to pull in a deep breath but could not. It didn't help matters any that Emma had ruthlessly yanked her corset a good inch tighter than usual to make her waist look infinitesimal in the wedding gown. She could only breathe shallowly in the top of her lungs.

"Have you had anything to eat today?"

Margaret shook her head. She'd been too nervous to stuff anything down. "I wasn't hungry."

"Yes, and no doubt you're laced up so tight you can't breathe," Stone went on sourly. "Damn women and their vanity."

Margaret turned startled eyes on him. It was highly improper for a man to discuss a lady's corset. Of course, they were married now, but still...why, she hardly knew him. Color stained her cheeks and she didn't know what to say. She glanced away. At least his words had surprised her right out of her trance. Her mind was beginning to function again.

"I want you to at least eat something at the reception," Stone commanded. "It would be rather embarrassing to have my bride faint dead away right after the wedding."

Margaret smiled a little. "All right. I'll try." Her grin grew. "However, I suspect tongues are already wagging about our hasty departure from the church. I can't imagine what people will think."

Andrew chuckled. "Why, quite rightly, that the groom was eager to have his beautiful new wife all to himself."

It was such a charming statement that Margaret couldn't stop herself from staring at him in surprise. He chuckled again at her expression. She thought how much younger and more handsome he looked when his face lightened like that, and she wondered why he went around looking so dour all the time. Then she realized that she was staring and she looked back down at her lap, embarrassed.

She studied the narrow gold ring on her finger; her lace glove had been slit at the finger so that he could slip it on her. The ring felt strange, it looked strange. She wondered if she would ever get used to being Mrs. Andrew Stone. A shiver ran through her; she felt almost as if she'd somehow lost herself.

Andrew pulled the surrey to a stop in front of her aunt's house and came around the side to help her down. They walked inside, and Andrew insisted that Margaret drink a glass of punch and eat something before the guests started arriving. Margaret downed the sweet punch quickly; she was very thirsty. But she found that she could make herself eat only a little.

Before long, Aunt Charity arrived with Emma, Zach and Annie, and within minutes after that, the guests began to stream in. Margaret stood and greeted her neighbors and relatives and the men who worked for her husband, all spruced up in their Sunday best. It seemed to go on for hours. Her feet hurt, as did her back, and before long she felt weary to the bone. She wished she could get away and lie down for a moment. She wished her face didn't ache from the effort of smiling.

Aunt Charity came over to them. "It's time for you to lead out the dancing, child." She carefully avoided looking at or speaking to Andrew, as she usually did.

Margaret had never felt less like dancing. She sighed and turned toward Andrew. Then she remembered his limp. He hadn't even wanted to dance at the engagement party; he surely wouldn't want to take the first waltz around the floor by themselves, the object of everyone's eyes.

"I cannot," she said quickly. "I'm too tired."

Her aunt stared at her, bug-eyed. "Too tired! Surely you're joking."

"No. I'm quite weary."

"But it's expected."

"I'm sorry. I don't want to. Just tell everyone to start dancing."

"Margaret Ellen Carlisle! I will not stand for this kind of silliness."

Andrew's arm slid around Margaret; his hand was firm against her waist. His voice cut into her aunt's speech, crisp and commanding, "Mrs. Winstock. Need I remind you that Margaret's name is now Stone, not Carlisle. I think you'll see, upon reflection, that you no longer have the right to demand anything from her."

Aunt Charity stopped in midbreath; her mouth gaped in astonishment.

"Mrs. Stone is exceedingly tired, as she said. However, I think what my wife is doing is attempting to spare me embarrassment. My injury generally prevents me from taking a turn on the dance floor."

Aunt Charity's eyes dropped to his leg, then quickly back up, and she colored. "Oh—excuse me. I didn't think. Of course. Well, I'll, uh—"

"No. It seems a shame to rob a bride of her first dance as a married woman. It is tradition, after all."

Margaret glanced up at him, surprised. He was gazing down at her questioningly.

"Well? Would you rather bear with my clumsiness than miss the first waltz?"

She hesitated, then smiled. "Yes, I should like to dance, if you're sure it's all right."

"It may cost you a few bruised toes, but that is all."

Her smile grew. "Thank you."

Andrew took her hand and led her into the sitting room, cleared once again of furniture, and the guests gathered in a circle around them. The fiddler and the piano player struck up a waltz, and Andrew turned and took her in his arms. They began to move to the music. His hand at her waist was firm, guiding her expertly, and Margaret suspected that he had once danced quite well. Even now, he was not difficult to dance with, his steps were a trifle slow and smaller than normal, that was all.

She smiled at him. "You've been lying to me. You're not a clumsy dancer."

He raised his eyebrows. "No?" He thought of the way he had once whirled around the room with Damaris, his steps as joyous as his heart. "It's hardly what I'd term graceful."

"I've danced with worse."

That rare, reluctant grin touched his mouth. "I won't ask you when."

It was odd to face him thus, so close, with so many people around watching, to feel the weight of his hand at her waist, to look into his eyes. She had never danced with him; he was a stranger to her. Yet she was married to him. Tonight she would sleep in his bed. Her chest tightened, and she glanced away, afraid that he would read her thoughts in her eyes.

His masculinity surrounded her. He could hurt her if he wanted; there would be nothing to stop him. She belonged to him now. Fear knotted her stomach and she wished desperately that it was over. Anything was worse than this waiting.

The fear didn't go away; it lasted through the rest of the reception and through the goodbyes, even through the long ride out to the Stone ranch. Laura, deadly silent, rode in the seat behind them. She had hardly said two words to

Margaret the whole afternoon. Margaret was certain that
the child hated her and would never accept her. But that
worry couldn't even begin to touch the cold well of fear
that had grown inside Margaret at the thought of the night
before her. She knotted her hands in her lap and watched
the countryside go by, willing herself to be brave and
strong.

Behind them rode the men from Stone's ranch who had
attended the wedding. Margaret felt rather odd to be riding in procession this way. But she had heard that Andrew
never came to town without at least one of his hired hands
along. Some of his men looked like the gunmen she'd
heard they were, especially one, who had cold, flat eyes of
a strange yellowish color. A man who had done nothing
wrong wouldn't feel the need of such protection, would
he? At last they turned in at the ranch entrance, but it was
still a long ride until they reached the main house. It was
dusk by the time they got there. The house was large, at
least twice as big as her aunt's home. It was made of white
native stone, two stories tall, with a porch running all the
way across the wide front. A section on either end had
been added on, running perpendicular to the rest of the
house.

The house did not sit by itself. There were a couple of
houses not far away, one long and the other small, as well
as a large barn and numerous sheds. There were also several corrals; most were empty but the one closest to the
barn held several horses. The Stone ranch was obviously a
large operation.

Andrew helped her down from the surrey, and one of the
men led the horses toward the barn. Margaret glanced
around her and saw that the horses and riders were all
scattering, going to the barn or corral or the long house,
some simply riding away. Now only the little, silent Laura

was with them. The front door opened, and a heavyset woman with iron-gray hair appeared in the doorway.

"Good afternoon, Herr Stone, mein Frau." The stiff woman bobbed a curtsey while managing not to lose any of her dignity.

"Fräulein Hoelscher," Andrew replied. He turned to Margaret. "This is Laura's governess, Fräulein Hoelscher."

"How do you do?"

"Vell, tank you. I am fery pleased to meet you. Com here, Fräulein Laura. Ve vill get you out of de vay, *ja*?" The girl went to her, and she clamped a hand around Laura's wrist, leading her into the house.

Margaret was suddenly alone with her husband. She glanced at him uncertainly.

"Well." He, too, seemed nervous. "Shall I show you the house?"

"Yes, please." She wasn't about to tell him that the house was so big it overwhelmed her. She didn't really want to see it; she wanted only to jump into her bed back home and pull the covers over her head.

She made her legs move forward with him. At the doorway, he stopped and bent down to scoop her up into his arms. The movement surprised her, even though it was customary to carry the bride over the threshold, and she gasped a little, one hand going instinctively up to clasp his shoulder. His arm was hard as a rock beneath her; she could feel the heat of his body through her clothes. She was trembling; she thought he must feel it. She looked at the side of his face, at the way his crisp black hair curled down behind his ear and over his collar. He turned his head and looked at her. He was only inches away; she could touch his face if she reached out, smell the scent of his skin, feel the brush of his breath. Her throat closed up.

Andrew carried her into the house and set her down. The house was big and silent around them, shadowy in the gathering gloom. Margaret shivered.

"Are you cold?" Stone closed the door behind them.

"No. I'm all right. Well, maybe a little."

He shrugged out of his frock coat and draped it around her shoulders. It hung ludicrously on her, but she felt warm inside it. It smelled pleasantly of tobacco, horse and masculine cologne, the scent of him. Margaret pulled it more tightly around her, holding it closed in front of her.

Andrew lit an oil lamp that stood on a table by the front door and held it up. "Perhaps we ought to put off the tour of the house until the morning, when you can see better."

"All right." Her heart began to hammer. That meant that there was nothing to delay them from going to bed.

"I'll show you your room, then I'll get your bags." He took her by the elbow and led her up the stairs and down the hall. A door stood open, and he stepped back to allow her to enter, handing her the lamp.

Margaret walked around the room slowly. It was large and dark. There were two windows and each was hung with heavy drapes of dark green velvet. The bed, built of mahogany with thick, knobbed posters, was covered with the same green material. There was a vanity table, velvet chair, chest, dresser and a spindly-legged table, all made of the same rich dark wood. Margaret felt weighed down by the heavy, dark things. Perhaps it was because it was nighttime, she told herself. The room would probably seem brighter in the morning.

"If you don't like it, you can change whatever you want," Andrew told her. "I didn't know what you would like."

She turned, forcing a cheerful smile. "No, this is fine."

"Good." He hesitated, then turned and left. Margaret set the lamp down on the small table and sank into the chair beside it. The chair was stiff and studded with buttons; she thought with longing of the padded rocking chair that sat in her bedroom at home. No, at Aunt Charity's house. This was her home now.

She felt like crying. The room was strange and she felt little and lost in it. She closed her eyes for a moment, forcing back the tears. Then she stood up purposefully and walked to the dresser. She had to get through this without crying. She pulled the pins from her veil and lifted it from her head, laying it down carefully on the dresser top.

In the mirror, she could see her pale reflection, her face almost as white as her dress, her white-blond hair falling in thick crimped waves down over her shoulders, caught at the sides with faux-pearl-studded combs. She began to undo the tiny white buttons that fastened her cuffs. Her fingers were cold and clumsy; it seemed to take forever to undo them all. She reached for the buttons in the back, but she could touch only the first two. She would need help to unfasten her dress. The realization made her slightly panicky. Would she have to rely on Andrew Stone to help her undress? Would he actually see her underclothes? Even her bare flesh?

Her pulse raced and she found it hard to breathe. It felt as if her tight corset were squeezing the life from her. Why had Emma insisted on pulling it so tight, just for vanity's sake? She struggled to reach more of her buttons, but could succeed in loosening only one more.

The door opened and Andrew walked in, carrying her two bags. His gaze went to her hands, fumbling with the buttons of her dress. Margaret blushed.

"Are you having trouble?" His voice came out huskier than usual. He set down the bags and closed the door behind him. "I'll help you." He started forward.

Margaret's heart skipped into double time. He came around behind her. Her hair, as soft and pale as corn silk, lay spread across her back, blocking the buttons in question. Andrew reached out to take the silken mass in his hands and lift it aside. He could not resist running his hands down her hair, feeling it catch on his rough skin, feeling the glorious softness of it. He gathered it up and pulled it to one side and over her shoulder. He was reluctant to let it go. His hands went to her shoulders, touching her as lightly as a caress. Margaret shivered all through. He bent and nuzzled his face into her hair.

"You smell so sweet, like spring," he murmured. His heart was hammering now, his blood racing. He straightened and began to undo the buttons. There were many of them, and they were small and round, resembling pearls. It seemed to take forever for his clumsy fingers to work them out of their fragile loops. He wanted to curse at the frustration. He wanted to grasp the cloth and rip it down, sending the buttons flying. But he forced himself to do neither.

Margaret put both hands on the front of her dress, holding it up over her breasts as the sides began to part and sag downward. She knew she must be a fiery red all over. She could hardly breathe. There was a faint buzzing in her ears.

He had the buttons undone halfway down her back; she could feel the air on her skin above her chemise. She shivered.

"Cold?"

She shook her head. "No. I—I'm scared."

He paused, frowning. "Of what will happen tonight?"

She nodded, unable to say anything. Strange black specks were beginning to dance before her eyes. Andrew put his hands on her shoulders again and turned her around to face him. He gazed down into her eyes. "I promise I shall hurt you as little as possible."

Margaret made a low, moaning noise, and her eyelids fluttered. She fainted.

Chapter Seven

Instinctively Andrew reached out to catch Margaret as she fell.

"Well, I'll be damned." Was he so frightening that a woman would faint at the mere thought of his making love to her?

He lifted her into his arms and carried her to the bed. Beneath her dress was something hard and stiff. Of course. Her corset. She'd laced it too tightly, as so many women did in their vanity. He rolled her onto her side and unfastened the little buttons that ran down the back of her dress. Then he pulled the dress off her shoulders and arms.

Her torso was bared to his sight, clothed in the armorlike corset and a flimsy cotton chemise. The stiff corset pushed up her breasts so that they almost spilled out of her chemise, nipples visible through the sheer cloth. Andrew's mouth went dry.

He recalled himself to what he was doing and reached behind her back to undo the laces. Quickly he stripped the laces from their holes and tossed the corset aside. The cotton chemise beneath was damp and glued to Margaret's skin, an almost nonexistent covering. He lifted it gently away from her flesh. Beneath the cloth were angry red marks where the stays had dug into her tender flesh. He cursed under his breath and his forefinger ran gently down one red line. He hated the thought of anything hurting her.

Andrew went to the washbasin and poured water from the pitcher, then dipped a rag into it and wrung it out. He brought it back to the bed and ran the cloth gently across Margaret's cheeks and down her throat. He moved it slowly across her chest, onto the soft mounds of her breasts. God, she was lovely. Enticing.

He felt like a lecher, sitting here ogling his wife's unconscious body. Yet he couldn't seem to tear his eyes away, couldn't stop his hand from gently smoothing the wet cloth over her skin.

Margaret's eyes opened and she gazed at him blankly. Then her eyes cleared and the color returned to her pale face. "Oh. Oh, dear." She struggled to sit up. She glanced down and saw her state of semidress, and her cheeks blazed red. "Oh. I—what happened?"

"You fainted."

"I did?" She raised a hand to her forehead. "I felt so peculiar."

"You should have," he retorted, his voice harsh with restrained passion. "You had your damn stays laced so tight you couldn't breathe."

Margaret didn't think it was possible to be any more embarrassed, but she was. Here she was with a man, virtually a stranger even if she was married to him, her dress pulled halfway down and only her chemise to cover her, and he was talking about such intimate things as corsets!

"I don't want you doing it anymore, do you understand?"

"Yes. I mean, no. I won't do it anymore." She hesitated. "Won't do what anymore?"

"Wear one of those contraptions. Women are the vainest creatures on earth. They'd rather not be able to breathe, rather faint all over the place, than have their waist an inch or two larger."

Margaret frowned. "I don't think that's very fair. It isn't as if women did it because they wanted to! It's pure torture."

"Then why put yourself through it?"

"Why, to...because—because of men."

Andrew thought of the way she had looked in her wedding gown, her waist reduced to nothingness, and how he had thought his hands would fit perfectly around it, how he had wanted to try to see if they did. Guilt flickered across his face. "Perhaps a man does like the way a woman looks in one." He cleared his throat. "But, I should hope, not to the extent of asking a woman to be on the verge of passing out all the time. Besides, there's no pleasure in putting your hand on a woman and feeling solid whalebone instead of soft flesh." His eyes slid down her body. "I don't know many men who wouldn't rather have the pleasure than the appearance."

Margaret stared, her eyes huge in her face. She couldn't imagine what she could say to that. His words had sent prickles all over her body in the strangest way.

Andrew stepped back, tearing his eyes away. "I bet you still haven't eaten anything, have you?"

"Not much," she admitted.

"I'll get you some dinner."

"Oh, no, you needn't do that...."

He glanced at her quizzically. "You'd rather starve?"

"No, of course not. It's just—well—I don't know." She had never had a man prepare or bring her any food, not even her father. It seemed strange.

Andrew turned and left and Margaret seized the opportunity to hop out of the bed and skin out of her dress and petticoats as quickly as she could. She tore open one of her bags and pulled out the first nightgown she could find. She didn't care what she looked like; she just wanted to be done before her husband got back. She couldn't stand the thought of undressing with him in the room! It would be too embarrassing.

She managed to remove all her clothes, even her stockings and the new kid half boots, put on a cotton nightgown and hop back into bed before Andrew returned to the room, carrying a large tray.

He paused for a moment, then set the tray on the dresser and turned back to close the door. It took him that moment to collect his wits, which had scattered completely when he'd walked into the room to find Margaret sitting up in bed waiting for him, wearing a lacy nightgown. He had expected to find her weeping and distraught. Instead, she seemed far more composed than he.

He crossed the room with the tray of food and set it down gently on her lap. This close to her, he could see how the lace merely shadowed the skin of her chest and how the Empire waist cupped her breasts. She was small to have such full, firm breasts. The points of her nipples pressed against the delicate satin. His hands itched to reach out and cover her breasts. He had full right to. And he'd learned long ago that being gentle and tender with a woman only led her to take advantage of a man. He should establish the pattern of their marriage tonight. He should make it clear that he would not be maneuvered or cajoled or taken advantage of.

Margaret smiled up at him. "Thank you. It's very kind of you."

He shook his head. "You're hungry. You need to eat. There's nothing very marvelous about getting out a hard-boiled egg and a few slabs of meat."

It was more than that, Margaret thought, but she didn't say anything. Instead, she just dug into her food with gusto, suddenly realizing how hungry she was. Without the corset squeezing her stomach, she found it was decidedly empty.

"Mmm, it's delicious." She ate quickly, hungrily. He watched her, enjoying the dainty, precise movements of her fingers as she cut the meat or picked up a slice of cheese. His eyes slid up to her mouth, watching the soft pink lips open and the little teeth sink into the meat.

He felt the claws of desire dig deeper into his gut. "I'm going to my room now. Is there anything else you want before I leave?"

Her eyes widened. "What?"

Now she'd done it, Margaret thought. She had disgusted her new husband by fainting before they even got into bed. It would be enough to make any man angry, and Andrew Stone was less than a patient or tolerant man. Now he was going to leave her! Tomorrow morning he might very well repudiate her. She could see herself back at her aunt's house in less than a day, disgraced, doomed to the life of an old maid.

Suddenly her appetite was gone. Margaret set the tray down on the table beside the bed. "What did you say?"

"I said I was going to my bedroom now."

"No please." She held out her hand and he was amazed to see that it trembled slightly. "I'm sorry. I was foolish. You're right. It was doubtless the result of my vanity in tightening my—uh—garment too much. Honestly, I have never fainted before."

He looked puzzled. "I'm sure not. And you will feel better in the morning."

"I feel better already."

"I don't understand. I should think you'd feel relieved that I don't intend to make you share my bed tonight."

She shook her head. "No. I was just being silly earlier. I know that every woman has to—I mean, it's something that happens, and I—I will be fine. I promise, I'm not about to engage in hysterics."

That was obvious, and he was already surprised by that fact. "Of course not. But you were quite frightened of it earlier."

"It was silliness. Nerves. It has been quite a rush to prepare for the wedding and I'm a trifle on edge."

"It was fear," he cut in flatly. "I don't understand why you are so eager to explain it away."

"Because I've started our marriage so poorly. Already I've disappointed you. I've failed." Tears sprang into her big eyes, turning them a shimmering green.

"You haven't failed." Andrew sat down on the side of the bed and took one of her hands in his. "Whatever the people around here think of me, I am not a brute. I desire you tonight; that's quite true. A man usually desires his wife on their wedding night. But I don't have to act on that desire right now. I am capable of waiting. And I don't think you have *failed* just because you're feeling uncertain and a little scared." His eyes looked straight into hers. "I think it would be better if you lived here awhile and got used to the idea of marriage. Got used to *me*."

Margaret stared at him, adjusting her mind to the change. Why, he was not repudiating her, but offering to hold back, suppress his own desire, just because she was nervous. Surely this could not be the man Damaris had told her about, the one who humiliated and hurt his wife. A smile broke across her face like sunshine. "That is kind of you. But I would rather go ahead and get it ov—"

She stopped abruptly, realizing how blunt and uncomplimentary her words sounded.

His eyebrows lifted. Then, to her amazement, he laughed. "Get it over with? You never warned me what a blow you could deal."

"I'm sorry. I didn't mean that the way it sounded."

"Yes, you did. We both know it." Andrew sighed and looked down at her hand in his. He stroked his forefinger down each of her fingers in turn, his face thoughtful. Regretful. "I don't know why it is that the thing which brings a man such pleasure should be something his wife doesn't enjoy. Yet that seems to be the way it is."

Margaret had given him permission. He should just take her to relieve the desire that had been bubbling in him for weeks. Then, at least, the first time would be over for her—the strangeness, the pain. It didn't matter if he waited, if he introduced her slowly to sex; she would still lie stiff beneath him, gritting her teeth and waiting until he was through. He had learned that with Damaris.

Andrew looked into her eyes. For an instant he imagined those eyes darkening with desire, that mouth tilting up to meet his kiss. He made a frustrated noise deep in his throat and jumped to his feet, dropping her hand. "No. I can't. Whatever you've heard about me, I'm not an ogre. I can't force myself on an unwilling woman. A scared woman. We will wait."

"Wait?"

"Yes. Perhaps after a while, you won't be so scared of me." He had wanted her to be scared of him, scared enough that she wouldn't dare be unfaithful to him, yet now, looking into those huge eyes, he found he could not frighten her. He turned her hand over and raised it to his lips, kissing her palm gently.

Margaret gazed at him in wonder. Already the tight bands were loosening around her chest. "It's not true, is it?"

"What's not true?"

"You won't hurt me, will you?"

"Hurt you!" He frowned. "I shall try not to. But, you know, the first time there is likely to be some pain. There is little I can do to keep that from you."

"The first time?"

"Yes. The first time I make love to you. When I take your maidenhead."

Margaret blushed clear up to her hairline, but she had to know. She couldn't let embarrassment stop her. "But only that once?"

"Yes. I—" He stopped. "Didn't anyone tell you about this? Prepare you?"

"Yes, Aunt Charity talked with me. She told me that it was my duty to bear it, that it was a woman's lot in life. She didn't—she didn't really say what it was I had to bear."

Andrew muttered a word under his breath. Margaret suspected that she should be glad she couldn't quite hear what he said. He rose and began to pace the room. Finally he stopped and turned to her. "So you have absolutely no idea what is about to take place?"

Margaret shook her head. "No. I'm sorry."

"Never mind. It's not your fault. It's that damn harridan that raised you—I beg your pardon—your gracious aunt."

A giggle rose to Margaret's lips. "I think you were right the first time."

His mouth twitched into a smile. He wanted very much to kiss those lips, to feel her laughter against his mouth. He had to put his hands in his pockets to keep them from reaching out to her. "I can see that it is up to me to teach you."

He returned to the bed and once again sat down beside her. Margaret jackknifed her legs under the covers and wrapped her arms around them, resting her chin on her legs. Andrew was reminded of a child settling herself to learn a lesson. Andrew rubbed a sweating palm down his trousers leg. He felt like a fool, explaining such things to an innocent. Worse yet, he couldn't stop a rush of desire, too, at speaking so intimately with her.

He cleared his throat. "I—well, the way it is with a man is that he feels certain things when he looks at a woman. He wants to—to kiss her." His eyes went to her lips. "To touch her. Everywhere." His eyes dropped down her body. "To see her without clothes."

Margaret blushed at his words, yet a warmth started up deep in her abdomen, too. "Every time you see a woman, you feel that?"

"No!" He looked startled; then a grin crossed his face. "Not every time. Not every woman. A woman who appeals to you. The woman you want to share your bed. Your wife."

"You mean—you mean that is how you felt about me when you saw me? You wanted to..."

His eyes came up to meet hers; they were piercing. "Yes. That is how I felt. How I feel. I want to kiss you. Touch you. Look at you."

Margaret swallowed. "Oh, my." Her voice was small.

"I'm afraid it is the way men are made. I cannot help but feel desire for you."

The liquid heat in Margaret's abdomen spread, grew hotter.

"And when a woman marries, she gives herself to her husband."

"Then he has the right to—to do those things?"

"Yes. They go to bed together. They kiss and touch, and the more they do, the more he wants her." Just speaking of it, his heart was slamming in his chest. He curled his fingers into his palms.

"Like what we did that day in the garden?"

"Y-yes." His voice shook a little on the word. Heat flooded his loins. "Just like that. Like this." He leaned over and brushed her lips lightly.

Margaret's lids fluttered closed. A pulse leaped in her throat. When his lips left hers, her tongue stole out to touch her lips, as though to capture the taste of him there. Andrew suppressed a groan.

"But that wasn't scary. Not exactly. It was...exciting. I liked it."

He bent over her again, bracing his hands upon the bed, and kissed her. His lips lingered this time, tasting her lips fully. Margaret let out a little sigh of pleasure. His lips were so warm and soft, so velvety. How could anything this nice lead to something frightening?

Gently his lips moved against hers, urging her mouth to open, and when it did, his tongue slipped inside. It did not surprise her this time, but there was the same rush of excitement, the flash of heat in her stomach. Andrew's tongue explored her mouth in a leisurely way, tickling, teasing. Instinctively her own tongue met his. He made a noise. His breath surged hot against her cheek.

His arms went around her and he bore her backward. She was imprisoned by his arms and the weight of his body pressing into her, but Margaret felt no fear, only a delicious, hot heaviness all through her. He kissed her again and again, breaking the fusion of their mouths only to change the slant of their kiss. His body was burning, encircling her with heat, and Margaret found that almost as intoxicating as his kisses. Margaret was dizzy and breathless and she hoped he would never, ever stop.

Finally Andrew lifted his head. Disappointment rippled through Margaret. She opened her eyes. He loomed above her, his face flushed, eyes glittering. There was the strangest tingling, restless sensation in her lower abdomen, and instinctively she squeezed her legs together.

"And how," she breathed, unaware of the way her lambent, dazed eyes affected him, "how does he touch her?"

His eyes grew even brighter. He lifted one hand and ran it lightly down her cheek. Her nerves were alive to his touch. His fingertips slid down over her jaw onto the soft flesh of her throat and slowly back up. He buried his lips in her hair, rubbing his face against the silken strands. His mouth moved to her ear, nuzzling, nipping, tasting.

Margaret felt his tongue trace the whorls of her ear, and she trembled under the force of the sensations rushing through her. Unconsciously she moved her lower body against the bed. She ached inside in a delicious, mysterious way. She wanted to relieve the ache, to satisfy it...but not quite yet. First, she wanted to feel it longer.

Andrew's hand flattened out across the plain of her chest, his fingers spread wide. His thumb brushed the swell of her breast. Andrew kissed his way from her ear to her mouth. His breath rasped. His mouth was like fire. He kissed her deeply, consumingly. Margaret wrapped her arms around his neck, kissing him back. He moved over her, supporting his weight on his forearms, his lower body pressing her into the feather mattress. Margaret felt covered by him, wrapped around by him, and it was a delicious, protected, exciting feeling. Her hands clenched in his shirt, bunching the material. She wanted to rip at it, tear it away so that she could feel his bare flesh beneath her fingers.

It was a shocking thought, but she didn't pause to analyze it, any more than she tried to understand why her body longed to arch up against him. She was driven by pure, simple desire, and all she could do was be swept along on the sensations of the moment.

His lips left her mouth and traveled down her throat. He murmured her name, and just the sound of it in his husky, passion-heavy voice sent desire pulsating through her. His hand curled around her breast, caressing it through the thin material of her nightgown. He rubbed his thumb across her nipple and the nub tightened. Margaret felt as if her body was ripening beneath his touch, the breasts swelling and nipples growing, hardening, all of her opening up to him.

Andrew's hand slid lower, bunching up her nightgown until he had pulled it up to her waist. His hand slipped beneath it onto the naked skin of her stomach. Margaret, surprised by the intimate touch, tightened instinctively. His hand stilled on her flesh. Then, with a groan, he broke away from her and sat up.

Dazed, Margaret opened her eyes. "Andrew?"

He shook his head, unable to speak. He was turned slightly away from her and she could not see his face. She sat up, one hand reaching tentatively for his arm. "What is it? Did I do something wrong?"

His laugh was short and humorless. "No. No, you did everything right. But if I go on, I won't be able to stop."

"That's all right."

"No. I promised I wouldn't make love to you tonight." He sighed, shoving both his hands into his hair, and closed his eyes.

"Oh, but, please—this isn't all you wanted, is it?"

He cast her an amused look. "No. There's a lot more I want."

"Then go on. It's all right."

Andrew hesitated. He wanted very badly to yield to the temptation. She was so lovely, her face flushed and her eyes glowing, her mouth wide and slightly swollen from his kisses, that he wanted to take her at her word and lay her back on the bed again. Nothing had ever affected him like her honest, untutored response. She had enjoyed his kisses; he had felt it, tasted it. She couldn't be playacting, as the whores he'd known over the years had; she was too unknowing for that. And there had been none of Damaris's stiffness in her—until right at the last, when he had touched her naked skin.

If Margaret was given the time and opportunity to become accustomed to his touch, perhaps she would lose her stiffness and react with the same innocent enthusiasm she had shown earlier. Perhaps she could enjoy their lovemaking. A hope long dead flickered to life in him. He refused to crush that hope by forging on past the point of her comfort. If he went ahead, she would let him—*after all, hadn't she been trained by her dragon aunt to be dutiful?*—but her enjoyment would stop. He'd be damned if he would ruin the chance of a lifetime of shared passion just to satisfy his desire tonight.

"No. You need time. I want you to—to know me, trust me."

Margaret stared at Andrew in frustration. This was decidedly annoying. She didn't want him to quit; she enjoyed what they were doing, and she felt dissatisfied. Her body was heated, and there was a strange, throbbing ache between her legs that she knew instinctively only *he* could take away. But a lady would certainly not ask him to continue, would not plead with him to satisfy her. A lady did not even enjoy what they were doing; Aunt Charity had been quite clear on that. The fact that she had been enjoying it meant that she was unladylike. It didn't surprise her; Aunt Charity had, over the years, scolded her for countless actions that were not genteel.

But she didn't want Andrew Stone to realize that she was not a lady inside. That was one thing she had had drummed into her head in countless ways by everyone she knew; a man might have base desires for any woman, but a man loved and respected only a lady. And her husband's love and respect was something she wanted more than the immediate gratification of her fledgling passion. Only a husband's love brought a woman a decent, safe and comfortable life.

"Oh." Margaret simply looked at him. He found it very hard not to reach for her, not to pull her up hard against his chest and start kissing her again.

Stone made himself turn away. "Well, good night, then. If you need anything, my room is right next door." He gestured toward the next room.

Margaret nodded. His room. Was this, then, *her* bedroom? Would they have different rooms? Not share a bed? She didn't understand it. Her mother and father had slept in the same bed; she had just assumed that was the normal way with a married couple. Perhaps it was not.

She watched Andrew walk out of the room without even looking back at her. Sighing, Margaret settled back in her bed, pulling the sheets up to her neck. The wedding night she had feared was over. None of the vague horrors she'd imagined had transpired. She was relieved. She was also confused and restless. And she didn't understand the man she had married at all. She wondered if she ever would.

Chapter Eight

The next morning Margaret awoke much later than usual. The sun was already high in the sky. Guiltily, she jumped out of bed, washed at the basin and dressed. She opened her bedroom door and stepped into the hall. The house was quiet as a tomb. Her heels sounded abnormally loud, even muffled by the long runner. She went down the stairs almost on tiptoe, intimidated by the heavy silence. The house might have been completely uninhabited, for all the noise in it.

She wandered through the downstairs, feeling rather like a snoop. She had to keep reminding herself that it was her home now and she had the right to go anywhere that she chose. Finally she stepped into what was obviously a dining room. The furniture was massive and dark, as was all the furniture in the house. She found it a trifle overpowering. Andrew's taste in furniture surprised her. She would not have thought him a man who cared much for ornate things.

Margaret crossed the room and pushed open the door in the opposite wall. A short hallway led to another door; she was in a butler's pantry. At the other end, the door opened into the kitchen. She stuck her head inside and found, at last, another person.

A plump woman in a simple, full skirt and scoop-necked blouse stood with her back to Margaret, chopping busily away with a huge knife. Her hair was as black as midnight and hung down to her hips in a single thick, loose braid, interwoven with a bright ribbon. She hummed as she worked, her entire body moving with her exertions.

"Excuse me..." Margaret began, and the woman whirled.

"*¡Señora!*" A broad grin creased her round, brown face, revealing a broken tooth. A flood of Spanish issued from her.

"No. I'm sorry." Margaret held up her hand, vainly trying to stop the flow. "I don't understand you. I'm afraid I don't speak Spanish."

"Ah, Meezes Stone," the other woman said, much more slowly. "My name ees Carmela. I am nice to meet you."

Margaret blinked. "Why, thank you, Carmela. I'm very pleased to meet you, too. You cook for Mr. Stone?"

"*Sí*, I cook." The broad grin flashed again. "*Mi hija, Rosa—*" She paused, then went off into Spanish again, making wide sweeping gestures.

"Rubs? Cleans? Rosa cleans?"

"*Sí.*" Carmela beamed.

"Well. That's nice." Margaret smiled back, not knowing what else to say. She glanced around the kitchen.

Carmela gestured toward the counter, where she was preparing something, and looked questioningly at Margaret. She spoke in Spanish, then began to make scooping gestures with her hand, bringing it up to her mouth.

"Eat?" Margaret ventured.

"*¡Sí!* You eat?" Carmela beamed.

"Would I like something to eat? Yes, that would be nice, thank you."

"*¿Café?*"

Coffee. That was easy enough. *"Sí. Café. Con leche, por favor."*

Carmela's grin grew even broader. She began to talk in Spanish again as she bustled about the kitchen, starting Margaret's breakfast.

"No. I'm sorry. I'm afraid I've exhausted my knowledge of Spanish." Like most people who lived in Texas, Margaret had picked up a few Spanish words here and there, but nothing more. "*Yo no...comprendo.* Is that right?"

Apparently it was, for Carmela glanced back at her in disappointment and gave a little nod. Margaret looked around. She wondered where it was proper for her to sit. Should she go to the dining room or just take a seat at the large kitchen table? At home—Aunt Charity's house, that is—they ate breakfast and other informal meals at the kitchen table, using the dining room table only for dinner or company. But this house was so much bigger and everything seemed so formal. She didn't want to look as if she didn't know how to act as Andrew Stone's wife should.

Finally, she sat down at the kitchen table. She preferred this sturdy, plain oak table and the hominess of the kitchen to the formal dining room. Carmela seemed to approve her choice, for she smiled as she placed a cup of coffee, creamer and sugar bowl on the table. She added a plate of *pan dulce*, round Mexican sweet cakes, then went to the stove to prepare breakfast. Before long, she brought Margaret a plate of scrambled eggs and sausage that was large enough to satisfy a starving man. Margaret stared at it in dismay. She took a bite of the eggs. They were spicily hot. She ate two more bits and went to the sausage. It was just as spicy, but she was more used to spicy sausage and she managed to eat a decent amount of it. Hoping that she wouldn't offend Carmela, she left the eggs and let one of the sweetcakes suffice for the remainder of her breakfast.

Then, smiling and thanking Carmela, she left the kitchen and started back up the stairs to her room, unsure exactly what she should do. There were the garments in her bags to unpack, but most of her clothes and possessions would be arriving by wagon in a few days, when Annie and Zach moved out to the ranch, too. She had noticed several places where Rosa's housekeeping was not up to her standards, and she could set about dusting and cleaning, but she suspected that both Carmela and Rosa would take that as an insult. It was going to be difficult enough to communicate with them without starting off by criticizing their work. Straightening up the house could wait for a little while.

She went into her bedroom and put away her clothes. Then she glanced around the room. The furniture was just as dark and heavy as it had looked last night. She had hoped that the room would appear more welcoming by the light of day. She sighed. At least she could pull back the heavy drapes and let the sunshine in.

She stood for a moment looking out the east window. She could see the barn and corrals from here, and beyond them the land stretching on out of sight. It was a pleasant view to her. She had always loved the land. The muted colors of the ground and vegetation and the piercing blueness of the high-arching sky were beautiful to her. She loved the ancient, sturdy live oaks, the twisted, scrawny cedars, the feathery mesquites. She even liked the scrubby chaparral brush and the thorny pear cacti. Her soul answered to the limitless stretch of land. She could remember when she was a little girl finding her mother crying one day, and when Margaret asked her why, her mother, born and bred in Tennessee, could only say "It's so ugly. So empty. I wish I could go home."

Margaret had been shocked. Texas, harsh and hot, was home to her, and she couldn't imagine considering it ugly. All the years she had had to live in town with Aunt Charity, she had felt cramped and restless.

She turned away from the window and wandered into the hallway. The door to the next room stood open, and she strolled past it, casting a studiedly casual glance into it. It was empty, so she stopped and inspected it more thoroughly. This must be Andrew's bedroom. A pair of men's boots stood against the far wall, and a man's coat was slung over the back of a chair. The furniture was less ornate than that in her room and was made of oak. Even though there was a decidedly masculine air to the room, Margaret liked it better than her own. It seemed more comfortable, less likely to send one into a fit of the glooms.

Margaret stepped inside. The dresser was bare, except for a miniature portrait and a set of heavy masculine brushes and combs. She bent down to look at the portrait. It was of his daughter.

"Can I help you?"

Margaret whirled guiltily. Andrew Stone stood in the doorway. She blushed to her hairline. "I—I'm sorry." What would he think of her snooping in his room?

"Sorry? For what?" He walked toward her.

Her eyes widened a little. Was he joking? "For being in your room. I have no excuse. I was just . . . curious."

She waited, bracing herself. But there was no anger on his face, and he said only, "No need to apologize. I've nothing to hide. You are the mistress of the house. I would say you have the authority to be in any room you wish."

"Oh." She didn't know what to say. She wouldn't have suspected that Andrew Stone would be so easy-going about anything.

"I came back to the house to see if you were awake. I thought you might enjoy a ride around the ranch with me. Get a look at your new home."

"Yes." A grin flashed across her face. "I would like that very much." She started toward the door. "I'll go change into riding clothes."

Andrew reached out and caught her elbow. "Just one thing."

"What?" She looked up at him anxiously.

"This." He bent and kissed her gently on the lips. "We haven't even said good morning."

"Good morning." Margaret wondered if her voice sounded as breathless as she suddenly felt.

"Good morning. I trust you slept well."

"Very well, thank you." She wasn't about to reveal how long it had taken her to go to sleep or that she had tossed and turned.

"Good." He kissed her again, this time a peck on the forehead, and moved out of her way. "I'll wait for you outside."

When she came down in her spanking-new riding habit a few minutes later, Margaret saw Andrew in front of the barn, saddling a horse. Beside him was a man saddling another horse. Margaret walked toward them a little shyly. She had never worn a riding habit before. When she had learned how to ride, she had been just a girl and she and Annie had both ridden in their regular skirts. Since then, while they lived with their aunt, she had had no horse to ride.

But Aunt Charity had included a riding habit in her generous allotment of new clothes. Margaret thought the rather mannish cut of the jacket gave it a jaunty, intriguing look, and she liked the straight skirt without the voluminous petticoats she usually wore. Best of all was the wide-brimmed hat that shaded her face. It resembled a cavalry hat and was pinned up on one side with a swooping blue feather that curled over and down to her eyes. She had never worn anything half so dashing, and Aunt Charity had protested loudly that it was a ridiculous hat for a young girl to wear. But Emma had been adamant that it looked the most fetching of any hat she'd tried on, and Margaret had been determined to get it. Now, when Andrew looked up and saw her and straightened reflexively, a look of admiration and desire mingling on his face, Margaret was very glad that she had insisted.

"My dear." Andrew came to meet her, reaching out to clasp her hand. Margaret smiled, giving her hand willingly into his. It was funny how nice it felt to have Andrew's large, masculine hand surrounding hers, warm and rough. "You look very fetching," he told her in a low voice.

"Really?" Margaret asked ingenuously, her eyes lighting up. "It's new. Aunt Charity bought it for me. Do you know, she turned quite nice about the whole marriage there at the end? She even got me several new dresses."

"How very generous of her." Andrew's voice was heavy with sarcasm. Apparently Margaret thought that she could continue to play the unmercenary innocent, pretending that she didn't know he had paid her aunt the money she had refused to take. He wondered if she actually thought he would be fooled by it.

Margaret glanced at him, surprised by his tone. "Well, yes, it was. I realize that it wouldn't be much money for you, but my aunt is not a wealthy woman. It was a considerable expense for her."

Andrew glanced at her. "Margaret, please. Why keep up the pretense? Your aunt is not a wealthy woman, true. That's why I offered you the money in the first place. I knew it would be a burden on her to provide the parties and dresses and everything you'd need. But I can see no point in our continuing with this charade."

Margaret gave him a puzzled stare. What on earth was he talking about? "I—I'm sorry. I don't understand. What charade?"

"The money, my dear, the money which you refused and had your aunt so cleverly accept. It was a practical matter. I don't think any the less of you for taking it. What bothers me is your doing it in an underhanded way. I told you. I don't like deceit."

Margaret stopped dead still. "I beg your pardon. What did you just say?"

He stopped, too, looking at her. What was her point in keeping up this game?

"Are you telling me that my aunt took the money from you?"

"Yes. She threw out a few broad hints about how expensive it was to put on an appropriate wedding, and I gave her the money."

"And you think I planned that? You think I refused the money from you so that I would look sweet and honorable, then had my aunt take it?"

He frowned. "Yes."

Margaret pressed her lips together and her eyes flashed. "You have a fine opinion of your wife, sir. I don't understand why you married me when you obviously consider me such a cheap, conniving—" She made a strangled noise of rage and whirled around to stalk off toward the house.

Andrew stared, then ran after her. "Margaret! What the hell do you think you're doing?" He grabbed her arm, pulling her to a stop.

"I don't want to go riding with you. I don't want to have anything to do with you. How could you think I'd do that! I didn't know Aunt Charity asked you for money! She didn't tell me! I thought *she* was paying for everything. I even thanked her profusely for the dresses. Oooh! The nerve of that woman. I don't know whether I'm madder at her or you!"

"You didn't know? You had nothing to do with her asking me?"

"No! No! Oh, how humiliating! I can't believe I married a man who thought I was deceiving him! Taking money from him, like a common—" She broke off, her voice trembling with rage.

Her anger was like a spark to the tinder of his passion. Andrew wanted suddenly, voraciously, to kiss her, to pull her down right there in the yard and plunge into her. She wasn't lying. He was sure of it. She was as honest and beautiful, as clean in her anger as a flame.

"Wait, don't go." His fingers turned caressing on her arm. "I'm sorry. I was a fool." He took a step closer so that they were almost touching and stared down into her eyes. Their emotions were so intense they crackled between them like heat lightning. Looking up into his eyes, Margaret knew what he wanted to do. And some wanton something deep inside her responded to it; she half wished he would sweep her up into his arms and carry her back into the house. "I should have known it was your aunt, not you."

Unexpectedly, her arm went limp in his grasp. She looked away. "No, I'm sorry. It is I who should have known. I know Aunt Charity. It was foolish of me to think that she provided for me out of the generosity of her heart. I guess I wanted to think that she loved me deep down inside." She looked back up at him, blinking away tears. "I'm sorry. I can see how it must have appeared to you, her asking you for money right after I'd turned you down so righteously. But I truly didn't know. I didn't want her to do that. I—I'll pay you back."

He smiled. "How? With my own money?"

He had her there. She had nothing of her own. "I'm sorry."

"Don't be a fool. I wanted you to have the money. I wanted you to have the dresses and the parties. It was my right and my duty to provide them. And, having seen you in the new gowns, I can assure you that it was also my pleasure."

Her eyes widened a little at the last statement and she had to smile. "Thank you."

"I never cared about the money. It was just the thought that you were playing a game with me. You're my wife and whatever I have is yours, also. Don't worry about that little bit of money."

He bent and kissed her softly on the mouth. His lips wanted to linger, but he knew he did not dare or he would be in danger of picking her up and taking her back up to his bedroom. He doubted she'd ever forgive him for a public scene like that. "Shall we forget all this and start over again?"

"Yes. I'd like that."

"Good. Come and meet my foreman." He took her arm and led her back toward the horses. He felt suddenly lighthearted. She had not lied to him. She hadn't sought his money, all the while pretending that she had not. There hadn't been greed and deception in her heart.

The other man, who had finished saddling the horse long ago and had been watching them with interest, straightened as they approached.

"String!" Andrew said. "I want you to meet my wife. Margaret, this is String McAlister, my foreman and right-hand man. String, this is Margaret Carlisle Stone."

"Miz Stone." The other man tugged at his hat. "I'm pleased to meet you."

"I met you the other day at the reception," Margaret said with a friendly smile, extending her hand to him.

He grinned. "Yes, ma'am, but I didn't expect you to remember me with all that was going on."

String was older than most of the men who worked on the ranch, a wiry, slim man with the leathery skin of one who had spent most of his life outdoors. He had an open, friendly face and twinkling brown eyes, and Margaret had liked him the moment she met him. There was no trace of the South in his voice, and she suspected that he, like her husband, came from the North.

"Did you serve with my husband?" She hazarded a guess.

The man's face lit up delightedly. "Now, how'd you know that?" He glanced toward Andrew. "This lady's too sharp by half for you. You're right, ma'am, I did serve under the colonel. I was his sergeant when he was a raw lieutenant. I had to take him under my wing or he'd a likely killed himself."

"You old coot," Andrew retorted good-naturedly. "I was the one who had to pull you out of the stockade, as I remember."

The older man made a dismissive gesture. "A complete error."

Margaret smiled, enjoying their banter. It was nice to see Andrew at ease with someone, laughing and joking, without the tenseness that was usually on his face, the careful, guarded look of someone who didn't trust anyone.

As they were talking, another man stepped out of the barn. He was dressed in denim trousers, like most of the men, but without the leather chaps that the others wore. Margaret presumed it was because he didn't go out to work all day on horseback as the others did. She wasn't sure what he did, but she had seen him several times this morning, just strolling around the yard or standing on the porch of the bunkhouse, smoking a cigarette. He was the man who had usually accompanied Andrew into town and had stood waiting for him outside when Andrew called on her. Zach swore he was a gunslinger, and Margaret was inclined to think that her brother was right. He wore a low, strapped-down leg holster, and there was something cold and deadly in his odd yellowish eyes.

He stopped when he saw them. ''Mr. Stone. Miz Stone.''

''Whitman.'' Andrew could hardly not introduce him. ''Margaret, this is Whitman. He works here, too.''

The man nodded toward her and stepped forward to shake her hand. Margaret found that she was reluctant to give it to him, but she mustered up a false smile and offered her hand.

''Mr. Whitman.''

''Ma'am.''

She turned toward Andrew brightly. ''Shall we go?''

''Of course.'' He gave her a leg up into the saddle, then swung up onto his own horse, and they started off.

''I like String,'' Margaret said.

''He's a good man.''

''But that other man, that Whitman...something about him gives me the shivers.''

Andrew glanced at her. "Don't worry about him. He's just here to protect you. You needn't have any dealings with him."

"Is that necessary?" Margaret asked a little timidly. "I mean, do we need so much protection?"

"Yes," he answered shortly, and Margaret quickly dropped the subject.

They rode at a steady, gentle pace until they came to the Escollo River, the western boundary of Andrew Stone's land. Here Andrew drew his horse to a stop and sat, looking down at the river. It was broad and green, and the vegetation grew thickly on its banks. Huge cottonwoods and spreading, gnarled oaks shaded its sides. It was a peaceful scene, a fresh, green gem set into the harsh land. There must be times, Margaret knew, when it swelled and raged, but right now it was slow and somnolent.

She glanced at Andrew. There was something softer in his face as he gazed at the river. "It's beautiful, isn't it?" he asked quietly, not looking at her. "I remember sometimes during the War, I'd think about this spot and I'd tell myself that when it was over, I'd come home. Somehow it helped."

"When you were wounded?" Margaret ventured.

He glanced at her, surprised. "Yes. I thought about it most of all when I was wounded."

"I'm glad it helped."

"Are you?"

She looked puzzled. "Of course. Why wouldn't I be?"

"I don't know. I don't know why you should care one way or the other."

Margaret frowned. "You mean because you were on the other side?"

He shrugged. "I guess. And because you don't know me. Because our marriage is only the arrangement that it is."

"I don't like the thought of any person in pain. I would like for anyone to have something to help them get through it. I wouldn't wish an injury to someone I disliked, let alone a whole army of people I didn't even know."

"That's what war's about, though."

"Well, I didn't have any say-so about the War that I recall," she retorted sharply. "I didn't start it. I didn't continue it, and all I ever got out of it was losing my father. War is something men throw themselves into without any thought to the women who love them."

"Sometimes there are principles that compel us to go to war."

"Principles!" Margaret sent him a brief, flashing glance.

"Yes. Such as freedom."

"That's what you fought for?"

"Yes."

"Funny, that's what my daddy said he was fighting for. He said the people of a state had the freedom to choose their own destiny, that there was no way a Texan was going to let some old fools in Washington tell them they couldn't secede. So there you were on one side and him on the other, and you were both fighting for the same principle. That makes a lot of sense, doesn't it?"

Andrew smiled faintly. He hadn't imagined Margaret firing up about anything. He liked the spark in her eyes and the color in her cheeks, even the touch of acerbity in her voice. "I take it you wouldn't fight for any musty old principles?"

"I wouldn't take up a gun about it, no."

"What would you take up a gun about?"

"The people I love," she responded without hesitation, and she turned her head to look at him, her eyes unwavering. "My family, my home."

He wondered if he was included in that group or if he was a stranger, merely the means by which she was able to take care of those she loved.

Andrew looked away. "Where did your father fall?"

"The Wilderness." Tears filled her eyes.

"I'm sorry."

"It was his choice. He believed in his principles." She closed her eyes and the tears splashed down onto her cheeks.

The sight of her tears pierced Andrew and he edged his horse closer to her, reaching out to lay a gentle hand on her arm.

Margaret attempted a wobbly smile. "I'm sorry. I shouldn't be bitter. You must think I'm terrible."

"No. Not at all. Why would I think that?"

"Because—" her chin trembled, and she set it determinedly, pausing to recover her composure "—because I sound angry at him."

"There's nothing wrong with that."

"To be mad at a person because he died?" She cast him a disbelieving look. "That's hardly loving or generous."

His hand slid down her arm and clasped her hand. Even through the leather of her glove, she could feel the warmth and strength of his hand and it was somehow comforting. "Maybe not, but it's not so bad, either."

"I don't know. It seems wicked to me. When I saw his name on the casualty list, it was as though he'd cheated me, betrayed me. I was angry at him! I wanted to throw things, to smash them. I wanted to jump on a horse and ride like the devil was after me. I was furious with Daddy for dying and leaving me, leaving us. As if he'd done it on purpose." She glanced at Andrew uncertainly. "I've never told anyone that. I was too ashamed."

He squeezed her hand. "You're not wicked. I can't imagine you being wicked." He didn't stop to think about how deeply and positively he felt that, he, who only weeks before would have claimed that any woman had the seeds of wickedness inside her.

Margaret looked up at him and smiled. "Thank you." He was gazing at her with gentleness, kindness. Suddenly she knew, without any doubt, that he could not have done whatever horrible things Damaris had accused him of. "You're a good man." She leaned over to him and brushed her lips against his. "I'm not scared. Not of you."

Andrew's heart began to race. Did she mean she did not fear him in bed, that he need wait no longer to make love to her? He could feel the tamped-down desire beginning to surge in him. He cupped her chin, his fingers softly stroking her cheek. "I would never try to hurt you."

"I know." Her eyes were calm and trusting in a way that twisted his heart.

He kissed her gently, tasting the sweetness of her lips. He wanted to sweep her off her horse and make love to her right there. But he could imagine her fright and dismay if he did. She might be inviting him into her bed, at least tentatively, but she certainly wasn't asking that he pull her off her horse and take her in the rough field.

They straightened from their kiss and for a moment, looked at each other. Tonight, he thought. Tonight he would go to her room. And if she didn't stiffen up while he was kissing her, if she didn't pull away . . . then tonight he would make her truly his wife.

Margaret and Andrew didn't return from their ride until late in the afternoon. As Margaret was changing, she realized with a touch of shame that she hadn't seen Andrew's daughter today. Worse than that, she hadn't even thought about her. She wondered where Laura could have been this morning; the house had been so quiet—surely there hadn't been an eleven-year-old girl anywhere in it. She glanced at the clock. There was still time before supper. Since she had missed lunch, she had planned to steal into the kitchen for a bit of food to keep her going, but she decided instead to find Laura. She had the uneasy feeling that it wasn't going to be an easy task to win Laura's liking; it would make it much worse if the girl thought she was snubbing her on the very first day of her residence.

She went out in the hall and past her husband's room. Most of the doors stood open, and the rooms beyond were obviously unoccupied. Margaret was amazed all over again at the size of the house. There would be room for Zach and Annie to each have a room, with plenty left over for guest rooms. If they ever had any guests, that was. That was another thing she was going to have to tackle.

Finally, at the far end, she came upon a set of rooms that were lived in. The first, and smallest, was spare and neat, so neat in fact that she would have had trouble telling it was occupied if it hadn't been for the hairbrush and mirror lying on the dresser. The next room looked to be a cross between a sitting room and an office, with a small desk and several shelves of books, as well as a couple of comfortable chairs, a small table and a heavy trunk. On shelves along one side sat an array of porcelain dolls in pristine condition. Connecting to it was a bedroom, again quite neat, though with more signs of occupancy than the other. A hat was tossed across a chair and a book lay open on the bed. The bed had a tester with a single deep ruffle around the edge, but aside from that, the room seemed very lacking in frills for one of a girl of eleven. Even Annie, tomboy that she was, had preferred bedspreads and curtains with ruffles and had kept flowers on the dresser and pictures on the walls.

Margaret wondered where Laura was. Just as she was turning to leave, she heard measured footsteps on the stairs and in the next moment, two heads came into sight. One was the dark one of Laura Stone; the other was blond, mingled with gray, the hair pulled back tightly into a coronet of braids. It was the German governess Andrew had introduced Margaret to last night. The pair reached the top of the stairs.

"Gud afternoon, Frau Stone," the governess said in her accented voice.

"Hello, Miss Hoelscher. Laura. It's nice to see you. Have you been out? I must confess, I haven't heard a sound from you today."

Miss Hoelscher secretly pinched Laura on the arm and Laura started, then curtsied. "Good afternoon, ma'am."

"Now answer your new mooter, Fräulein."

"What? Oh. No, ma'am, we weren't out. I mean, well, we were behind the house, practicing my painting."

"Where there's no mess to be cleaned up. How practical." Margaret smiled. "Do you enjoy painting?"

Two lines appeared between Laura's eyes. "I'm afraid I'm not very good."

"I should like to see your work sometime."

"Of course. If you want to."

"If you vill excuse us, Frau Stone, the fräulein must clean up. Den I tought I vould bring her to de sitting room. Vere you can visit, *ja*?"

"Yes, that would be nice. I'll see you in a bit, then." Margaret felt awkward, almost as if she'd been dismissed by the other woman, but she tried to smile at Laura. There was no visible response from the child.

She went downstairs and chose the room that looked most like the one the governess would term the sitting room; it was more comfortable and not as ornate as the room closer to the front, which Margaret assumed must be the formal parlor. A few minutes later, Laura appeared in the doorway, Fräulein Hoelscher behind her.

"Now, Fräulein, you sit and talk vit de Frau." She turned toward Margaret. "You vish me to stay or leave, Frau Stone?"

"I believe I'd like to talk with Laura alone, please." She hoped uneasily that the other woman wouldn't take offense. She could see nothing in the governess's face as she nodded and left the room.

"Well, Laura . . ." Margaret began brightly, turning to the girl and forcing a smile. What was she to say to her now? She wished Emma were here. She could always find something to say. Or Annie. She would soon have everyone laughing. "How was your day?"

"Fine, ma'am."

Margaret was at a loss once again. Laura's dress and pinafore were awfully plain for a girl of her age and station in life. She wondered why Andrew had her dress that way. Of course, he wore those plain black suits, but why would he want a girl to dress so somberly? That, she thought, would be another of her projects. She seemed to be acquiring them quickly.

"Fräulein Hoelscher said I was to call you 'Mother,'" Laura said, breaking into her thoughts. "Am I?"

Though Laura was sitting quite still and proper, her hands folded in her lap, her back straight and her face polite, Margaret could see the stubborn dislike in her eyes. Clearly, calling Margaret "Mother" was something Laura had no desire to do. Margaret thought about how she would have felt if her father had remarried after her mother died and she had been told to call such a woman "Mother." Her stomach knotted even at the thought. And her mother was dead, at least; Laura's was still very much alive, even if she never saw her.

"No, dear, I wouldn't think so. I mean, if you wanted to call me Mother, I would be honored, of course. But you hardly know me, after all, and I'm only ten years older than you. Not enough to be your mother. Why don't you call me Margaret—or Maggie. That's what my brother and sister call me. I hope that's what I can be for you, an older sister."

She could see the tension ease in the girl's shoulders. "All right. Thank you. Will you tell the Fräulein you told me to? I don't think she'd think it was proper, my calling you by your given name."

"Yes. Of course." Margaret paused. Laura gazed back quietly. She obviously wasn't much more of a conversationalist than Margaret herself. Finally Margaret said, "Zach and Annie are coming out here to live soon. That's my brother and sister. You met them at the wedding."

"Yes."

"I hope the three of you will be friends. I am sure it will make it much less lonely out here."

"Yes, ma'am."

"Annie is fifteen and Zach is thirteen, so they aren't much older than you."

"Yes, ma'am."

Margaret was beginning to wonder if the girl could say anything else. She had such a solemn face and grave eyes. There was something closed about her features; Margaret couldn't tell what she was thinking, as she could with Annie. She wasn't sure if Laura was simply shy or if she disliked her.

She continued to prod the stilted conversation along, hoping that eventually she would find a topic that interested Laura. But while she smiled a little when Margaret mentioned horses and riding and looked proud when she mentioned the girl's father, Laura didn't wax enthusiastic about anything. It was a relief when Fräulein Hoelscher came to the door thirty minutes later.

"It is time for de fräulein to eat now," she announced.

Laura rose obediently. "Good night, ma'am."

Margaret stood up, too. She would liked to have taken the girl's hands, but she felt that Laura would have recoiled. "Please, call me Margaret." She turned toward the governess. "I told Laura that I would prefer she call me by my name."

"As you vish, madam." Miss Hoelscher nodded.

Margaret let out a sigh of relief when they were gone. No doubt Laura was a model child, and no doubt Fräulein Hoelscher was a wonderful governess. But couldn't the woman ever smile? Couldn't Laura just once look as if she enjoyed something?

Margaret leaned back against the chair and closed her eyes. It was in this pose that Andrew found her sometime later, dozing in the large wing chair, her legs curled up under her. There was something sweet and angelic about the way she looked; he almost hated to awaken her. He went to her and lightly touched her hair. His fingers slid down over the silky silver-gold mass and onto her face. He touched her smooth cheek and traced the outline of her lips. The deep, hot ache that had been his constant companion the past few weeks started up in him again.

Margaret's eyelids fluttered open and she gazed at him blankly for an instant before her eyes cleared. Then she smiled slowly and sweetly. As always, her smile was a shock to Andrew's senses. He wanted to go down on his knees in front of her chair and take off her clothes, kissing and caressing every inch of her tender white flesh as he did so. The erotic picture burned in his mind and he could think of nothing to say; he could only stare down at her.

Heat started in Margaret's abdomen as he continued to look at her; there was something in his eyes that made her feel like melting wax. She wondered if he were about to resume his "lessons" of the evening before, and her pulse quickened. She reached up her hand toward him and he took it. His skin was searing.

Andrew tried to recall the mundane things they should do now. It was, after all, hours yet until bedtime. He could hardly stand here panting over her all evening. He cleared his throat. "Uh, it's...uh, Carmela has supper ready, I think."

"Oh." She was distinctly disappointed. "Of course."

She rose lithely to her feet and took his arm to walk into the dining room. They ate at the formal table in solitary splendor. Margaret paid little attention to her food; her stomach was too knotted with excitement. They made a few attempts at conversation, but both of them found that their minds were too much elsewhere to be able to keep any discussion going.

"I trust our ride today wasn't too tiring for you," he said. He looked at her mouth, so soft and luscious, and thought about kissing her.

"No, it was fine. I enjoyed it." She thought of his hands sliding down over her body and her breasts tingled, her nipples tightening.

There was silence. His gaze dropped down her throat to her breasts. He thought about unbuttoning her dress another two or three buttons, until he could see the softly swelling mounds of her breasts.

"I, uh, talked with Laura this afternoon," Margaret said. She remembered his kiss, his tongue thrusting into her mouth. She wanted to taste it again. She wanted to feel his breath hot upon her skin, his teeth teasing at her earlobe.

"Did you? Good. That's nice." Andrew pictured himself undressing her, peeling off each layer of civilized clothing until she stood completely naked before him.

"Yes. I—enjoyed it." There was a hot, pulsing ache between her legs and she surreptitiously squeezed them together. Would he come to her tonight? How could she make sure of it?

Again their conversation ground to a halt. And so it went throughout the whole meal. It was a relief when supper was finally over and they were able to leave the table. They strolled back to the sitting room. It was still too early to retire. Margaret sat down and folded her hands in her lap; she wished she had some sewing or knitting to keep her hands occupied. Andrew wandered aimlessly around the room.

"I—uh, if you will excuse me, I believe I'll step outside and have a cigar."

"Oh. Of course. But why don't you just smoke it in here?"

He glanced at her. "You don't object?"

Her eyebrows went up. "Why should I? It is, after all, your house."

"It is yours, too, now." He shrugged as he went to the large box on the table and removed a thin cigarillo. "A house is always the lady's domain."

"Then you will not object if I change a few things?"

"Of course not. Change whatever you like."

"I felt a bit uneasy about taking over the reins of the household—changing the housekeeping or anything."

"Do what you want. If you want something done differently, just tell Carmela."

"That may prove to be a little difficult."

He chuckled, rolling the cigar between his fingers. He snipped off the end and lit it. "I've had that problem with Carmela myself."

"I think I shall have to learn Spanish."

He glanced at her, surprised. "I've found it helpful. I've learned enough to get by with her and some of the Mexican hands. But I've never known you Texans to care overmuch whether you could communicate with them."

"My, my," Margaret said softly, her accent suddenly thicker and more liquid. "Here I was thinking it was only the people of Huxley who were so quick to judge their fellow man."

His eyes narrowed. "Are you trying to tell me I'm as narrow-minded as the people of Huxley?"

Her eyes widened innocently and her voice practically dripped with honey. "Why, no, I was merely pointing out that the people in this town seem to know so very much about you and what you do and think—and here you know all about them, too."

For a moment Margaret thought that she had gone too far, that her sense of humor had betrayed her into antagonizing this man upon whom she was utterly dependent. But then Andrew grinned as he blew out a cloud of smoke and laid his cigar in the ashtray. "Why, you little minx. You plan to keep me on the straight and narrow, don't you?"

"I don't know about that." Her voice turned serious and she jumped up to go to him. Her eyes were big and entreating. "But I would like to make your daughter accepted in Huxley, as you wanted me to."

"Yes?"

"And I think that in order to do that, you're going to have to socialize with them and not—not let your contempt be so obvious."

"Contempt?" He looked genuinely surprised. "I don't hold the people around here in contempt."

"Perhaps you don't realize it. But it's in your voice, your face."

"You think so?" She nodded. He hesitated, gazing at her seriously. "But not—not when I look at you. Is it?"

"No. I don't think so."

"You aren't sure."

"Sometimes, particularly when we first met, there was something in your eyes. I thought that you disliked me, but then I decided that it was all women you disliked."

"I don't dislike you. I—" He cast around for a way to express it that wouldn't hurt her feelings. "I have some mistrust of women. But it's not contempt for you. Or lack of caring."

That was another way of saying that he cared for her, wasn't it? Impulsively Margaret reached out and took one of his hands in hers. It was large and rough between her two hands, and it sent a frisson of excitement through her for him to let it lie quiescently captive to her, his power leashed for her. "I want to be a good wife to you, Andrew. I want to create a good home for you and raise your children well."

Andrew looked down at her. She was so beautiful, so soft. There was something warm and comforting about his hand resting between hers, yet at the same time it stirred him.

Margaret saw the glow in Andrew's eyes, and felt a corresponding heat start deep within her. Would he make love to her tonight?

"God, you're lovely," he breathed. He was afire for her, as eager to have her as a lad coming into manhood. He couldn't remember when he had last felt this hungry, this anxious about a woman. It had been years. Since Damaris.

He stiffened and his hand dropped away from her. He stepped back. Damaris had been pliant and sweet at first, too, when she was trying to enchant him. It wasn't until she'd had her claws in him good and deep that she had turned cold and scornful. After he had made love to her.

"Andrew?" Margaret's voice was puzzled. A moment ago the very air had been sizzling with his passion. Now he was as remote as a stranger.

In that she was wrong. The desire still burned inside him, hot and high. But he controlled it. He looked at her coolly. "Yes?"

She could think of nothing to say. "I—" She shook her head and stepped away, brushing her damp hands over her skirts. "Nothing." She was hurt and dismayed. "I believe I'll retire now. I am a little tired, after all."

Andrew heard the hurt in her voice and he steeled himself against it. He knew how good some women were at playacting. He couldn't take the chance of believing her; it could mean the loss of his soul. That was something he knew all too well. He'd already had the heart torn out of him once. "All right. I will see you in the morning."

Then he wasn't coming to her bed tonight. Margaret turned away to hide the pain his words brought her. She had thought he was wild with passion for her, yet he obviously didn't even want her. "Yes. Good night." She swung away and left the room quickly.

There was a knot in Andrew's chest and another one in his stomach, and his loins ached. He hated himself for falling in so easily with Margaret's honeyed words and sweet looks. He hated himself for having exiled himself from her bed tonight. He hated himself for being unable to take his pleasure with her without having any deeper feelings, as he had intended when he came up with the idea of marrying her. He swung around and slammed his fist into the wall. He hit it again and again, hardly feeling the pain. He wished he could beat out all the confusion inside him.

Finally he turned away and, after kicking a small embroidered stool halfway across the room, he flopped down in a chair. He stared moodily across the floor. He wished he could relieve the twisting, clawing desire for her. He wished he could go back and start this evening's conversation again. Most of all, he wished he could stop his mind from seeing, over and over, the surprised, wounded look in Margaret's eyes before she turned and walked out the door.

Chapter Nine

Once again, the next morning when Margaret awoke, she went downstairs and ate a solitary breakfast. She would be glad when her brother and sister came, she thought; at least then she'd have someone to eat with. Laura had had supper last night in her room. Did she eat all her other meals there, as well? Margaret wondered if that was because she and Andrew were newlyweds and Miss Hoelscher was politely giving them their privacy or if it was customary. She had heard that in some wealthy Eastern families, it was the custom for the children to dine alone in the nursery with their nanny or governess. Would her new husband expect Zach and Annie to dine separately, as well? It seemed a lonely, bleak prospect.

After breakfast, Carmela introduced Margaret to her daughter, Rosa, who did most of the cleaning in the house outside of the kitchen. Rosa was as short and wide as her mother and possessed the same round, smiling face. Fortunately, she knew much more English than Carmela, so Margaret was able to explain to her what she wanted done.

"I need to learn Spanish," she told Rosa after she'd set out the work to be done. She unbuttoned her sleeves and began to roll them up. "Do you think you could teach me some words?"

Rosa stared at her oddly. "Of course, *Señora*."

"Good. I imagine we could do it as we worked. It would be handy, don't you think?"

"As we work?" Rosa looked at Margaret's rolled-up sleeves. "You mean, you will clean, too?"

"Why, of course. We need to get everything squared away this first time, and that's too much work for one person. When Annie gets here, it'll go even faster. Now. Where are the aprons and the cleaning supplies?"

Rosa was obviously stunned. However, she led Margaret into the kitchen where she donned a practical long apron that covered most of her dress. Then they set to work, with Carmela helping them whenever she wasn't busy in the kitchen. They dusted the furniture and polished it, then cleaned every piece of glass, from mirrors to the china cabinet, and finished the day by washing the windows.

"Tomorrow," Margaret said, "we'll take out the rugs and beat them and wash and wax the floors."

Rosa rolled her eyes in her mother's direction. The new *señora* was a nice woman, but she was certainly a taskmaster. One might almost wish that the colonel had remained a bachelor.

"Now, Carmela, I was wondering if you might make me one of my favorite dishes?" Margaret asked tactfully, with Rosa translating for her.

"Sí, Señora."

"Wonderful." Margaret beamed at her. "I will show you how to make it. You're such an excellent cook, I'm sure you will catch on immediately."

She led her into the kitchen, where she set about teaching her how to batter and pan fry steak and whip up creamy smooth mashed potatoes.

That evening when Rosa set down the steaming platters in front of them at the table, Andrew blinked in surprise. He had grown used to Carmela's Mexican food and had long ago given up trying to explain to her what he wished to eat. But now, looking at the potatoes, steak and creamed peas, his mouth watered. He turned to Margaret.

"You've worked miracles." He was a little uncomfortable around Margaret after the way he'd turned away from her last night. He'd spent half the night tossing in his bed, bitterly castigating himself for being such an idiot. He had been afraid that when he saw her again, she would be cool and aloof, punishing him for the rejection.

But Margaret, who never was one to hold a grudge, had worked out her resentment in the day's heavy housecleaning. Then a hot, soaking bath in the slipper tub in her room had eased out the soreness of her muscles and left her feeling relaxed and happy. So she merely smiled and said, "Thank you. But it wasn't a miracle, I'm afraid. I asked Carmela to make a special dish for me, and I showed her how to do it. With Rosa to translate, it wasn't any problem."

"Well, it was something I was never able to accomplish." He took a bite. "Mmm, delicious." He paused. "I'm sending a wagon tomorrow to pick up the rest of your things and to bring your brother and sister back."

Margaret's eyes lit up. "Oh, thank you! It will be so wonderful to see them."

Andrew experienced a strange little pang at the thought that she was so happy to have someone else in the house with them. Yet at the same time, the joy in her face made him feel larger than life, even heroic. "It will be nice to have your family here. It will help fill up the emptiness."

Margaret thought of Annie's exuberance and capacity for noise making. "Maybe more than you realize." She hesitated. She didn't want to offend Andrew again, as she somehow had last night. But this was the perfect opening for her concerns. "Will Annie and Zach eat with us, or will you expect them to eat with Laura?"

His eyebrows lifted. "I don't know. I hadn't thought about it. I suppose they would be good company for Laura. Still, they seem rather old to be eating in the nursery. Would you like to have them at our table?"

She nodded. "I—perhaps it isn't what you're used to. But I'm accustomed to dining with my family, and it's—much livelier."

"Then they shall eat with us." He thought of the dining room humming with talk and laughter, and it seemed a pleasant vision.

"Perhaps Laura could, too. At least sometimes."

"You'd like her to?"

"Well . . . yes." She wasn't sure how she should answer. He had turned so inexplicably cold last night; she was afraid of taking some misstep that would cause him to do it again. He might think it plebeian of her to want to have children at the dinner table.

"All right." He smiled. "Then she shall. I'm sure Laura will be pleased to hear it. She's been wanting to sit with the adults for a long time now."

"She never ate with you before?"

"No." He thought of the long months and years past, of silent, solitary meals and a bitter, pervading loneliness that had at last driven him to seek another wife, despite his vow never to remarry. "Fräulein Hoelscher took it as a matter of course that her charge would eat with her in the nursery, and I, well, I assumed that it was best."

"I saw Laura last night and tonight. Miss Hoelscher brought her in before supper to visit with me."

"How was your visit?" Margaret could see the tightening of his fingers on his fork, the sudden rigidity of his back and arms.

"Fine. Laura is a quiet little girl."

Some of the tension left him. "Yes. I trust she behaved well."

"Oh, yes. Very. But the routine is rather formal, and I thought she might feel a little constrained. It—might be nice to spend time with her in a more natural situation."

"I'm not sure what you mean."

"I don't know when her lessons are, and I certainly didn't want to interfere with them, but I thought if she and I did something together during the day, take a ride, maybe, or just—" she made a vague gesture "—I don't know, do *something* together, we could get to know each other better."

Andrew looked at her. "You manage to surprise me every time I talk to you."

Margaret looked puzzled. "I don't understand. What do you mean? How did I surprise you?"

"When you started talking about Laura, I thought you were going to complain about having to visit with her so much, and now here you are asking to spend more time with her. It's very kind of you."

Margaret's eyebrows shot up. "Complain? About having to spend less than an hour a day with a child? Why would I complain about that?"

"She's not your child, after all. God knows, her mother never wanted to spend even that much time with her."

Margaret stared. "What?" He must be exaggerating. A mother not want to spend even a brief time every day visiting with her child? That couldn't be true.

He made an impatient gesture, dismissing the topic. "Never mind. I shouldn't have mentioned it. I have no desire to discuss my former wife. Especially not at the dinner table—it spoils my appetite." Scowling, he picked up his knife and fork and attacked the meat on his plate.

Margaret burned to ask more questions. She wanted to know the truth about Damaris Murdock and Andrew. If Mrs. Murdock actually didn't want to spend time with her child, then maybe it wasn't that Andrew had kept the child from her out of meanness or spite. Maybe everyone had been wrong to assume that he was cruel enough to deny a child and mother the chance to see each other. But the look on Andrew's face didn't invite any questions. He would probably snap her head off if she brought up the subject again.

She clasped her hands together in her lap, summoning up courage. "Mrs. Murdock does not want the child, then? Is that why Laura lives with you?"

The look he turned upon her was pure steel and Margaret immediately regretted her insistence on talking about it. But he did not blast her with his anger. He said only, in clipped tones, "Laura does not live with her mother because Damaris is not a fit mother with whom to live. And Laura does not see her for the same reason. I would not let my daughter near her. But Damaris has certainly never indicated any desire to visit with her daughter, let alone take care of her. Does that satisfy your curiosity?"

His words shocked Margaret into silence, though embarrassment reddened her cheeks at his last sentence. He thought she was nothing but a vulgar busybody. She said stiffly, "I am sorry. I didn't mean to intrude on your—your feelings. But it did seem to me that as your wife I had some interest in your daughter and in what the situation was between her and Mrs. Murdock. If it was presumptuous of me, I apologize.''

She turned her attention back to her plate. She was startled when Andrew reached out and laid his hand on her wrist. ''No. I apologize. I shouldn't have said what I did. You have a right to know, and I should have told you already. Unfortunately, my temper often gets the better of me when I'm discussing that topic.''

Margaret raised her eyes to meet his, touched by his apology. She knew that Andrew Stone was a man for whom apologies were hard—and rare. A small joy was blossoming deep inside her at the thought that there was a reason why Andrew kept his daughter from her mother, that she and all of Huxley had been wrong in assuming he was heartless.

Andrew had expected Margaret to be sulky or angry after he'd snapped at her. When he saw instead her glowing eyes and the wisp of a smile on her lips, he felt suddenly lighter and freer. His own mouth curved up and he spread his hand out over hers. He found himself wanting to tell her how beautiful she was, to bring her hand to his mouth and cover it with slow, soft kisses, working his way up her arm. He could feel the desire building in him at just that touch. God, he wanted her. He'd been ten kinds of a fool last night for turning away from her. He wondered if Margaret had been irritated by his actions—or merely relieved.

Margaret gazed at him, her big eyes questioning, her lips slightly parted. He thought of kissing those lips, of tracing them with his tongue, opening them to him. He remembered the other night, when she had seemed to respond to him, when he had felt her chest rising and falling with rapid breaths against his and had seen her eyes dark and velvety with passion, her lips soft and moist and red, like bruised rose petals.

He wanted to climb right across the table after her, to brush everything heedlessly to the floor and pull her onto the lace-covered table beneath him. It was an image so vivid, so sensual, that his blood thundered through his veins. He swallowed thickly and his other hand gripped the arm of his chair, as though to hold him there and keep him from acting out the fantasy.

He pulled his hand from hers with effort and forced himself to focus on his plate, to eat and drink as if everything were normal. As if he weren't drowning in desire, weren't conjuring up lustful images of taking his wife right then and there, like a brute.

The food might have been sawdust for all he tasted of it. He couldn't speak. Across the table, Margaret watched him, puzzled. For a moment he had been warm, even kind. Then there had been that breathtaking moment when he had looked at her, his eyes bright, hot and glittering, his body tensed. For an instant she had thought he was going to come out of his chair and kiss her right there. She had actually wanted him to, the heat surging through her body in answer to his look. But then he had pulled back and continued eating silently, never looking at her, almost as if she were not there, until she began to wonder if she had imagined the brief flare of passion in his eyes.

Margaret ate little, not interested in her food. She didn't think she would ever figure out her husband. He blew hot and cold, confusing her. She was ignorant enough about marriage without his adding to her confusion, she thought with some resentment. Why didn't he tell her straight out what he wanted of her?

They finished dinner and the two of them retired to the sitting room in the same awkward silence. Margaret crossed her hands in her lap and struggled to think of something to say. Andrew stared at the floor, the wall, the furniture, anything but her. His gaze returned again and again to the clock on the mantel and Margaret wondered in irritation why he was so all-fired interested in what time it was. Did he feel obliged to sit and socialize with her for a certain number of minutes because she was his wife? It was obvious that he didn't want to be there with her. She set her jaw.

She glanced at the clock, too. It was early yet for bed, but she couldn't stand to sit here another minute and watch him fidget. She rose to her feet. "I believe I shall retire."

His head snapped up and he looked straight at her for the first time since they'd entered the room. Margaret was amazed to see the intense fire in his eyes. Andrew stood up, too. Why was he looking at her like that? It made her feel weak and molten all over, unable to move from the spot. Her hand came up to her chest. It was hard to breathe.

It took some effort to pull herself together and leave the room, picking up a candle to light her way. It was easier once she was out of the reach of his eyes, and she hurried across the hall and up the stairs. Once in her room, she set down the candle and flung herself into a chair, burying her face in her hands. Her breath was coming too fast, her pulse racing. She felt hot and eager, frustrated and angry. What was Andrew doing with her? What did he want? She was in a turmoil.

After a time she got up and lit the oil lamp with shaky hands. She crossed to the window to draw the curtains, and her hands paused on the cloth as she looked out. The night was dark and moonless, the stars glittering coldly in the black sky. The barn and animal pens were dark shapes across the yard. A boot heel scraped upon the porch below her, and Andrew stepped off the porch into Margaret's line of vision. He strolled aimlessly out into the yard, the red tip of his cigar glowing in the night, and stood for a moment, looking out across the distance. Then he turned and gazed up at Margaret's window.

Margaret gasped and stepped back quickly. He had seen her! Now he would probably think she was spying on him or something, that she was interested in where he was and what he was doing. And she wasn't. She wasn't! Furiously she began to undress, unbuttoning her dress and flinging it onto the chair, then jerking off her petticoats and underclothes one by one and throwing them after it.

She didn't care what Andrew Stone did or how he felt about her! If he wanted to ignore her, fine. After all, it wouldn't be any skin off *her* back if he stayed clear of her. It would be *wonderful* if he didn't come to her room, if he didn't insist on his marital rights. It would bring her a great peace of mind, in fact. She sat down and untied her shoes, jerking at the laces, which seemed determined to thwart her. Her efforts resulted in a knot in the second set of laces that grew tighter and harder the more she struggled with it, until finally she yanked at the shoe with all her might, tearing it off her foot. She stood up and flung it across the room, where it bounced off the wall with a satisfying thud.

She felt like screaming. She wanted to curse and stamp her feet. Why did she feel like this? Why was she buzzing with irritation and dissatisfaction? Why were her nerves sizzling under her skin as though they might break loose at any moment and go shooting off in all directions?

There was a knock at her door and she turned just as the door opened. Andrew stood in the doorway, one hand still on the knob. His eyes dropped to her body and stayed. Margaret's breath caught in her throat. She thought about the fact that she was standing there in front of him wearing only her chemise, pantalettes and stockings, and she knew that she should have been embarrassed. Well, she was; heat flooded up her face. But, strangely, she didn't make a move toward her night robe. Despite the embarrassment, there was something wonderfully exciting about it, too. She realized with some amazement that she actually enjoyed having his eyes roam down her body. And the heavy-lidded expression on his face sent delightful, sparkling shivers through her. She was aware of a crazy desire to run her hands over her body in front of him, pressing the cloth against her skin.

Andrew stepped inside, closing the door after him. He was dressed in only his trousers and shirt, open at the throat. Margaret's eyes went to the tanned slash of skin the shirt revealed. She thought about pressing her lips against the hollow of his throat, and she blushed at the licentious freedom of her thoughts. Did women want such things? Was she wicked to stand there brazenly, letting him look at her in only her underthings, thinking about kissing his throat?

He came closer, and Margaret simply stood, waiting. He stopped inches from her. "You are beautiful," he breathed.

Andrew was already hard and aching when he came into the room, but the sight of Margaret in her thin underthings flooded him with an even fiercer desire. And the way she stood, letting him look at her without squealing and trying to cover herself or jumping for her robe, inflamed him almost past the point of reason. He had had whores who had done that, of course, even undressing before him to arouse him, but they had done it in a careless, cold way. But Margaret—Margaret had blushed, yet she'd remained where she was, almost as if she enjoyed having him look at her.

Andrew reached out and unbuttoned the top button of her chemise. Her eyes fluttered closed and a funny little sigh escaped her lips. He bit back a groan at the exquisite pleasure of seeing that combination of shyness and pleasure. Slowly his fingers unfastened the buttons, moving lower and lower until finally the sides fell completely apart. Gently he parted the material, exposing her soft, smoothly rounded breasts, centered by large, pink-brown nipples. Her eyes flew open in shock. She saw Andrew gazing avidly at her breasts. His eyes were hot, his mouth softened by desire.

She knew she should have been blazing with humiliation at this invasion of her modesty, but, curiously, she was not. A fire far hotter than that of embarrassment moved through her, making her skin glow. Moisture came between her legs and an ache began to pulse there. She knew she wanted him to look at her...look at her forever. More than that, she wanted him to touch her. Had she been bolder, she would have reached out and brought his hand to her breast, but she was too naive and inexperienced to do that. She could only wait and hope, excitement clenching her stomach.

Andrew pulled the chemise off her shoulders and dropped it on the floor. His hands went to the drawstring of her pantalettes, his eyes all the while feasting on her breasts. Margaret was surprised to find that her nipples puckered and tightened under his eyes, drawing up into pointed little buds. She wanted him to touch her there, and she was sure that that was wicked, but she didn't care, if only he would do it.

But he did not. He just looked with a heat that was almost as tangible as a touch as his fingers untied the drawstring of her pantalettes and began to draw them down. Margaret drew in her breath sharply and he paused. He glanced up at her and saw astonishment in her eyes, quickly diluted by excitement and hunger. He swallowed. She wanted him to undress her, even as she felt the shock and surprise of his doing it.

Andrew's fingers slipped inside the cloth of the undergarment and her skin jumped at the touch. He spread out his fingers caressingly, feeling the incredible satin smoothness of her skin, the sharpness of her hipbones beneath it, and he moved his hands downward, shoving the cloth down with them. Her creamy white skin was revealed inch by inch until finally the loose garment fell freely to the floor. She was naked then except for the dark stockings and the garters that held them up. Andrew found the picture she presented overwhelmingly erotic. The dark stockings slashed across her white flesh; the pink satin and lace of her garters encircled the firm, shapely thighs beneath the stockings.

He throbbed, so swollen with desire he thought he must take her now or burst, but Andrew forced himself to do nothing but gaze at her fully. He looked at her breasts, the tips provocatively tight and hard, as though waiting for his hands, his mouth. He looked at the soft white flesh on her stomach, narrowing in, then blossoming out again into rounded hips. His eyes dropped to the thatch of hair between her legs, almost as pale as the hair upon her head, and involuntarily his hand stretched out to touch the soft, springing curls.

Margaret gasped and jerked at his touch. She had never in her wildest dreams imagined a man touching her there! Yet she found that amazingly, wantonly, she was glad he had touched her, that she actually wanted to move her legs apart to let him touch her further.

His fingers slipped between her legs and he touched the slick wetness there. Shame flooded Margaret's face and she closed her eyes. *What must he think of her?* Yet, incredibly, pleasure, even pride, washed over his face when he touched her and a long shudder ran through him.

"Oh, Margaret. Margaret." His voice shook. He dropped to one knee in front of her and quickly rolled down her stockings, garters and all. His hands lingered caressingly on her skin. He would have liked to kiss the tender flesh of her thighs, to sink his lips into them and gently nip with his teeth, but he knew that would be too much for her.

He stood up and began to tear off his own clothes, so eager to feel her naked skin pressed against his that he cared nothing for popped buttons or a rip in the cloth. Margaret watched him reveal his hard, muscled chest and flat stomach, her eyes sweeping over the taut contours of his muscles. Dark, curling hair sprinkled his chest and grew downward in a V to his stomach. She had never seen a man's naked chest and arms before, had never expected that there could be a kind of hard beauty to them. Certainly she hadn't guessed that looking at his bare torso could make her throat close up and her insides melt like wax.

His fingers went to the buttons of his denim trousers, and Margaret reddened with embarrassment. She turned her head aside, hearing but not seeing as he pulled the heavy material down his legs. Her curiosity grew too much and after she heard his clothes drop to the floor, she could not refrain from peeking back around at him. His legs were long and lean, his hips narrow, the hipbones sharp beneath his skin. A curving scar curled down across one pelvic bone and onto the softer flesh of his abdomen. But Margaret saw these things without registering them. Her sight, her consciousness was filled with only one thing: the thick, thrusting evidence of his desire. Her eyes widened and she would have gasped if she could have found the breath. But all she could do was move backward on suddenly shaking legs until she ran into the footboard of the bed and could move no farther.

Andrew cursed himself silently. He'd been a fool to undress so openly and abruptly in front of her. He'd been too pulsing with his own desire, too influenced by the appearance of desire in her so that he had forgotten how naive and young she was, how inexperienced and even frightened she would be at the taking of her maidenhood. Now he'd scared her, horrified her.

"No. Don't." He took her hands, hating himself for the sudden stiffness in her. She leaned back from him a little. "I shouldn't have—I'm a fool. But, please, don't look like that. There's no need to be frightened."

Now Margaret understood where the pain came in, why her aunt had told her she must endure it patiently and Damaris had spoken of hurt. "I can't," she whispered, turning her head away and blushing a fiery red. "It's too— you're so—" She looked up at him, tears pooling in her eyes. "You will tear me apart."

"No. No. I swear." He raised her hands to his lips and gently kissed them, holding her eyes with his, willing her to be calm. "It's not true. It happens all the time. I wouldn't hurt you." He sighed. "I'm sorry. I should have undressed in the dark. I was too eager. I didn't think about the fact that you have never seen a man."

"It—it's all right." She took a breath. "I'm fine now. Really." She pulled her hands from his and turned away. Quickly she walked around the bed and pulled back the covers to get in.

Andrew wasn't foolish enough to think that Margaret's action indicated any eagerness to continue their lovemaking. She was probably seeking the fastest way to cover her naked body. Andrew blew out the oil lamp and followed her to the bed. He crawled in beside her and slid his arm beneath her head, drawing her to his side and holding her.

Softly he pressed his lips against her hair. "Relax, sweetheart." He kissed her again. "I won't rush you." He hated promising that, the way his blood was pounding through him and his body was on fire for her. But neither could he take her this way, stiff and resistant, merely bearing her duty grimly. Not when he had felt her so pliant and warm in his arms.

He stroked her arm with his other hand and kissed her gently, his lips moving over her hair and onto her forehead and cheeks as he spoke in a low, quieting tone. "Don't be scared of me, Margaret." He pressed his lips against her temple, lingering, drinking in the faint rose scent in her hair. "Meg. Does anyone call you Meg?"

"Sometimes. My sister and brother. But usually they call me Maggie."

"Meg. I like Meg. It suits you—sweet and warm." He smoothed his hand over her hair and down her back. He wished he were better with sweet, seductive words. He wanted to soothe her, calm her, make her melt again with passion as she had earlier until she no longer thought of her fear. But, even more than that, he wished that he could express how beautiful she looked to him, how much he wanted her, how it filled him with delight to gaze upon her naked form—all the tangled, heated emotions that swirled inside him.

His lips trailed along her jaw, butterfly light, and ended finally on her mouth. He felt her begin to relax then, and her lips pressed back, opening to him. It sent a jolt through him and he wrapped both arms around her, rolling Margaret onto her back. He kissed her thoroughly, his tongue invading her welcoming mouth. A little hesitantly, her tongue met his, winding around it; he groaned, deepening the kiss. Tentatively Margaret's hand came up to his shoulders. When she felt the bare skin beneath her hands, she jerked them back, startled and a little scared, but then they crept back to rest on his shoulders.

Andrew's skin was smooth beneath her touch, faintly damp with sweat—and burning. His muscles bulged beneath his skin and instinctively she caressed their curves. She suspected guiltily that touching him like that was something a lady should not do, but she couldn't keep from doing it; it sent fire all through her body. He made an indistinguishable noise deep in his throat and his skin was suddenly hotter beneath her hands. Andrew pressed her into the soft feather mattress, covering her with his entire body.

It was new and startling to feel his bare body all up and down hers—the heat and smoothness of his flesh, the rasp of curling hairs, the weight and strength of his muscles. There was that hardness, too, pressing and swelling against her, so huge and urgent. She tensed, but gradually, as he continued to kiss her, she relaxed. The textures of his body, the dampness, the heat were all exciting to her senses. He rubbed against her, awakening every inch of her skin. The hairs of his chest teased at her nipples and they hardened in response. Her breasts felt strangely full, almost swollen, and the taut nipples ached. Margaret twisted under him, yearning for something, though she had no idea for what.

Andrew slid down her body, his lips trailing fire over the tender skin of her throat and onto her chest. His mouth touched the upswell of her breast and Margaret gasped. His mouth on her breasts surprised, even shocked her, but more than that, it set every nerve in her body clamoring. He moved his hands slowly down her arms, fingers spread wide, as his mouth moved lower. His lips savored the pillowy softness of the orb, the delicious smoothness, opening to let his tongue flicker out over her skin in dancing, teasing patterns. Margaret could not stop the groan that escaped her throat. She felt the faint scrape of his teeth, a delightful counterpoint to the softness of his tongue and lips. He reached the aureole of her nipple and he paused to trace the circle with his tongue. Margaret arched up involuntarily, her breath hissing in.

Andrew's arms went beneath her, thrusting her chest upward, and his mouth settled slowly, luxuriously, on the engorged pink nipple. Margaret groaned, her head falling back, and gave herself up to the utter pleasure. He suckled gently as his tongue flicked over the hard bud and twined around it, playing with it until Margaret thought she would go mad from the intense pleasure.

"Drew," she breathed, scarcely able to say anything else.

He lifted his head and gazed down at the button of flesh, reddened and pointed from his ministrations, glistening with moisture. He bent and kissed it lightly, then moved across to her other breast. He cupped it in his hand, his brown fingers gently pressing into the soft white flesh, plumping her breast up, then burying his mouth in it. He kissed her over and over, at last pulling her nipple into his mouth and working the wonders on it that he had on the other.

Margaret moved restlessly, helplessly, on the bed, digging in her heels and clutching the sheets beneath her fingers. She had never in her life felt, indeed had never even imagined, such an intense assault on her senses, a pleasure that was so overwhelming it bordered on pain. She wanted to cry out that she could not bear it. She wanted to burst into sobs. She wanted to beg him to continue.

As his mouth feasted on her breast, his hand dropped down to caress her abdomen and upper thighs. It moved ever closer to the thatch of hair low on her abdomen until finally his fingers tangled in it. His fingers slid between her legs, finding the moisture there. Margaret was embarrassed for him to feel the thick, undeniable evidence of her swift and compelling desire. He would be bound to think her forward and bold, not a proper lady at all. Yet he did not seem repelled by it, for his fingers did not leave, but moved slowly over those intimate satiny folds, caressing and exploring.

Then his finger moved up inside her, and at the same moment he pulled deeply on her nipple with his mouth. A huge tremor of desire surged downward into her loins and exploded there. More of the strange moisture gushed forth. A groan rose up from deep inside Margaret. She could not help it, but she blushed at these involuntary betrayals of her body. Andrew would think now that she was no lady.

But he looked up at her and she saw no sign of repugnance on his face. It was flushed and stark, the skin stretched tightly across the bones, and his eyes blazed with an almost unholy passion. Though she had never seen such a look before, she knew somehow that it was the face of a man teetering on the brink of his control.

"I have to have you," he muttered hoarsely. He moved her legs apart and settled himself between them. Slowly he guided himself into her. She felt the tip of his manhood probing her soft recesses, moving gently into the flesh. Suddenly it wasn't scary anymore; Margaret realized that it was what she wanted more than anything else, that it was this for which her entire body ached. She arched up, opening herself to him completely.

Andrew groaned and plunged into her fully. There was a brief, tearing pain, and Margaret muffled a cry, sinking her teeth into her lower lip. He paused, holding himself taut and still above her. He bent his head and kissed her neck. "Are you all right?" he whispered.

Margaret nodded. The pain had been sharp and swift, leaving behind a low, dull ache. But there was also the intense satisfaction of having him inside her, filling her, that made the soreness seem negligible. Andrew lifted his head and saw her looking up at him, her eyes soft and shining. It was too much for him. A long shudder passed through him, and he began to move within her, thrusting rhythmically. His fingers dug into the sheets on either side of her, and his muscles were taut with the effort of holding back and moving as gently as he could, so as not to hurt her tender flesh.

Margaret lay with her eyes closed, still and silent, her whole being concentrated on the tumult of sensations, wholly new, that he was creating within her. She had never known anything as wild and stormy and delightful. She felt as though she might shatter at any moment. Then he plunged deep within her and a cry escaped from his lips.

He collapsed upon her, and Margaret wrapped her arms around him tightly, holding him to her as though he sought comfort. There was something about him so vulnerable at that moment that she instinctively moved to protect him. His skin was damp and cool with sweat; his skin quivered in the aftermath of his violent seizure. Margaret smoothed her hands down his back quietingly and gently kissed his shoulder. His skin was smooth and salty; she liked the taste of it. The thought crossed her mind that it would be enjoyable to traverse his body with her lips as he had done hers, and she wondered if that would be too shocking a thing to do.

Andrew half groaned, half laughed and rolled over onto his back, keeping his arm beneath her head. Margaret glanced over at him. His body glistened with sweat. His eyes were closed and his face utterly relaxed. Gone were the tight lines about his mouth and forehead, the frequent frown. His face was peaceful, almost smiling, and he was more handsome than she had ever seen him.

His eyes opened and he looked at her. He smiled and reached out a hand to caress her cheek. "Thank you," he whispered.

Margaret smiled and turned her face a little to place a kiss in the palm of his hand. For a moment he looked at her, a light in his eyes that she could not fathom. Then he pulled her down beside him, cradling her to him and rained kisses over her hair, cheek, neck and shoulder. "God, you're beautiful. So beautiful. So sweet."

And, with Andrew holding her to him tightly, they drifted off to sleep.

Chapter Ten

Margaret opened her eyes. She lay quietly, awash in a delicious lassitude. Her limbs were heavy, and there was a small, lingering soreness between her legs. She thought of the night before and a smile curved her lips. Andrew had made love to her. It hadn't been awful or scary at all; in fact, it had been downright pleasurable. She remembered his hands stroking her body and the delightful sensations that had run through her. She remembered his mouth on her skin, his tongue hot and wet. Margaret shivered deliciously and rolled over, pulling her pillow tight against her body and curling around it. She felt like giggling. She felt like grinning idiotically at nothing.

It hadn't been the way Aunt Charity had described, not in the slightest. Margaret wondered if that meant that she had more passion than a lady should. Was she naturally loose and wicked? It had been even less like what Damaris Murdock had warned her about. At the thought of Damaris, Margaret's chin set and her eyes flashed. That woman! She had lied to her, maliciously lied just to scare her. However fierce a man Andrew might seem, he had been understanding and gentle with her in bed. But Damaris had told bald-faced lies to her—and all the while she was doing it, her very manner of sweetness and concern was a lie!

Margaret was sure that Damaris had lied to everyone for years about what had happened between her and Andrew. The people of Huxley had been eager to believe something bad about a Yankee colonel, and no one had ever bothered to get Andrew's side of it—not that he would have stooped to justify himself, anyway. There was no telling what the truth really was, but after what Damaris had done to her, Margaret was sure that Damaris had been at fault, not Andrew.

Margaret snuggled up against Andrew's pillow. It smelled faintly of him and she smiled dreamily. She wished that he were still here, that he had remained in her bed all night and that she could wake up and look into his face. She thought of him smiling at her and leaning over to kiss her good morning. Even though he obviously preferred to sleep by himself, she had hoped that when he made love to her, he would stay with her through the night.

She sighed and rolled onto her back, staring up at the tester above the bed. Then she grimaced and sat up, shaking off the momentary loneliness. She wasn't going to spoil her good mood by thinking about what *didn't* happen, when what had happened was so wonderful. After all, there could be all kinds of reasons why he had gone back to his own bed. He might be a light sleeper or was so used to sleeping alone that he couldn't sleep any other way. Or maybe he snored and didn't want to keep her awake. Margaret had to giggle at that thought.

The important thing was that his leaving her bed didn't necessarily mean that he didn't care for her. Margaret paused, thinking. Was it that important that he cared for her? Of course, she wanted him to; a loving husband meant greater security for her and her siblings. It meant he would be kinder and more generous, easier to get along with and not as harsh when she made mistakes or did something he didn't like. She had tried to be pleasant and attractive so that he would like her.

However, deep down, she knew that she was talking about something deeper than a mere husbandly fondness. She desired more than security and a lack of trouble. She wanted—passion! She yearned to feel again the way she had last night when Andrew had looked at her with hot eyes and she had known all through her that he wanted, really *wanted* her. At that moment, she had felt desirable, beautiful, special. She had felt . . . loved.

Margaret sat up at that thought, pulling her knees up and resting her chin thoughtfully on them. Did she want Andrew to love her? It wasn't part of their bargain. She didn't love him. Did she? Excitement sprouted in her chest and she found herself grinning. She thought of Andrew and the way a smile rushed to her lips whenever she saw him or heard his voice. She thought of how often she thought about him and how eagerly she awaited his return home at night. Could it be that she was beginning to love him?

She giggled to herself and hugged her knees more tightly. Surely that wouldn't be a terrible thing, to fall in love with one's husband . . . provided that he loved her in return, of course. Otherwise, it would mean a lonely and unhappy life. Andrew didn't love her; he hadn't deceived her on that score. But Emma had assured her that she could get him to love her, even if he had started out wanting to marry her for purely practical reasons. She wondered if Emma was right. She had never thought of herself as being able to entice a man into loving her.

Margaret hopped out of bed and went to the mirror above her bureau. Her hair was tousled and tangled, flowing wildly over her shoulders, and her green eyes were huge in her face. Was she pretty? She wasn't sure. She hadn't thought of herself as pretty before she met Andrew. But somehow she didn't look so pale anymore. There was a new vivacity and color in her face and when she smiled, her eyes sparkled. Her hair was that awful pale color, of course, but Andrew seemed to like it. She thought about the way he had buried his face in it last night, murmuring that it was like silk. She smiled like a cat that had gotten into the cream.

Maybe once she had been a pale wallflower. But her looks had improved tremendously over the past few weeks. However she looked, what was important was that Andrew thought her attractive. He desired her; she had seen it clearly in his eyes. According to Emma, if a man desired you, he was halfway to loving you already. She couldn't flirt with men the way Emma could; she didn't know how to be entrancing. But Andrew had wanted her. And she was able to please him in bed, no matter how unskilled she was. Surely, with those advantages, she could bring him to love her.

Margaret felt as if she were teetering on the brink of something wonderful, awesome and scary. She didn't know what would happen or how it would feel. But she knew she wasn't about to draw back from it.

Margaret washed and dressed, then braided and pinned her hair into several loops at the nape of her neck, a style she had found to be practical and neat, as well as softly feminine. Then she started downstairs. She found she couldn't keep a smile from popping back onto her lips. So she was smiling when she rounded the corner and stepped through the door of the dining room to find Andrew sitting at the table, a cup of coffee before him.

"Oh!" Margaret came to an abrupt halt, her skirts swaying, and suddenly it was difficult to breathe. "Hello. I—I didn't expect to see you here." It occurred to her that her words sounded rude, and she hurriedly explained, "That is, I mean, you're usually gone when I come down." That didn't sound any better.

Andrew didn't notice any rudeness; he didn't even see the nervousness in her manner. He was too aware of the way his own heart had started to pound as soon as he heard her footsteps in the hall and the way his mouth had gone dry and his mind blank the moment Margaret appeared in the doorway.

She was beautiful, a lovely soft vision. He wanted to run to her and kiss her, to pull her into his arms and squeeze her tightly against him. Instead, he just rose to his feet and stood there awkwardly, drinking in the sight of her.

"Good morning." His voice was soft and caressing. He had to touch her, so he came around the table and took her arm to escort her. As they walked, his hand slid down her arm until their hands were clasped. Andrew didn't even notice it until she stopped beside her chair and he had to release her hand.

Andrew seated her and went to his chair, ringing the bell for Carmela as he sat down.

"I'm not usually here at this hour." Andrew realized that he should explain his presence at the table; she would think it odd. "But today I had to catch up on my record keeping, so I didn't go out with the men." He didn't mention that he had racked his brain to come up with an excuse for staying in the house—an excuse other than that he wanted to see his wife this morning.

Last night had left him blissfully drained, utterly satisfied. He had wanted to curl his arms around Margaret and hold her all night long. It had taken a tremendous effort to slip out of bed and leave her there, but the night had been too sweet, too good, to ruin it with stiffness or recriminations the next morning. Damaris had always hated to have him sleep the night through with her. Though Margaret was obviously different from Damaris, she would surely want him there even less, given the loveless nature of their marriage. So he had gone back to his room, but when he had awakened this morning, he had had to see her.

"I've eaten breakfast, but I thought I'd have another cup of coffee." Nor did he tell her that the reason he had decided he needed more coffee was that the breakfast table was where he was most likely to "accidentally" bump into her.

"I see." Margaret couldn't have cared less about his explanation. She was simply glad he was there.

At that moment Carmela waddled through the swinging door from the kitchen, a pot of coffee in her hand. *"¿Café, Señor?"* She saw Margaret. "Ah, Señora! I not know—you want breakfast?"

"Yes, Carmela, please."

The woman poured them both coffee that was strong enough to stand a spoon in and returned to the kitchen. Margaret took a sip of hers and winced, then quickly added another spoonful of sugar and a large dollop of cream. She had taught Carmela how to make eggs just as she liked them, but she had made no headway with her concerning the coffee. Carmela insisted that the men liked it that way. Maybe they did. Certainly it would wake them up.

"I should get up earlier, so that Carmela wouldn't have to make two breakfasts," Margaret commented. If she got up at the same time Andrew did, they could eat breakfast together every day.

"I'm sure she doesn't mind. There's no need to pull yourself out of bed at the crack of dawn." He would love to see her at that time, her face still slack from sleep, her eyes huge and dreamy, her hair mussed. Just thinking about it brought a tightness to his groin.

"I'm used to rising early. But here, there isn't enough noise to wake me up. The hen house is too far away. No tree full of birds at my window." But if Andrew slept with her, she would wake up when he arose.

Andrew smiled at her. He wanted to lay his hand on her arm, to stroke his fingers down her cheek, just to touch her some way. If he didn't watch it, he told himself, he would turn into as big a fool about Margaret as he had been about Damaris. He curled his hand around his cup, almost as though to keep it from wandering to her. What he didn't know was that he couldn't hide what lay in his eyes and face—the ease and contentment that smoothed out the lines of his forehead, the warmth of incipient desire in his eyes.

Looking at him, Margaret was aware of a tingling starting between her legs and her thoughts went back to the night before. The tingling developed into a spreading warmth. It surprised and shocked her that she could feel this way in the morning—it didn't seem proper. Wasn't it only done at night? And there had been so little provocation, merely a look in Andrew's eyes. She glanced down, a blush spreading across her cheeks. What if *he* knew what she was thinking about!

Her blush told him that he had embarrassed her with his amorous gaze. He cast about for some innocuous topic. "Your brother and sister should be here early this afternoon."

"Good. We can show them the ranch, and—that is, if you're not too busy. Would you mind?"

"Of course not." He saw no reason to reveal that he would do almost anything she asked to keep that sparkling look on her face. It filled him with warmth to hear her say "we" as if they were an entity and to include him in her plans with her family. Of course, they wouldn't be able to find their way around the ranch on their own. No doubt that was reason enough to include him.

He laid his hand over hers on the table. He traced his finger down each of hers; he didn't think he could get enough of touching her. His voice dropped. "Are you—do you feel up to riding?"

Margaret's cheeks reddened as she thought of the soreness their lovemaking had left with her. "Yes. I'm fine."

"Good. I—I hope I didn't hurt you too much."

"No, oh, no," she hastened to assure him. It was embarrassing to talk about it, yet she had to reassure him. "You were very gentle. Thank you."

He had been staring at their hands as he talked, but he looked up at her face in surprise when she said that. The last thing he had expected from his bride was thanks. Strangely, it started up his lust again. Or perhaps it wasn't so strange, he thought; everything about this woman seemed to stir his lust. He hadn't dreamed it would be this way with Margaret.

He wanted to pull her onto his lap, he wanted to run his hand over her body, caressing the line of breast and waist and hip. He wanted to slip his hand under her dress and slide it up until it reached the damp heat between her legs. Andrew swallowed. She had been so wet and ready for him last night. Had he dreamed that? It had almost undone him, filling him with such lust that it had been all he could do to keep from plunging himself crudely into her and taking her in a storm of desire. He couldn't have imagined that dew of passion. It had been as real as the way she had groaned when he touched her or the way she had arched up against him. She had felt pleasure; she had desired his touch, his body.

Andrew wanted to tell her how she affected him and what he wanted to do to her. He couldn't, of course; that would shock her right out of the room, probably. But, sweet Heaven, she made him feel randy. As if he were sixteen again—or the young army lieutenant, straight out of West Point, who had ridden through Huxley and seen a young, red-haired beauty step out onto the porch of the general store.

That thought was enough to douse his rising ardor. What had happened with Damaris would *never* happen again. He had spent too many long and bitter years becoming immune to that kind of helpless passion. He wasn't about to let some big-eyed chit of a girl turn him into a weak-kneed, cuckolded idiot again.

He rose abruptly, pushing back his chair with a harsh grating noise. "I must get back to work."

Margaret stared at him, confounded by the sudden change in him. What had she done? Had she spoken too boldly about last night? But all she had done was thank him!

"No doubt you'll want to get your brother and sister settled in today. Tomorrow I'll show them the ranch, if you'd like."

"Yes, that's fine. If you want to." Her voice was small and pale and she felt suddenly insignificant and undesirable. Why had she been so presumptuous as to think that he felt anything for her? That she could ever bring him to love her? It was ridiculous.

Andrew strode out of the room without even a goodbye. When Carmela brought in Margaret's breakfast a few minutes later, Margaret was barely able to shove down a few mouthfuls of it, and she had to reassure that good woman over and over again that there had really been no fault with her cooking.

Later her spirits rose a little as she and Rosa prepared Zach's and Annie's bedrooms. She had decided to give them the two rooms at the other end of the hall, across from Laura and her governess. The poor girl ought to enjoy having some youthful company for a change. Margaret and the sturdy Mexican woman had already taken the feather mattresses off the beds and changed the down in them so that they were plump and fresh. This morning they made up the beds and swept the hardwood floors, beat the braided rugs and waxed the heavy mahogany furniture until it gleamed. Margaret opened the drapes wide, so that at least there would be some light in the rooms to counteract the gloomy furniture. As soon as her trunks arrived today, she would replace the dark velvet bedcovers with some of the brightly patched quilts that were part of her hope chest. Then the rooms would look almost normal.

Early in the afternoon, Margaret heard the sound of the wagon approaching and flew down the stairs and out onto the porch. Annie and Zach sat on the high seat of the wagon beside the driver, and when Annie saw Margaret on the porch, she began to wave vigorously. The wagon pulled up in front of the house, and Annie scrambled down immediately, not waiting for the driver to help her. Zach followed almost as eagerly.

"Maggie! Maggie!" Annie flung herself into her sister's arms, nearly knocking the breath from her. "Oh, I'm so glad to see you. I've missed you something terrible. Our room's so lonely without you. How are you? Are you all right?" She stepped back, holding Margaret at arm's length to study her. "You look different."

Margaret smiled, shaking her head. "I'm the same."

"No." Annie shook her head. She couldn't put her finger on it, but Margaret seemed older somehow, and prettier. "I don't know what it is. But you look awfully good, so I guess it doesn't matter. You must be happy."

Was she? This morning she would have laughed and nodded in reply. But why had Andrew stalked off like that this morning? He had left the house and she hadn't seen him since then.

"Of course I'm happy," Margaret replied. She wasn't about to reveal any of her doubts to Annie, who would immediately, loyally, blame Andrew.

She turned and smiled at Zach. "Come on, you're not too big to give your sister a hug!"

He grinned almost shyly. "Nope." He stepped forward and pulled her into his arms in a bone-cracking hug.

"My goodness!" Margaret laughed breathlessly. "You're getting so strong!" It wouldn't be long before he was a man. How strange it was to think of her little brother growing up.

The driver of the wagon and his helper began to take the trunks down from the wagon bed and move them into the house. Margaret followed with Annie and Zach. "Are you all ready for a tour of the house?"

"Oh, yes!" Annie's eyes grew huge and round. "Isn't it gigantic? I never dreamed it would be this big."

"Me, neither," Margaret confessed. She took each of them by the hand and led them into the house.

She led them through the house and introduced them to Carmela and Rosa, then took them upstairs to meet Laura and her governess, ending up at their bedrooms.

"Well? What do you think?" Margaret asked, going back and forth between Zach's room and Annie's. "Do you like them?"

Annie turned around slowly. "It's big. I've got plenty of room to spread out in." She went to the window. "And look out there! I can see everything!"

"It's the nicest bedroom I've ever been in," Zach admitted, strolling into his sister's room. "Thank you."

"Yes. Thank you." Annie flew across the room to squeeze her sister. "It's beautiful, and I know I'm going to like it here lots better than Aunt Charity's."

"That's condemning with faint praise," Margaret replied jokingly, but it warmed her heart to hear them praise the rooms. Perhaps the furniture was more massive and dark than any of them would have liked, but they were luxurious surroundings, and Annie and Zach would grow up here without any want. She had done the right thing for them, and that, after all, had been her main object. She would have to remember that when she was feeling blue because her husband wasn't fond enough of her.

Andrew didn't return until late that evening. She had waited dinner until Carmela had complained that it would be ruined, adding that Señor Stone had probably eaten out on the range with the men, as he often did. Then she had sat down to eat with Annie and Zach alone. Andrew didn't come in until after dinner, when they had retired to the sitting room. Margaret was embroidering and Annie and Zach were engaged in a lively game of checkers when Andrew appeared in the doorway. His clothes and boots were covered with dust, as was the hat he held in his hand. But he had evidently taken off his hat and stuck his head under the pump to wash his face, for it was clean and his hair was wet.

"I'm sorry," he apologized. "We didn't stop until sundown, and then it was a long ride back to the house."

He had cursed himself all the way home for getting so caught up in the work that he hadn't left earlier. Margaret would have every right to be angry with him for not being there for supper the first night her brother and sister were in his house. He also had to admit that he had stayed out because he was nervous at the thought of being with Margaret with the members of her family around, afraid that she would be different, that he would feel excluded. It had been obvious from the first moment he met them that her sister and brother hadn't wanted Margaret to marry him. Besides, his manner had been less than polite when he'd walked out on her this morning at breakfast. Most women, certainly all the ones he'd ever been around, would have treated him to a cold shoulder when he came in tonight.

But Margaret just jumped up, smiling. She had been afraid that Andrew was mad at her and staying away because of that. It was pleasant to hear him apologize for being late. "It doesn't matter. You look as if you've been working hard. Are you tired?"

"A little." He nodded.

"You know my sister and brother."

"Yes. Hello, Miss Carlisle." He tipped his hat to Annie, then stripped off his heavy leather work glove and extended his hand to Zach, who stepped forward to shake it. "Zachary."

Annie giggled. "Miss Carlisle!"

"Annie!" Margaret said sharply and shot her a stern look.

"Have I said something wrong?" Andrew glanced at Annie and then at Margaret.

"No. Of course not. It's just that my sister is such a hoyden she's unused to being addressed politely." Margaret spoke her last words pointedly toward Annie.

"I'm sorry." Annie tried to pull her face into solemnity. "Nobody ever calls me Miss Carlisle." She looked up at Andrew doubtfully. This man was such a silent, stern looking one that he made even her feel a trifle uneasy. "Couldn't you call me Annie, like everybody else does?"

He smiled. "Of course. If you wish it." He turned toward Zach, a question in his eyes.

"Just Zach'll do."

"Good. I hope that you will call me Andrew."

It seemed a great liberty to take with a man so much older than they were—and so wealthy and influential—but it also pleased them.

"Are you hungry?" Margaret asked solicitously. "Shall I get you a plate of food? I'm sure Carmela set something aside for you."

"No. Don't bother," he told her, surprised and warmed by her concern. "I ate earlier, out with the hands."

"Then sit down." Margaret put a hand on his arm to guide him toward a chair. "You must be very tired."

"Yes," he admitted, but he glanced askance at the cloth-covered chairs. "But I'm all dirty. I'll ruin the chair."

He was right, of course. Frankly, Margaret couldn't have cared less if he had ruined one of the dark, heavy things, but it wouldn't have been polite to say so. She smiled and said, "Then come with me." She held out her hand and he took it. Margaret smiled toward her brother and sister in goodbye and led Andrew out of the room.

Andrew followed her with alacrity as she led him up the stairs and along the hall toward his bedroom. Excitement began to build in him. He couldn't believe that Margaret, sweet and naive as she was, meant to suggest anything lewd, but just the idea of her leading him into a bedroom was enough to start desire pounding through his veins. She whisked him into his bedroom and pushed him down onto a leather chair.

"There. That'll be easy enough to clean." She smiled and knelt in front of him, startling him.

"What are you—"

But before he could get the words out, Margaret was tugging at one of his boots. Amazed, he watched as she pulled it off and set it aside, then picked up his stockinged foot and placed it in her lap. She began to knead it with her expert fingers. Andrew couldn't stifle a groan as her fingertips unerringly picked out the sorest places and began to work on them.

"Where did you learn that?"

She chuckled. "My mother used to do this for my father when he came in from the fields. He always said his feet ached as much as his arms after a day's work." She shrugged. "I watched her and later, after Mama died, I'd do it for him sometimes." A shadow crossed her face. "I didn't do it often, though, because it made him sad. I think he couldn't help thinking of Mama."

Drew groaned again as she reached a particularly sore spot and she glanced up anxiously, her hands stilling. "I'm sorry. Did I hurt you?"

"No. Just the opposite. It feels almost too good."

Margaret chuckled again. "Now, how can something feel too good?"

He looked down at her head, earnestly bent over his feet as her fingertips dug into him. "I don't know." He could hardly tell her that even while her rubbing eased out the soreness and stiffness of a day spent in boots, it was also sending erotic sensations shimmering up through him. The thought of her kneeling down before him and engaging in such a humble task, just to make him more comfortable, filled him with awe and pride. But the magic she worked on his nerve endings, the submissive position, even the tenderness she displayed, also filled him with lust. Damn!

Margaret finished one foot and went to the other. Andrew closed his eyes, awash with pure physical pleasure.

Animalistic he might be, but he wasn't about to forego the enjoyment. He just hoped she wouldn't happen to glance at his lap and realize the effect she was having on him.

All too soon, Margaret stopped and rose to her feet. Andrew's eyes fluttered open, and he had to struggle to keep from protesting. She moved behind the low-backed chair and put her hands on his shoulders and began to rub his back and shoulders, moving up to his neck and head and down onto his arms. Andrew made a noise of pure primitive enjoyment; it was all he could do not to rub his head against her like a cat.

Her fingers were firm and supple, sometimes digging into his muscles, at other times gently, soothingly stroking. He had never felt anything so marvelous—or so seductive. He hoped she would go on forever. But he knew that if she continued much longer, he would drag her down to the floor with him. How could something be so soothing and at the same time wind him up tight as a watchspring with desire?

Margaret placed her palms on either side of his head, fingers spread out through his hair, and tilted his head back until it came to rest upon her breasts. She massaged his temples with her fingertips, moving onto his face, smoothing over the hard bones. Andrew relaxed even further, letting his head sink into the pillowy softness of her breasts. Her fingers eased the ache in his head caused by hours of sun and work and smoothed out the strain. And with every stroke, every subtle movement, she stoked the fire of his passion.

He was unaware of it, but Margaret was no more immune to the sensations of her skin rubbing his than Andrew was. She looked down into his face as the tension drained out of it and found she wanted to bend over and kiss the vulnerable skin of his eyelids and brush her lips over his. She smoothed her fingers over his eyebrows and down along the line of his nose. She thought about touching him all over his face, even down his neck to the collar of his shirt, and it made her go breathless and warm inside. She longed to kiss his forehead, his cheek, his hair, and she wondered how he would react if she were to do such a thing. Would he enjoy it? Or would he find her unattractively bold? Vulgarly forward?

Her hands slid down his neck, rubbing, and onto his shirt. "Your shirt is wet."

"Mmm-hmm. I stuck my head under the pump when I came in."

Margaret wet her lips. She hoped she wouldn't go too far and disgust him; she hoped he would believe her ruse. Her hands slid around to the front of his shirt and began to undo the top button. "Why don't you take it off, then? It'd make it more comfortable—not having that wet cloth next to your skin."

Andrew made no reply. He couldn't. All the wind seemed to have left him the moment he felt her soft hands on his buttons. His teeth sank into his lower lip. He couldn't respond like an animal or she would stop the wonderful things she was doing.

Margaret's fingers slipped down to the next button and the next. She was tempted to slide her hands in under the shirt and smooth her fingers down his skin. An ache formed deep in her abdomen, heavy and pulsing. She wanted to feel his skin beneath her sensitive fingertips, wanted to learn the texture of the hair and flesh. She wanted to touch the small brownish buds of his masculine nipples. Would they tighten and grow hard as hers did at his touch? Would he feel the way she did if she placed her lips on them? She was afraid to find out; that didn't seem like anything a proper wife would do. He would probably be disgusted. And yet . . .

Margaret pulled the shirt down off his shoulders onto his arms. Andrew shrugged it off impatiently. She began to knead the knotted muscles of his shoulders with her hands, and he made a muffled noise and leaned forward, exposing more of his back to her touch. Firmly Margaret dug her thumbs and fingers into him, working out the soreness. But she also noticed the smoothness of his skin beneath her fingers, the curve and bulge of his muscles, the clean line of neck, shoulders and back. Her fingers gradually slowed and her touch became more caress than massage. Her hands drifted over his back, touching the sharp outcropping of his shoulder blades, the hard line of his spine, the thick pads of muscles. Margaret wasn't aware of what she was doing or the way in which her touch had changed. She was lost in looking at him, in feeling him beneath her skin. She thought of kissing the tanned expanse of skin and she swayed forward a little, drawn by her vision.

She realized what she was doing and jerked her hands back. Her cheeks flamed with embarrassment. What would he think of her?

Andrew rose slowly and turned. There was no condemnation in his face, no contempt or disgust. There were only the sharp, hard lines of desire, the blazing blue of his eyes eating into her, the heat that flooded up his throat and into his face. He reached out and took her arms in his hands, pulling her toward him. She went easily.

But he stopped, holding her from him. "No. Wait. I'm filthy. I'll get you dirty."

"I don't care," she replied honestly, and closed the gap between them.

His arms went hard around her and pulled her up into him, lifting her off her feet. He kissed her passionately, his lips digging into hers, his tongue raking her mouth. Margaret felt immediately, searingly, alive all over her body. Every nerve ending tingled, every inch of skin burned. Andrew walked her toward the bed, reaching out with one arm to slam the door closed as they passed it. He kissed her again and again, his mouth probing, hot, desperate. Margaret answered him in kind, clinging to him tightly. She wrapped her arms around his neck, aware of a desire to wrap her legs around him just as tightly. Her impulse would have embarrassed her if she had stopped to think about it, but she had no time or interest for thinking. All she wanted was to feel his body pressed into hers, his mouth consuming hers.

''Drew, Drew,'' she murmured breathlessly between his kisses, and just the sound of her voice calling his name shook him with passion.

They fell backward onto the bed, struggling to undress as they kissed and caressed and rolled across the bed. Taking off their clothes would've been a difficult enough process under ordinary circumstances, given the voluminous folds of her skirts and petticoats, but it was almost impossible when neither of them could tear themselves away from the other long enough to finish the job. Finally Andrew managed to unbutton enough of her bodice to pull it down to her waist, and he roughly yanked her chemise down with it, impatient to see the lovely white globes. He covered her breasts with his hands, titillated by the contrast of their exquisite whiteness beneath his browned skin. He squeezed them gently and stroked and caressed, arousing the sensitized flesh until Margaret arched up off the bed, begging mutely for the touch of his mouth.

It was an appeal he couldn't keep from responding to, and he bent, taking one nipple into his mouth. He cupped both hands around her breast as he suckled it, kneading and stroking until Margaret thought she must go mad from the doubled delight of his hand and mouth. She laced her fingers through his hair, whimpering with each new dazzling sensation. He seemed to take forever with her breast, worshiping it with his lips and fingers, while the tension mounted in her almost unbearably, gripping her with tendrils of fire. She twisted restlessly beneath him, aching to feel his skin against hers all the way down her body and frustrated by the clothes that lay between them.

Andrew loved the involuntary sounds that escaped her lips, moans and little sobs that spoke far more clearly than any words could that she delighted in his lovemaking, that she was as caught in it as he was. He tore his mouth away from her breast finally, and the nipple, damp from his kisses, prickled at the touch of the air upon it. He watched, his breath rasping in and out of his throat, as the small bud roughened, and the sight of it sent another stab of hunger through his loins. He bent and took the nipple between his lips, pulling gently, teasing, then releasing it with a kiss as Margaret moaned softly.

He closed his eyes, fighting back the rage of desire that almost took him at the sound of Margaret's passion. Slowly, deliberately, he took her other nipple in his mouth and began to work the same magic on it. He rucked up the skirt and petticoats that covered her legs and slid his hand up her thigh to the joinder of her leg. The cotton of her underclothes was wet with the evidence of her readiness for him, and he smiled against her breast. He began to rub his fingers over the dampness, pressing the cloth against her, and the moisture increased. She moved her hips impatiently against his hand.

He yanked down the underdrawers, snapping the drawstring in his haste, and slid his fingers into the slick, moist warmth. He moved unhurriedly, circling, sliding, slipping into her. His fingers moved in time to the pull of his mouth on her breast, and she thrust up into the cup of his hand again and again.

Margaret was in a daze of passion, hardly aware of what she was doing. Nothing seemed important or real except the strange, wild feeling growing in her abdomen, a feeling as if she were racing headlong toward something wonderful. She was consumed with an intense anticipation. Andrew's fingers stroked her rhythmically, and with each movement the anticipation heightened until the pleasure became almost unbearable. She felt as if she might shatter into a million pieces, might fly completely out of her skin and mingle with the black void of the night. Then, abruptly, astonishingly, ecstasy thundered through her, wiping out all other thought and feeling. She arched up, crying out, as the pleasure took her, bursting in her loins and sweeping out over her body.

Then it was gone, leaving her limp, exhausted and trembling, utterly warm and peaceful in a way she had never felt before—had never even imagined existed. Her eyes, clamped shut tightly in the shock of the storm, fluttered open now and she looked up at Andrew, her eyes velvet soft and lambent, filled with love. She was too stunned to speak or even to reach out to touch him, but her eyes spoke more than enough of her wonder and gratitude. In that moment Andrew Stone was her whole life, and she thought that there was nothing she wouldn't do if he asked it.

But Andrew had not yet come to his own release, and the glowing look in Margaret's eyes only made his desire increase. He had loved watching the pleasure take her, knowing with a kind of pride and awe that he had brought her this. It had swelled his own yearning to the bursting point, and now, the way she gazed at him almost shoved him over the edge. He moved between her legs quickly and sank into her, hard and slow. He was watching her face and saw Margaret's eyes widen in surprise.

She had thought she was capable of feeling no more pleasure, but she found out she was wrong. Andrew was hard and huge inside her, satisfying her in a way that nothing else could. She released a shaky sigh of bliss. He began to move within her.

She moaned. Could there be still more pleasure? It was hard to believe, but it was undeniably true. Every time he pulled back, then thrust, tingling sensations shimmered through her. And, incredibly, that knot of desire, that anticipation, was building again. She wrapped her legs around him, pulling him into her, and he began to pump harder and faster, racing toward their goal. Just as he buried his head in her neck, muffling his groan, and bucked wildly against her, another explosion of pleasure slammed through her. For one wild, white-hot moment, they were joined together, intertwined in ecstasy and lost to everything else.

Chapter Eleven

They lay in silence for a long time afterward, stunned by the beauty and intensity of what they had experienced. There was nothing adequate to say to the moment, nor were either of them capable of pulling their thoughts and feelings together enough to make a coherent sentence. Instead, they simply lay, still twined together, now and then lazily running a hand down the other's arm, as though to reassure themselves that this was real and not a dream. Andrew pressed a kiss to Margaret's hair and to her damp temple; he nuzzled into her silky locks, breathing in her scent. There were feelings in him that sang of love, but he closed his mind against them, keeping himself solely in the sensual realm. He refused to think; he would only enjoy.

Margaret did not bother to try to separate her thoughts or feelings from the physical enjoyment she had just reached. It was enough for her simply to drift in a haze of bliss, without analyzing anything. At this moment there was nothing else for her except this man and this room. Without thought or decision, without hesitation or doubt, she had become Andrew Stone's woman, his wife in every way as well as name. She did not stop to consider whether she loved him; she simply lived it.

Andrew dozed for a few minutes, snuggled against her, his breath ruffling her hair. Margaret lay quietly, not wishing to disturb him. Sometime later he awoke and with a sigh, pulled his arm from around her and rolled out of bed.

"I better wash up now. I'm so dirty I've probably already turned the sheets black."

Margaret smiled and wiggled in the bed a little. "There is something a little scratchy in here."

"I'm surprised you didn't kick me out. I must smell like a horse."

"Not entirely. There's a little aroma of cattle, too."

He glanced back at her and grinned. She looked pretty and sweet, lying there, the sheet demurely pulled up to her arms. She also looked devastatingly desirable. He couldn't imagine a man alive who wouldn't respond to the picture she presented. And there hadn't been a word of reproach from her for the way he'd come to her, still covered with the dust of the ranch. She only smiled and joked with him.

Andrew wrapped his bedrobe around him and went downstairs to haul up water for his tub. Margaret lay, propped up on her elbow, watching him, as he took off the robe and stepped into the tub. It no longer made her blush to see his naked body. After the way she had responded to his lovemaking, she thought she had gone past feeling shame. She smiled reminiscently, thinking of the intense, thunderous joy that had seized her earlier. She had never dreamed that a woman could feel anything so sensual or shattering. Everything she'd ever heard was that women were above such carnal pleasures as occupied men's thoughts. Obviously she wasn't.

Even now, watching Andrew stretch and step into the tub, a tendril of desire curled low in her abdomen. His body was beautiful in a hard, masculine way, and she enjoyed watching the play of muscles beneath his firm skin, the long, powerful line of thigh and back. In fact, she thought, her eyes caressing him, she wanted to touch that body again. She wanted to run her hands over his back and onto his muscled buttocks, then lower still, to the hair-roughened legs. She wanted to know the texture of every part of him.

She watched Andrew lather the soap and begin to wash. As he rubbed the soapy rag across his arms and chest, she imagined what it would feel like to take that rag in her own hands and wash his body herself. Her heart raced at the thought and heat began to prickle within her. She would like to bathe him, to have him lean back against the tub and let her minister to him. She thought of stroking the rag across his chest and sliding lower...

Margaret swallowed. Thank Heavens Andrew was turned away from her and could not see the hungry course of her eyes or he would know exactly how brazen she was. What would he think of her if he knew she would like to touch him all over? She feared that he would decide that she wasn't a lady at all, not a fit person to be his wife or his daughter's mother. After all, everyone knew that a man who truly loved his wife put her up on a pedestal; a lady was supposed to be something of a saint, not one who reveled in the pleasures of the flesh.

But perhaps Andrew already knew that about her. He couldn't have not realized how much she had enjoyed the pleasures of the flesh tonight. He might not care if she was a lady. Perhaps it even brought him pleasure when she enjoyed it, too; he had certainly seemed to reach as great a peak tonight as he had last night, maybe even more. Was it possible that he might like her to touch him? After all, she had loved feeling his hands on her. Could a man be that different? Wouldn't his skin, too, quiver beneath her touch?

Just thinking such delicious, lascivious thoughts was bringing back that pulse of desire between her legs, and she squeezed her legs together. Did people ever do what they had just done more than once a night? Did they do it at any other time? She tried to imagine what her Aunt Charity would say about the thoughts she was having and she had to stifle a giggle.

Aunt Charity's reaction mattered very little to her now. What mattered was how Andrew would feel about her. She would hate for him to think her crude or low. Before, she had wanted them to have a pleasant marriage, for him to be kind to her. Now—well, now she wanted far more than that. She wanted him to love her and not just a little bit, but with all his heart and soul. She wanted to be the center of his days, the light of his life. For that was exactly what he had become to her. Over the course of the time she had known him, she had grown to care about him more and more until tonight, when her passion had exploded, blowing away all doubt and fear. She no longer wondered if she was falling in love with her husband. She loved him. She loved him more than anything else on earth. That was why it was so important to bring him to love her, too. She dared not risk doing anything that would disgust him or turn him away from her.

Margaret chewed doubtfully at her lower lip. If only she knew what to do. What he wanted. Her instinct was to lavish her love on him, to treat him with all the sweetness and generosity that was inside her. She wanted to coddle him, to please him in every way she could. Yet doubts assailed her. He was no ordinary man, and theirs was no ordinary marriage. Andrew had married her for a purpose, and if she did what she wanted, she wasn't sure that she would be what he had married her to be. Of course, she didn't *want* to play that friendly, unloved role of the wife he had envisioned. But neither did she want to turn him completely away from her. It would be so much easier if only she had the surety of his love.

She sighed and flopped back on the bed, closing her eyes. Vaguely, she heard the sounds of his washing, then getting out of the tub and drying off, but she paid little attention, too caught up in her thoughts. But then he came around to her side of the bed and her eyelids flew open. He stood beside the bed, looking down at her, and Margaret gazed back up at him silently. She would have liked to jump up and throw her arms around him, he looked so good to her, standing there all clean and scrubbed, his hair wetly slicked back, his skin still damp. But she was scared to, so she just lay, waiting for him to take the lead.

"It's getting late. You must be tired." He reached down and ran a gentle finger along her cheek.

He wanted her to go back to her room now, she realized, and she looked away. She had to fight back her tears.

Andrew, watching her, saw the look of disappointment that had flashed into her eyes before she turned her head away, and hope surged up in him. Could it be that she did not want to leave him? Could it be that she would like to stay in his bed, cuddled up beside him all night? He struggled to keep his voice even. "Do you want to go back to your room?"

Margaret glanced at him, unsure what to say. She realized that she could not lie to him, no matter what he might want her to say. Her heart would not let her deny even that much of her love. "No," she whispered. "Not unless you would prefer it. I—like it here." She looked away again, unable to meet his eyes for fear of what she might see there.

Andrew swallowed. Emotions tore at him, trying to get out, and it was all he could do to keep them contained. *Damn it, he wasn't going to give this woman that kind of power over him.* So he said nothing, but merely bent down and brushed his lips against her forehead. He walked around the bed and climbed in on his side, sliding over beside her. He slipped his arm beneath her, pulling her to him. "I'm glad."

Margaret looked up into his face and a sunny smile broke across her face. "Really? I thought you liked to sleep by yourself."

He shook his head. "No. I didn't think you would want me to impose myself on you that way."

Margaret giggled. "Impose?" She snuggled closer to him, rubbing her cheek against his shoulder and sliding her arm around him as far as she could reach. "It's no imposition. I like to have you close." She felt him tense beneath her, and she added hastily, "It's, uh, warmer and safer."

He kissed the top of her head. "You're always safe in this house. Or anywhere else. I'll see to that."

The tone of his voice, hard and determined, warmed her more than his words. It made her feel as if she was dear to him, someone he would always protect, whatever the cost.

"Good night, Drew," she said softly, wishing she could kiss the smooth skin beneath her cheek, but she did not dare. She wondered if he liked her using his nickname; it made her feel closer, more intimate.

"Good night, sweetheart." He didn't even realize what he had said until he said it. It was too late to call it back then.

For the first time since she'd come to the ranch, Margaret did not awaken long after Andrew had breakfasted and left. This time when she opened her eyes, it was still pitch black outside, and the only light was from the oil lamp beside Andrew's shaving stand. He was standing before the small mirror, stroking the razor down his cheek, his face twisted to pull his skin taut. He had put on his pants, but wore his shirt unbuttoned and hanging outside his trousers. The galluses hung in loops down beside his thighs. His dark hair was tousled from sleep.

Margaret watched as he wiped the soap from his razor and returned the instrument to his face. Her newly found love stirred warmly in her chest as she watched him. He glanced toward the bed and saw her eyes open, and he smiled ruefully.

"I'm sorry. I was trying to be quiet so as not to awaken you."

She shook her head, smiling back in a slow, sleepy way that, though she did not know it, did peculiar things to his insides. "That's all right. I've been wanting to get up when you do. It seems strange to eat breakfast alone. Besides, there's plenty to do."

"You needn't work so hard. I can hire another maid if you need it."

"Oh, no. Now that Annie's here, too, we should have enough to do the work."

He frowned. When it had been only him and Laura in the house, it had seemed that Carmela and her daughter were enough to get the work done. But, now that he thought about it, there had been several more servants when Damaris had been his wife. And he had seen the change in the state of the house the past few days. Obviously he hadn't realized how things had been allowed to slide without a woman overseeing the house. "But you and your sister shouldn't have to do that kind of work. Hire whomever you need. I'm sure Carmela has a whole roster of relatives.''

Margaret grinned. "Yes, if what Rosa says is true. But I'm used to working. I wouldn't know what to do if I didn't.''

Andrew looked at her. He didn't know what a woman did precisely, either, but he was sure that he had never seen his mother or Damaris polishing the stair rail as he had found Margaret doing a couple of days ago. They had always been sitting somewhere, with only their hands or their mouths occupied. Of course, Damaris had managed to spend a good portion of her day on her toilette.

"I don't want you to tire yourself. I didn't marry you to scrub my floors.''

It was on the tip of her tongue to ask him flirtatiously why he had married her, but she stopped herself. As likely as not, she would hear an answer she didn't care to.

Margaret started to get out of bed, then remembered that beneath the sheet she was stark naked. It had been an entirely different thing last night to let him see her body in the heat of passion. But this morning, in the cool, rational dawn, it would be too embarrassing. She sat there for a moment, clutching the sheet to her bosom, wondering what to do. Andrew finished shaving and wiped the remaining bits of soap from his face, then turned toward her as he began to button his shirt. He must have seen her dilemma, for he reached down to the chair, picked up his own robe and tossed it onto the bed.

"It will doubtless be miles too big, but at least it will cover you.'' He smiled.

"Thank you.'' He turned away and she slipped into the robe and hopped out of bed, wrapping the robe around her and tying it tightly. Only the cloth belt fastened it, so that the neckline revealed rather more than was decent of her chest, and when she walked, her bare legs flashed beneath the robe. But, as he said, at least it covered her. And it was his, which somehow made her feel warm and secure.

He turned back, his shirt buttoned and tucked in, and his eyes ran down her, taking in the glimpse of leg and chest. With the long sleeves dangling below her hands and the hem trailing ludicrously along the floor, she presented a picture that was sweetly erotic to him. Andrew wanted to kiss her, a long, slow, deep kiss. That wasn't the kind of marriage they had, of course, but…but, Lord, she hadn't responded to him last night anything like the bloodless, businesslike marriage partner he had expected, either. She had cried out in a satisfaction as deep and wild as his own. She had twisted and moaned beneath him in passion. She had wanted to sleep the night with him. Margaret was a woman of heat and desire, of sensuality and hunger.

Andrew went to her. Almost involuntarily, he took her shoulders in his hands. The satin of his dressing gown was slick beneath his fingers and her shoulders were small and delicate under that. She was frail, he thought, and he was too big, too tough for her, too animalistic. But his thoughts couldn't control his desire; even her soft delicacy was stirring to him.

"You look beautiful in the morning," he told her, surprising himself. He had sworn not to give her the power of knowing her effect on him.

But Margaret smiled up at him, and he found he could not regret what he had said. "Thank you. So do you."

He chuckled. "Beautiful? I think not. I'm just an old Yankee with a limp."

"You're not old," she retorted, her face drawing up into such fierce lines that he had to smile again. "And you *are*—well, not beautiful, then, but handsome. You're very handsome. I even heard Mrs. Pickens say so."

"That Stars-and-Bars-waving old hen? She must have taken leave of her senses."

"If she ever had any."

Andrew let out a bark of laughter, and Margaret clapped her hand over her mouth guiltily. "I'm sorry. That wasn't kind."

"Kindness be damned. It was the truth." He traced the lines of her face gently with his forefinger and thought about picking her up and taking her back to the bed. Would she respond as she had last night? His breath came out a little unevenly. "Will you sleep here tonight?"

Her eyes widened, but she said only, "If you want me to."

"It's not a question of what I want. It's what you want. I would have you with me every night." Lord, there he went again; he couldn't seem to keep the truth from tumbling out this morning. She was too pretty, too warm, too recently in his bed.

"And I would be there."

Her simple words robbed him of speech, even movement, for a moment. Then he pulled her to him and kissed her with all the time and care he had wanted to use and told himself he should not. At last his head came up. His eyes were bright and his voice was a little husky as he said, "Have Rosa move your things today. Just push anything of mine aside. Take all the room you want." He paused. "Unless—perhaps you would rather we used your room?"

"No." She shook her head. "I like your bedroom better. Mine is too...fussy." She looked horrified at what she had said and went on hastily, "I mean, it is beautiful, of course, and I'm very glad you gave me such an elegant room, but it is more—more richly done than I am used to. I'm a simple woman."

He grinned at her rapid backtracking. "You said it correctly the first time. It's too fussy. Too ornate. Too overdone. Do you truly dislike it?"

She nodded a little shamefacedly. "I know it is very expensive and I'm sure quite tasteful, but I—"

"You are not like Damaris. Thank God for that. All the furniture in the house is to her liking. Get rid of any you don't like. Put in what you want."

Her eyes widened. "But that would be too costly."

"I can afford it. I hate the stuff anyway. I just assumed that, being a woman, you would like it."

"Not all women are alike."

"I'm beginning to discover that." His mouth softened sensually.

Margaret thought that she would like to stretch up and kiss his lower lip. She hesitated, but then reminded herself that Andrew had just been pleased that she was not like other women. She went up on tiptoe and gently pressed her mouth against his lower lip. He went perfectly still, and she dared to kiss his well-cut upper lip, as well. She went back down flat on her feet. Andrew stared down at her, his eyes smoldering. He bent and kissed her fiercely.

His hand came up and slipped inside the gaping neck of her robe to cup her breast. Margaret sighed with pleasure and melted into him. Andrew swept her up into his arms and carried her back to his bed. It was some time before they made it down to the breakfast table.

Later that morning Andrew took Margaret, Annie and Zach on a ride around the ranch. To Margaret's surprise, she found that Laura was included in the group. It had seemed to her that Andrew rarely even saw his daughter, let alone spent time with her. But later, during the ride, Laura shyly told her that she went riding with her father almost every day, but added, with a glance toward Zach and Annie, "We never talked this much, though."

Margaret noted that there was a glow to Laura's cheeks and a sparkle in her eyes that was normally missing. Laura, for the first time since Margaret had known her, actually seemed to be having fun. "Yes," Margaret commented dryly. "You'll find that there is a great deal of conversation when my sister is around."

"I like her." Laura blushed, almost as if this were an embarrassing admission. "She told me to call her Annie and said that she was sure we'd be friends."

"I hope you will be." Margaret smiled. Laura was rather pretty when she smiled and looked interested in things. She seemed almost friendly today. Perhaps it would bring her out to have Annie and Zach there. Emma had once said that she was sure Annie could make friends with a horny toad if there was nothing else around. "And with Zach, too."

An outright grin flashed across Laura's face. "Oh, yes. He's very nice. He told me he didn't mind that I was a girl."

"Mmm. That was big of him."

"Well, it *was* nice. Sometimes boys do mind. Rosa has lots of little brothers and they will never play with me." Her shoulders slumped. "Not that Fräulein Hoelscher would let me play with them." Then she brightened. "But she can't refuse to let me play with my own—well, I guess they're no relation, really, but you know what I mean."

"Yes, I do. There's no reason why your governess shouldn't allow you to play with Annie and Zach. After all, you can't spend your whole day studying, can you?"

"Oh, no. I don't. But even when I'm not, the fräulein is careful that I act as becomes a lady. She says I must not lose my breeding."

"Here among the heathen?"

Laura looked up at her, puzzled. "Pardon?"

Margaret shook her head. She had taken an immediate dislike to the German governess and her strict ways, but that was not something she should reveal to her stepdaughter. "Nothing. I was making a feeble jest."

"Laura!" Zach turned to look at her over his shoulder. "Annie'n I are going to race over to that lone oak! You want to come?"

"Oh, yes!" Laura urged her horse toward him impulsively, then remembered to look to her father. "Father? If I may?"

"Of course. I'd like to see all of you ride." There was a warm glow of affection in his eyes as he looked at her. Margaret realized that that was another thing she had been wrong about. Andrew Stone did care for his daughter, even if he rarely showed it.

The three youngsters took off at a run, and Margaret and Andrew followed them more slowly, watching them.

"Your brother and sister ride well," he commented.

"They love horses, especially Annie. She teased Daddy into putting her up on a horse when she was three. She wasn't a bit scared, either."

"Today has been different from Laura's usual rides with me. When we're alone together, it seems neither one of us can think of two consecutive sentences to string together. I don't think I've ever heard her talk as much as she has this afternoon."

"She likes Annie and Zach, I think."

"They're a good influence on her. All of you are. It must be a Carlisle trait—moving into people's lives and taking away the gloom."

Was that what she had done with him? Margaret glanced up at him, her heart beginning to thud, searching for some sign in his face, his eyes, that would tell her that he cared for her. That he could love her back, *would* love her back someday.

There was something there, some warmth or spark, different from what she saw when he looked at Laura. But she wasn't sure exactly what it meant.

Laura won the race, more accustomed than the other two to riding and to her mount, though Annie and Zach both rode with so much dare-devil abandon that they kept close to her. Afterward, the five of them rode on to the river and meandered along it for a time. It was October and the heat had at last died down, but it was not cool yet, just a pleasantly warm day, with a breeze blowing across the river. The live oaks were their usual dark and dusty green, but the cottonwoods and other trees were turning yellow and red, creating a palette of colors in the distant landscape. All in all, it was a good day on which to ride lazily, laughing and talking.

But as they came around a bend in the river, they gradually became aware of a peculiar odor. As they rode on, it became stronger and more rancid.

"What's that smell?" Annie piped up, never one to hide what she thought.

"I don't know." There was a strange look on Andrew's face. "It reminds me of..." He shook his head.

"Of what?" Margaret prodded, bothered more by the expression on his face than by the odor, which was growing ever stronger.

"Of the War," he replied shortly. "Never mind. It's crazy."

"It kinda smells like the time that raccoon got caught beneath the house and died and we couldn't figure out for a couple of days why it smelled so," Zach put in.

Margaret turned to him, startled. "You know, you're right." She turned back to her husband. "Andrew..."

But he was looking ahead, shading his eyes to see. "There are some of the men."

"Where?"

"I see them." Annie stretched up, also shading her eyes. "Over yonder." She pointed.

Unconsciously their pace picked up as they rode toward the small clump of men and horses. The wind whirled a particularly strong whiff of the smell into their faces, and Margaret covered her nose and mouth, almost gagging.

One of the men in the distance mounted his horse and rode to meet them. Andrew dug in his heels and his horse broke into a gallop. Margaret and the others spurred their horses after him. There was a curious leaden feeling in Margaret's chest, and without even knowing why, she was scared.

"Colonel!" The man who came to meet them was String McAlister.

They all reined up. Andrew's voice was sharp. "What is it?"

The other man swept off his hat in deference to the women present and looked at Margaret. "You don't want to go any farther, ma'am. It ain't something for a lady to see."

"What?" Margaret's stomach tightened. The smell was ghastly now, and all of them were holding their hands over their noses, trying to breathe without smelling anything.

She looked past where the men stood. There were mounds dotted here and there over the ground, and spikes rose from most of them. She gasped, realizing what they were, just as Zach exclaimed, "That's cattle! Those are cows lying over there. They're dead!"

That's what the mounds were, cattle lying on their sides, and the prongs sticking up were their long horns.

String nodded grimly. "That's right, son. You best take the ladies back to the house."

Andrew said tersely. "He doesn't know the way. They got here only yesterday. Send one of the men with them."

He signaled toward the clump of men, and one of them left the group. He, like String and the other men, had tied his bandanna around the lower part of his face to protect himself somewhat from the nauseating stench of the decaying animal flesh.

Andrew turned toward Margaret. "Meg, take the children back. Jackson'll show you the way."

"But what happened to the cattle?" How could that many die all at once? There must have been fifty of them out there. "Is it a disease?"

String emitted a short, unamused grunt of laughter. "Yeah, a disease named Tom Murdock."

"What? What do you mean?"

"I mean, somebody killed 'em, Miz Stone. Shot through the head, all of 'em."

"String!" Andrew's voice was low and hard with warning.

"Sorry, missus."

But Margaret was too aghast at the import of what he had said to even hear his apology. "You mean someone slaughtered them all? And left them? But why?" It made no sense. Stealing cattle was one thing; it might be criminal, but it made sense. But simply shooting a bunch of steers and leaving them to rot on the ground! "That's crazy!"

"Yeah. Mean crazy."

"Margaret, take the children." Andrew shot a meaningful glance toward Laura, who sat stiff and white on her horse, her eyes as big as saucers.

"Of course. I'm sorry." She reached out and touched Laura's arm. "Come on, sweetheart, let's go back to the house." She nodded toward Annie and Zach and wheeled her horse around to start in the direction they had just come. Annie and Zach followed her lead, curious though they were. While they were horrified and amazed, it was obvious that the younger Laura was much more deeply affected by the slaughter.

They rode back to the house in silence, the black cowboy named Jackson in the lead. The only thing in anyone's mind was the carnage back by the river, but one sharp look from Margaret had stilled Annie's questions. Zach dropped back to ride beside Laura and reached out once to squeeze her hand. She managed to give him a wan smile, despite the white shock that still stamped her face. Margaret was surprised to see her brother be that thoughtful; it was certainly something she'd never seen him do with Annie. But then, Annie would have scornfully shrugged off his hand and told him to mind his own business. Laura was an easier person of whom to be protective.

When they reached the house, Laura went upstairs immediately to her room, and Annie and Zach launched into a spate of questions.

"What did he mean, a disease named Tom Murdock?"

"Did he do it?"

"Why?"

"How'd they know it was him?"

"You think maybe it was Indians?"

Margaret flung up her hands, overwhelmed. "Annie! Zach! For goodness' sake, I don't know any more than

you do. Though I'm sure it wasn't Indians, Zach, so you
can wipe that eager look off your face. There haven't been
Indians in these parts for years, and you know it. As for
why and who, I don't know."

"But why'd he say Mr. Murdock, like he was the one
who did it?"

Margaret shook her head. "I don't know. I guess he
thought it was something to do with this—this thing between Mr. Stone and Mr. Murdock."

"The feud," Zach supplied wisely.

"It isn't exactly a feud, Zach."

"That's not what I heard. I heard one of Stone's hands
got shot last year in Bannister's place, and—"

"Zach! Hush up! I'll not have you repeating saloon talk
in my house, and in front of your sisters, at that."

"Yes, ma'am. But that's what I heard."

"Gossip. We haven't any idea what the cause of the
quarrel was or exactly how the shooting occurred."

"Well, it's a fact that neither of them, or any of their
men, come into town anymore alone. All of 'em pack
guns. Everybody says they hate each other."

"It's not our place to gossip about it."

"I don't know why not," Annie retorted. "I mean,
we're in the middle of it now, aren't we?"

Margaret sighed. She couldn't deny that.

"Come on, Maggie, tell us what it's all about, at least."

"I don't know!" She threw up her hands in exaspera-
tion. "I told you, I don't know any more about it than you
do!"

"You mean Stone hasn't explained it to you? Hasn't told
you anything about it? But you're married to him."

Margaret felt a blush stealing onto her face. Any normal wife would know, of course. It was a blatant admission of how little closeness there was between them, even

though they were husband and wife. She shared Andrew's bed; he had taken her to the heights of ecstasy. She had come, all unexpectedly, to love him. But she didn't know his secrets. He didn't share his thoughts with her. She might love him, but the feeling was not returned. To him, she knew, she was no more than a respectable mistress, a woman to receive his passion. He was as little likely to confide in her as he was in one of the whores who lived near the saloons. It was bitter as gall to have her brother and sister realize that.

"He's told me nothing about it," she said shortly. Looking at her face, Annie and Zach quickly dropped the topic.

Margaret went to her room to change and afterward, she felt so tired that she decided to lie down. Curtains drawn, she lay in the dark, her thoughts as gloomy as the room. She was in love with a man who didn't love her, a man who wanted to marry only to have a mother for his child, an entree for that child into the local society—and a convenient bed partner. Tears formed in her eyes. That was all she was to Andrew. The lovemaking last night that had been like an earthquake to her world, was no more to him than a release of a man's physical need. Damaris had been right, after all. Andrew could hurt her, very much. Only it wasn't her body that ached. It was her heart.

Chapter Twelve

Andrew tiptoed into Margaret's darkened room and to the bed. He stood for a moment looking down at her. She lay atop the bedcovers, dressed in her underthings with her dressing gown wrapped around her. Her hair was loose and spilling across the bedspread, a pool of silver against its darkness. She looked fragile and lovely, like a work of fine porcelain—and just as breakable.

He stretched out a hand and ran it softly down the side of her face. He hated that she had witnessed that scene of slaughter today. It must have sickened and frightened her. He had been as anxious to get her away from it as to get Laura and the other children out. Violence should not touch her in any way, and he swore that from now on he would make sure she was protected against it all.

He bent and brushed his lips tenderly against her forehead. Her eyes fluttered opened and she smiled. "Andrew."

"Hello." He returned her smile. "I'm sorry I woke you. I just—wanted to make sure you were all right." He wouldn't tell her of the knot in his stomach all the way back to the house, the sickness inside him that Murdock's hatred had turned so vicious. Nor would he admit that he had needed to come to her, even though Annie had told him she was napping, because he knew the sickness inside would ease as soon as he was with her.

He sat down on the bed beside her and caressed her forehead, then her cheek. "Are you all right?"

Margaret nodded. The dark, unhappy feelings she'd had earlier had fled at the sight of Andrew's face. Her heart rose up inside her as it always did when she looked at him. "I'm fine."

"I was afraid it had made you ill."

A shadow darkened her eyes. "It wasn't pleasant."

"I'm sorry you happened to see it. I didn't want any of that to touch you. I—I had thought I could keep it away from you. I will in the future, I promise."

"Keep what away from me?"

He made a negating gesture with his head. "Murdock. His anger." His face turned fierce. "You don't have to worry. I will protect you. Nothing is going to happen to you or Laura or your brother and sister, either. I'll see to it."

"See to what? Why should anything happen to us? I don't understand all this, Drew."

He sighed. "I know. I saw no reason to talk about it— it isn't a subject I enjoy. I thought you would never have to face it. You shouldn't even have to hear about it."

Was that why he had not told her? To protect her, not because she didn't matter to him? Margaret's spirits perked up even further and she scooted up to a sitting position. His hand curved over her cheek and under her jaw, and she took it between both of hers and raised it to her lips and kissed it softly. She had no idea of the tremor of mixed lust and tenderness that darted through Andrew at her gesture.

"I want to hear about it. It is something that affects you. Was it really Murdock? Why does he hate you so much?"

She continued to hold his hand, now cradling it against her chest, and the gesture warmed Andrew, and not solely with passion. It made him want more than ever to protect her. Yet, looking at her big, concerned eyes, he found he wanted to tell her about it, too.

"It started years ago, soon after I bought the ranch and settled here, before the War. The river divided Murdock's land from mine and it switched course. It's happened before. The banks are shallow and sometimes when the rains are heavy, it will begin cutting a new path. When that happened, it added some land to my side, land that had once been Murdock's. He wasn't pleased about it, and he suspected that I had somehow helped to divert it. I thought he was being ridiculous and told him so, and it caused ill feeling between us. We had never been friends, but after that, we weren't even on speaking terms. Then the War came and I left. After the divorce, when I returned here, I found that Murdock had married Damaris."

"That made a greater rift between you. I understand."

"Yes. I'm sure Damaris has done everything she can to poison his mind against me. Besides, I fought on the other side and Murdock's son, the one older than Cade, was killed in the War. Murdock was very bitter about it."

"He could hardly blame you for his son's death."

"No?" Andrew raised an eyebrow. "To most of the people around here, I am an embodiment of 'the other side.' I'm the Yankee, and it's far easier to hate a single man than a vague, amorphous people. I'm right here. I'm visible. And I'm alive and prospering, when their husband or son or brother is dead or crippled."

"But it isn't as if you were unscathed." Margaret curved her hand protectively over his knee, where his scar lay.

"Yes. I took a ball at Antietam. I have a limp when I walk. But that's hardly the same as a man who's lost his eye or his arm. Nor is it much comfort to a man who lay in a Reb hospital, suffering, without adequate medical supplies.''

"I wouldn't think there's that much difference in one pain from another, whether it's North or South. And your leg isn't all. The War cost you your wife, as well.''

He glanced at her, startled. A short bark of laughter burst from him. "Is that what you think? Is that the story—that Damaris divorced me because I fought for the Union?''

"That's what people say.''

"Fighting for the Union isn't grounds for a divorce, no matter what the good people of Huxley might think. Especially in Pennsylvania." He stood up and walked away from her, going to the window and shoving open the drapes. He gazed out the window as he spoke, and the blaze of sunlight on his face revealed the harsh lines and bitter set of his mouth. "Damaris didn't divorce me. It was the other way around. And it wasn't for patriotic reasons. It was because I came home after I'd been wounded, and she, not expecting me, was in our bed with another man.''

Margaret gasped and stretched out her arms vainly toward him. "Oh, Andrew, no!''

"Oh, yes." He turned toward her, his face like granite. "She didn't love me. She never did. She married me because I was wealthier than any man in Huxley and because, like most other men, I groveled at her feet. I thought she was the most beautiful woman I had ever seen. A veritable goddess. I wanted her. I loved her. I wanted to marry her and take care of her. I would have done anything for her, but she didn't love me, even a little bit. Damaris hasn't the slightest idea what love is. She's a bitch—a wicked, treacherous, lying, beautiful bitch.''

His words hit Margaret like a blow. Andrew had loved Damaris from the depths of his soul; even his very bitterness was an indication of how much he had felt for her. Whatever he felt for Margaret, might ever feel for her, it wasn't a fraction of what he had felt for Damaris. He hated Damaris just as much now, but even so, that was more emotion than he had for Margaret.

Yet, at the same time, Margaret quivered inside for the pain in his voice, for the unhappiness that Damaris Murdock had brought to him. She hated the woman. How could she have hurt Andrew so? Especially when he had loved her as he did. Margaret thought that there was a lot she would give to have him care even half that much for her. But Damaris hadn't cared; she had wrecked his life.

"She told me that she had never loved me. My touch, she said, had made her skin crawl. She had betrayed me right from the start, but I was too naive and in love to realize it. She had had innumerable lovers, and any of them, she told me, were preferable to me."

Tears spilled down Margaret's cheeks and she scrambled off the bed and rushed to him. She wrapped her arms around Andrew tightly, as if she could shield him from the pain that encircled him. He stood stiffly within her arms. "God damn her," she said in a low, hard voice, words she had never said in her life but that seemed the only thing to say about Damaris Murdock.

"It's not true," she told him fiercely. "Drew, don't believe her. Whatever she said, it's wrong and false. Wicked!" Her hands rubbed up and down his back comfortingly. "She must be a monster." She tilted her head back to gaze up at him. "Your touch is heavenly." Margaret grinned provocatively. "But perhaps that's the wrong word to use. Your hands on my body make me feel not heavenly at all..." She went up on tiptoe and kissed his lips lightly. "They make me feel quite sinful, in fact." She kissed him again and again, punctuating her words with brief, soft kisses all over his mouth and jaw and down onto the softer flesh of his throat. "I love the way your hands feel on me. I ache to have you touch me. Most women would get down on their knees and thank God to have the pleasure you gave me last night."

Normally Margaret would never have dreamed of revealing the things she was saying now; even thinking them was almost enough to make her blush. But she didn't consider embarrassment at this moment. The only thing in her mind was comforting and reassuring Andrew, making him realize that Damaris had been wrong in what she had told him.

She felt Andrew's skin flame into life beneath her lips. He made a noise and his body relaxed, and she knew that the pain was fleeing before the desire she aroused in him. She released him and her hands went to the buttons of his shirt. Boldly she began to unfasten them, acting without any self-consciousness or, indeed, any thought save that of proving to Andrew how wrong Damaris had been, how very much he aroused a woman. She moved down from button to button, and as she went, she placed her lips to the strip of skin each button revealed.

Margaret felt as much as heard Andrew suck in his breath at the touch of her lips, and his skin jumped each time she kissed it. She pushed his shirt off his chest, sliding her hands across him as she did so. She shoved the material back and down his arms so that it fell and hung at his wrists, still fastened at the cuffs. Spreading her hands over his ribs, she trailed kisses across his chest and stomach.

"You are beautiful," she murmured. "I love to look at you. I've wanted to kiss you here...and here. I want to caress you." She suited her actions to her words, running her hands over his back as her mouth explored his front.

His breath was harsh and rasping. Tentatively she kissed one flat nipple and he groaned. "Oh, Meg..."

She stopped and glanced up. He was gazing down at her with burning eyes. "Should I not?" she asked uncertainly.

"Oh, yes. Yes. You should."

She brushed her lips over the nipple again, delighting in the way it hardened against her lips. Her tongue stole out and flicked across it. Andrew jerked, then panted quickly. "No, don't stop. Please."

Margaret smiled in a deeply feminine satisfaction and settled down to enjoy his body. She drew the nipple into her mouth and sucked at it, her tongue all the while teasing and lashing it, at times so delicately it was a mere breath, at other times with a rough force. Her fingers dug into his sides, but that was not the satisfaction she sought, and so they crept lower and around to his buttocks. She squeezed gently, then harder when he responded with a muffled moan. Finally she went to work on the other nipple, her hands busy all over his body. His hands, hampered by the dangling shirt, rested on her hips, clenching whenever she reached some particularly vulnerable spot. His breath was harsh and rasping, coming out in pants, and she could feel the swollen rigidity of his desire pressing into her soft flesh.

"Does that feel good?" she murmured, pausing in her ministrations.

"God, yes. Don't stop," Andrew replied shakily, and his hands pressed her hips hard against him, grinding his pelvis into her.

''That's how it feels when you do it to me. So good.''
She began to trail kisses down his chest and across his
stomach. ''So sweet.''

She reached the waistband of his trousers, and she
stopped. Her hands came up to it and shakily began to
unbutton his trousers. Again he sucked in his breath, and
Margaret looked up to find him gazing at her with eyes so
hot she was surprised she didn't burst into flames on the
spot. His teeth dug into his lower lip in an effort to retain
control of his passion.

But Margaret found that she did not want him to keep
that control. She continued undoing the buttons and when
she was through, she slid her hand beneath the material on
either side and pushed it off his hips and down. His manhood sprang out free and hard and pulsing, straining toward her, and Margaret gazed at it in fascination.
Gingerly, hardly daring to breathe, she brought her hand
up to touch it. Andrew jerked and said her name in a way
that was part prayer, part curse. Cautiously she curled her
fingers around him, enclosing him, and an unintelligible
noise escaped him.

He jerked his hands free of the encumbering shirt, popping off the buttons unheedingly, and threw it aside. He
hurriedly pulled off his boots and stepped out of his trousers, picking Margaret up around her waist and walking
the last few steps to her bed. He lay down on the bed,
pulling her onto it atop him. ''Touch me again,'' he whispered, cupping her breasts through the cloth of her chemise. ''Please, just touch me.''

Margaret did so without hesitation. He lay quiescently
beneath her, letting her explore him as she chose. She
touched the roughness of hair, the hardness, the exquisite
satin softness. He tightened beneath her, every muscle
straining. Finally he could take it no more and he whisked

away her clothes and guided her back over him, straddling his hips.

"Ride me."

Margaret's eyes widened in amazement, but she understood what he was saying and she quickly did as he asked, sinking down onto the hard shaft. It filled her with a satisfaction so intense she had to clamp her lips tightly together to muffle her cry.

"Don't." He rubbed his thumb across her lips. "Don't hold it in. I want to hear you."

She moved upward until she was almost free and then slowly back down to the very root of his manhood. Almost sobbing, she repeated her actions, retreating and advancing again and again until finally a violent shuddering seized her and she clenched tightly around him, groaning out his name. He dug his fingers into her hips, holding her still until the inner convulsions subsided, and then he began to move beneath her, lifting her from the bed with his strong thrusts. Her flesh was so sensitized that the pleasure was almost too much and she gripped the headboard tightly, holding on against the sensations storming her body, until finally the sweet explosion took them both and they clung together, riding out the storm.

Afterward, they lay together, too dazed with pleasure to even speak. Soon Andrew drifted into sleep. Margaret propped herself up on her elbow and watched him. The lines of torment that had stamped his face earlier was gone, and he slept peacefully. Lovingly, Margaret traced the lines of his brow and cheek and jaw. She might not be as beautiful as Damaris Murdock, but she knew that she would be a better wife to Andrew. She would make him happier. Her small jaw set in determined lines. Whatever it took, however long it might be, she was going to make Andrew Stone forget Damaris. It scared her to think of how much he had loved the woman, how much he might still love her inside, no matter how much he hated her, too. But somehow, someway, she would push the other woman out of his mind—and out of his heart. She had wiped away that memory tonight, at least for a while. Margaret was certain of that. And she would keep on until eventually, Damaris was erased permanently.

Margaret might have been a quiet, even shy person. But anyone who knew her knew that once she set her mind to something, nothing would stop her. When she decided that she would make Andrew happy, she put her heart and soul into the effort. The first thing she did was make certain that he was comfortable. It wasn't hard for a man to be happy with a wife who made sure of his comfort.

Though she was too frugal to get rid of all of Damaris's heavy, gloomy furniture, she did replace the pieces in the sitting room, where they spent most of their time. She culled through the rest of it, banishing the ugliest pieces to the attic and covering much of the rest of it with crocheted doilies and lace runners. She sewed new curtains and drapes in lighter colors and materials for every window in the house, hiring the seamstress in town to help her. She opened up the music room, which had been closed up, and had the piano tuned. Both she and Annie played the piano, and she was determined that from now on this house would have music.

Andrew had told Carmela to bring in some more help, so she arrived one day with another daughter and a daughter-in-law to work as maids, and a son, who because of a shriveled leg, was unable to work on the ranch or a farm. Margaret put the son to work in the yard, planting several saplings and breaking the ground for the flower garden she intended to border the house in the future. After that, there was the porch and trim of the house to be painted a sparkling white and a wide porch swing to be made and hung.

Andrew noticed few of the individual changes Margaret made, but he gradually became aware that everything around him was more pleasant. The house seemed lighter and cheerier, more inviting. Meals were on time and carefully aimed at pleasing his palate. Everything was clean, and he no longer had to deal with any of the nagging little domestic problems that Carmela or Fräulein Hoelscher used to bring to him. Instead of the silence and gloom that once pervaded the house, there was now laughter and talk.

One evening Andrew walked in through the back door, stopping to pull off his dirty boots. The kitchen was filled with tantalizing aromas, and his favorite dessert, apple pie, sat cooling in the pie safe. Carmela was singing in a soft voice, and she turned and smiled at him. He went through the kitchen into the hall, letting the door swing shut behind him. He could hear Annie and Margaret in the drawing room, playing a duet on the piano and giggling at their mistakes. There was a pounding of feet above his head, and a moment later Zach and Laura raced down the stairs and out the front door. Laura, his subdued, even somber Laura, was shrieking and laughing.

Andrew stopped and leaned against the wall for a moment, soaking it in, breathing in the smell of food and the beeswax Margaret used on the stair railing and the dried rose sachets she stashed here and there, listening to the happy, homey sounds of a family. It had been only a month since he'd married her, yet she had managed to turn his whole life around. Now each day he found himself eager to reach home, not content until he could see Margaret's delicately pointed face and feel the warmth of her big green eyes on him. How had she done it? He felt peaceful and happy now, fresh and eager again, as if he were a young man, not a battle-scarred bitter man of thirty-six years.

Margaret stepped out of the drawing room door, Annie behind her, and saw him. She broke into a grin and hurried toward him, her arms outstretched. "Andrew!"

She wrapped her arms around his neck and went up on tiptoe to kiss him. He returned the kiss warmly, feeling the ever-present, ever-ready desire begin to stir in him. Lord, but she was delicious, her body soft in his arms, her mouth sweet against his. He thought about making love to her tonight, and he had to bury his face in her neck to hide what he was sure must be a thoroughly lascivious look. It seemed crazy that she could stir him so, but she did. The more he made love to her, the more he wanted her. She was passionate in bed, far more than just the compliant, docile wife he had envisioned her to be. She wanted to please him and never hesitated to try whatever he might ask of her. She might giggle or blush in an endearing way, but she was always willing, even eager, to explore new avenues of sensuality. They made love often and at all times of the day. Once, in a rush of hunger, he had locked the study door and taken her right there. But Margaret hadn't complained; she had found it exciting.

Andrew had never before felt so complete, so drained, relaxed and utterly satisfied as he did whenever they finished making love. He could lie with her all through the night, her warm body curved up next to his. Sometimes he woke up in the dark and simply lay there, holding Margaret and listening to the soft, even sound of her breathing.

Margaret coddled and cosseted him in a hundred different ways. She trimmed his hair and kept his clothes in perfect order. In the morning she brought up a steaming kettle to warm his shaving water. At night she rubbed away the ache from his tired muscles. If he had a headache, she gently massaged his temples and scalp until it disappeared. When he returned from his hard day of work, she would help him pull off his boots, then sit down on a stool and take his feet in her lap to massage them while he talked to her about his day and the ranch. After supper she often played the piano, and he would sit and listen, lazy and dreaming, soothed by the music. At other times, she would simply sit with him, sewing, as they talked, or she might read aloud to him.

If he was late coming in, she kept a plate of food warm for him, and if, occasionally he had to stay out so late that he came in after she had gone to sleep, she always woke up and hopped out of bed to find him a meal and talk to him. When he came in soaked with rain, she pulled the sodden clothes from him and wrapped him in towels, rubbing his hair dry. When once he came in covered with mud, she was quick to draw him a bath—and even took a rag and bathed him in a way that made it a bath he would never forget.

Andrew loved the care she took of him, the sweet way she spoiled him. The physical pampering and petting she gave him somehow healed the wounds of his heart and spirit, warming and soothing him. He felt wrapped up in her gentle love, a husband who was valued and special. She was always available to him and he knew it. She was ready to listen to him, to comfort him, to laugh with him. And she was ever willing—nay, even eager—for his touch.

Margaret had come into his life and changed it. She had lit it up, turning it sparkling like the sun on a dark river. Andrew knew that every day he was falling more and more in love with her. He tried to maintain his mistrust of women, he told himself that Margaret could be manipulating him for some purpose of her own, lying to him, twisting him around her little finger, as Damaris had done. No matter how much he enjoyed Margaret, no matter how suddenly and remarkably happy his life was now, Andrew knew he should keep a distance between them emotionally. There should be a wall around his heart; he had spent bitter years building it.

Yet somehow Margaret, with her sweet smile and gentle ways, had breached that wall. He found more and more that he could not hold himself apart from her. He wanted to talk to her about everything, wanted to be with her all the time. When he wasn't with her, he thought about her and missed her constantly, and when they were together, he felt complete and peaceful. It was a joy just to hear her laughter or see her lovely face. He wanted to buy her things. He purchased a cameo for her in town and ordered a string of pearls from Galveston. He wanted to see her face light up with love and happiness. Sternly he kept himself from murmuring all the sweet, silly words of love he thought of. But saying the words was merely a formality. His heart had already, without his volition, taken Margaret in. There was no longer a real question about loving or trusting her; she was a part of him in a way no other person ever had been. Though he might deny and debate it in his head, in his heart there was no doubt. He loved her.

Margaret linked her arm through his and walked with him into the sitting room, leaning against him in that loving way of hers that always melted him, even though he tried to hide his response. Annie smiled a greeting at him and left, running off to find Zach and Laura. She and the others had quickly learned that they might as well leave Margaret and Andrew alone in the evenings; they rarely noticed anyone else, anyway, and besides, it got so mushy whenever they were together that it was downright boring.

Andrew hardly noticed Annie's departure. His senses were focused on Margaret, who seemed to be especially fetching tonight. He wasn't sure if she had done something different to her hair or was wearing a particularly attractive dress—or if it was just that every time he saw her, she looked lovelier to him.

He sat down in his chair and pulled Margaret onto his lap. She made a halfhearted protest, giggling, that someone might see them, but she snuggled up against his chest with alacrity, laying her head on his shoulder. Andrew curved his arms around her, holding her, and simply sat, drinking in the sweetness of having her in his arms. He knew that if he brought up his hand and cupped her breast or ran his hand caressingly over her body, she would not fuss. She would lean back, letting him have his way, and he would see the desire gradually take over her face until her lips were parted, her features softened, her eyes glowing. Once, when they were sitting thus, he had even slid a hand beneath her skirts, caressing her through her undergarments. Margaret had just drawn a long, shuddering breath and turned her face into his shoulder, letting his fingers work their magic on her until finally she had uttered a smothered cry and tightened against him. He remembered the sense of pride and power that had flooded him, knowing that he could bring her to respond so to his touch. Even the memory was enough to make him harden with desire.

But he did not move to caress her now. He enjoyed the anticipation of holding off until tonight, of delaying the gratification, certain that it would come. At the moment it was enough simply to hold her.

"Andrew..." Margaret sat up, pulling away from him a little. Her face was uncertain, perhaps even a shade frightened. "I wanted to talk to you about Laura."

"Laura?" Andrew went still. Perhaps the bliss was coming to an end. Was she going to begin to complain about his daughter? To try to wean his affections away from Laura and solely onto herself? "What about her?"

Margaret swallowed. She was certain she was right, but Andrew's stony face didn't help her retain her confidence. "Yes. I—I would like to make some changes in her...daily routine. Well, actually, in her life."

"What changes?" His eyes grew warier.

"Well, I—I don't think it's good for a girl to grow up as she is doing. I hope you don't think it's presumptuous of me—truly, I don't mean to interfere. But when you first spoke to me about marriage, you said that you wanted a mother for your daughter, and this is how I would feel, what I would do, if Laura *were* my daughter."

"Do what?"

"I'd like to spend more time with her," Margaret said in a rush, carefully not looking at Andrew. "I would like to send her governess away."

Her words were so far from what Andrew had been afraid she was going to say that for a moment he was too stunned to speak. He could only sit and stare at her, mouth agape. "What? Get rid of Fräulein Hoelscher?"

Margaret nodded, sneaking a peek at his face. He didn't look angry with her for poking her nose into his daughter's affairs, only thoroughly astounded.

"All right." He couldn't understand why she had looked so tentative, so anxious, when she brought it up. "I leave the realm of nannies and governesses to you. Send her packing if you like. But shouldn't you hire another one first?"

"No. No, that's not what I mean. I'd like to not have one at all. Maybe this will sound strange to you. I imagine you were raised like Laura. But things are different here. I don't think Laura will live the kind of life for which her governess prepares her. When is she going to have to paint those little pictures that she dislikes so much? Perhaps she could learn Spanish. It might be more useful. A woman here doesn't sit around and do—whatever it is that wealthy women do back East."

"You want to discontinue her education, then?" He frowned. "At eleven years of age?"

"No! Of course not. Oh, this is coming out all wrong! I had it all planned out, and now I'm getting it tangled up. But I hate to see her cooped up in her room all day with Miss Hoelscher. Frankly, that woman's enough to turn anyone's blood cold. The fräulein lets her visit with me for an hour, but that's hardly any time at all. And it's so formal and stiff. Neither one of us are very good at saying much. Usually I just let her run out with Zach or Annie, which Fräulein Hoelscher doesn't approve of."

He blinked. "Why ever not?"

"The fräulein told me last week that if I let Laura run around with them, she would never grow up into a proper young lady, that she would be a wild hoyden, or worse."

Andrew cocked an eyebrow. "She dared to say that your brother and sister were not proper influences on her?"

"Yes, in essence, I think that's what she was saying." Margaret's chin came forward. "I rather lost my temper at that, I'm afraid, and I said some things to her that were probably quite impolite." She sighed. "But she did make me so angry when she implied that my own family wasn't good enough to associate with a young lady."

"I understand why you wish to remove her from our employ. I shall see to it this evening."

"It wasn't just that. If I thought she was good for Laura, I wouldn't want to punish her just for disagreeing with me or casting aspersions on my family. But she's wrong—I just know it! Laura never gets to go through a day with Annie or me, seeing to the cleaning and cooking, learning how to run a ranch. Those are things she'll need to know—either here or at her future husband's place. What good will being able to paint a watercolor do her then? She's so restricted. There's never any time for her to run and play or have fun with other children. Laura's such a solemn little creature. She needs to laugh more, to enjoy life. I think Annie and Zach would be good for her."

Andrew smiled and raised her hand to his lips, kissing the back of it gently. "I'm sure you're right. What a kind and generous person you are."

Margaret smiled, pleased by his words, if also a trifle embarrassed. "Not really. Anyone else would want the same things for her, I'm sure."

Andrew's smile faded, and he said abruptly, "Not her own mother."

"What?"

"Damaris has never had the slightest interest in her. She left her in the care of her nanny, and sometimes days, even weeks would go by without her looking in on Laura."

"Oh, Andrew, no! A mother couldn't be so unnatural!"

"No? You don't know Damaris." He shook his head, as though ridding himself of something unpleasant. "But there's no need to talk about that. Tell me, what do you propose to do with Laura if you don't want her to have a governess? How will she acquire an education?"

"Why, go to school, the same as Zach and Annie. She can ride in and back with them every day."

Andrew frowned. "I don't know . . . it could be dangerous."

"Dangerous! Riding to school and back? Annie and Zach do it every day, and so do the Hansen children, who don't live much closer to the schoolhouse than we do. It's far, I know, but—"

"It's not the distance I'm worried about. Or any natural dangers. It's Tom Murdock."

Margaret gasped. "Andrew! Surely he wouldn't do anything to a child! Why, she's his own wife's daughter. Maybe Damaris wasn't a wonderful mother, but surely she would raise a fit if anything happened to her."

Andrew let out a grunt of disbelief. "I wouldn't be too sure about that. She'd more likely be the one who planned it. I don't know. I used to think that no harm would come to a child. I had thought Murdock to be a man of honor. But lately things have gotten worse. The slaughtered cattle down by the river are only one thing—there have been others. Fistfights in town, a polluted stock tank, missing cattle, accusations. Every week now it seems as if there's something new happening. I've been uneasy lately about even letting Annie and Zach ride to the schoolhouse. I've considered sending one of the men with them, to make sure no 'accident' befalls them."

"I can hardly believe that's necessary."

He shrugged. "I'd rather provide for the possibility and be proved wrong than suffer the consequences for being foolishly trusting."

Margaret stared at him with wide, frightened eyes.

"In some ways, Laura might be in more danger than your brother and sister. Hurting them would cause you pain, but if Laura were to be kidnapped, Damaris would have the heir to my fortune in her hands."

"Don't say things like that!" Margaret pleaded, taking his hands between hers. "It couldn't be true. It just couldn't."

"I'm sure Damaris is behind everything Murdock does. I see her hand in the spitefulness, the meanness. I think she's upset that I've married again. Perhaps she thought that when I died, she would be able to get her hands on my money through her daughter. But now I have a wife. I could have other children. Laura is no longer my sole heir. I think that's why so many more things have been happening lately." He paused. "I've been shot at twice the last few months."

"No!" Margaret went white and her hands flew up to her lips. "No," she whispered again.

It touched him to see her fear for him and he squeezed her hand reassuringly. "Don't worry. I've taken care of it. I've drawn up a new will, leaving my fortune and the land in trust for you, with Laura receiving it after—"

Much to his amazement, Margaret swung at him and her open palm connected flatly with his chest. "What are you talking about! Taken care of it! All that won't help a bit to keep you alive! What good is it going to do me if you're dead?" She jumped up from his lap and stood glaring down at him, her hands planted squarely on her hips. "You're just plain stupid if you think that's any kind of reassurance to me."

"You'll be taken care of."

"I don't want to be 'taken care of'! I want you alive!"

Her eyes were so fierce, her chin so adamant that he had to chuckle. It was like watching a kitten protect its home. "Darling, calm down. I want you taken care of."

"Then that takes care of your fear, not mine."

"Once Damaris learns that she won't get a cent if I die, that you will receive all the money, it won't be profitable for her to get rid of me."

"If she can manage to have you killed, I can't imagine her hesitating to kill me, too!"

He shook his head. "No. I can't believe that Murdock would sink that low. He wouldn't harm an innocent woman." He sighed and rubbed his forehead. "It's the best I could think of. And I'm doing my damnedest to make sure that neither one of us is killed. That's why we never go into town without Whitman and several of the men. And why I'm going to send a man to escort Annie and Zach to school." He paused. "Two men. I'll let Laura go with them, if you think it's that important."

"The teacher is good, I think. I met her when Annie and Zach switched to Three Points from the Huxley school. Laura will receive a decent education. And she'll be meeting the people she will live around the rest of her life."

"That's part of what worries me. I don't want her ostracized or mocked because she's my daughter."

That statement brought Margaret back to him in a rush of sympathy. "Oh, no. No." She knelt before him, leaning against his legs and taking his hands in hers earnestly. "I would never encourage you to send her there if I thought that she would be ostracized. But wasn't one of the reasons you married me was for Laura to fit in with the people around here? To be accepted by them?"

"Yes, of course." Though he no longer even considered that in regards to his marriage to Margaret.

"Well, I think this is the best way. Annie and Zach will be there to protect her if any of the other children should try to tease her or exclude her. Believe me, they'll make sure everyone is nice, and they're always at the center of things, so Laura will be, too. And she'll simply grow into being accepted by the community.''

He smiled. ''I bow to your superior judgment.''

''And well you should.'' Margaret grinned back flirtatiously. She had learned that Andrew wasn't nearly as fierce nor as solemn as she had first thought him. He enjoyed bantering with her and seemed to find it amusing when she displayed a spark of impudence. ''That reminds me. I think it's time we started working *you* into the local society.''

''Me?'' He groaned.

''Yes, you. That's the best way of assuring Laura a place in it. I received an invitation today from Mrs. Elihu Barton. That's the banker's wife.''

Andrew grimaced. ''I'm aware of that. She's also a gossip monger and a mischief maker.''

''That's true. I'm sure she invited us out of vulgar curiosity. No doubt everyone's hoping to see me looking pale and miserable or, even better, sporting a few black-and-blue marks.'' Margaret sat back on her heels and grinned. ''And I'm looking forward to marching in there looking my grandest and happiest.''

He smiled and reached out a hand to stroke it down the side of her face. ''You couldn't look anything but beautiful.''

''That's because that's how I feel.'' She jumped lithely up and back into his lap, twining her arms around his neck and bussing him loudly on the cheek. ''Oh, Andrew. I am the happiest woman in this whole county. In the state, even.'' She hugged him closely, laying her cheek against his, and whispered, ''It's because I love you.''

His arms clenched around her tightly and he wanted to say the same words back to her. But they stuck in his throat, mired in the suspicion and hurt that lingered in him still. He loved her, too—far more than was good for him. But, somehow, to admit it would seal his fate. He didn't want to know how Margaret might change if she learned that she held his heart in the palm of her hand.

Chapter Thirteen

The horses' hooves thudded softly as the buggy moved along the dirt road. It was twilight, and the evening air was chilly, for it was December now, but Margaret was snug in her long woolen cloak. She sat beside her husband, their thighs brushing, and her hand rested on his leg. It was a beautiful night and she would have loved it, riding beside Drew and looking at the first pale stars winking into life in the sky above them if it hadn't been for the two outriders, one in front and one in the rear of the buggy, who accompanied them.

Both men wore pistols at their hips and carried rifles in the saddle scabbards, and they looked around them often, eyes watchful. Andrew, though he wore no pistol in a holster to mar his elegant evening wear, did have a rifle lying at their feet in the floor of the buggy. Margaret supposed that all the armament should make her feel safe, but instead it gave her the shivers. She didn't like feeling as if she couldn't ride into town without a gunman to protect her. The men rode with the children to school and back each day, too. It was enough, she thought, to make a child grow up peculiar.

She had seen the slaughtered cattle by the creek and heard the tales of increased quarrels and violence, and she agreed that it was safer to have protection than to risk going without it. Still, the hard-eyed guards bothered her, especially Whitman. The other day she had caught Zach hanging around Whitman near the barn, apparently learning from him the art of quick drawing a gun from a hip holster. Margaret had given Zach a blistering talking-to after she'd pulled him back to the house.

Andrew glanced at her and forced a smile onto his grim face. Margaret smiled back and squeezed his leg reassuringly. Drew hated going to this party of the Bartons so much that it was almost comical. What kept it from being funny was the fact that he had every reason to dread the event. After all, he had been hated, reviled and ostracized for several years by the very people who would be at the party. It couldn't be pleasant to attend a social event knowing that everyone's eyes would be sharp as needles on him, that every handshake or nod of the head would be stiff and forced, or that there would probably even be some who would turn away without a pretense of politeness.

Margaret frowned, worrying for the hundredth time whether she had made the right choice in urging Andrew to attend this party. She had been certain of it in the beginning. She wanted Laura to fit in with the people of Huxley as she grew older; she couldn't bear for the child to be cut out as her husband had been. It was one thing for a man to bear it, quite another for an impressionable young girl. She had reasoned that if she and Andrew cut through the rough times of integrating into that society, Laura would be able to blend in naturally and easily. It was logical, but as they grew closer to the date of the party, she had become less and less convinced that what she wanted to do was the right thing. She hated the thought of Andrew being snubbed by some old matron, or of all eyes focusing on him while the hiss of gossip ran around the room behind the cover of fans and gloved hands.

It had been bad enough when he had attended the parties in honor of their marriage, but at least then the guest list had been handpicked by Aunt Charity to be favorable to the Carlisle family, and, by extension, this man who was marrying into it. But this dance that Mrs. Barton was holding would not be weighted in even Margaret's favor, let alone Andrew's.

Andrew saw the shadow of worry and doubt in her eyes, and he covered her hands with his. "I'll be all right," he told her, humor lacing his tone. "Surely it can't be worse than facing the guns at Fredericksburg."

It pleased Margaret that he was trying to give her comfort. She turned her hand over and laced her fingers through his. "Perhaps not. But I never had to face those."

"Take my word for it. Even Miriam Barton hasn't quite their firepower."

"Thank you for doing this," Margaret told him earnestly. "You know, if it were just me, I wouldn't care if the rest of the town never saw us or spoke to us. I'd be happy keeping to ourselves out on the ranch."

That warmed him, though out of habit he tried not to let it show. "But we aren't by ourselves. You have a brother and sister."

Margaret shrugged. "Oh, Zach and Annie will do fine. I don't worry about them. Just living with us won't taint them in the eyes of Huxley. It's Laura for whom it will make a difference. I don't want her to be torn between being loyal to you and being accepted by them."

"And our children."

Margaret's color heightened. "Yes. And our children." She paused. "Would you . . . that is, would it be pleasing to you?"

"What?" He glanced at her and his face softened. "Having children?"

Margaret nodded.

"Yes, it's pleasing to me. Very much so. Perhaps you think I haven't been much of a father to Laura."

"Oh, no! I didn't mean that. Laura adores you."

"I'm afraid that's more testimony to her good nature than to my skills. Frankly, I've never known what to do with her. I knew Damaris wasn't much of a mother, and I tried to make up for it, but I was away in the War when she was little. Sometimes I think that I missed the most important times of her life. She's almost a stranger to me. We've always ridden together for an hour or so every day, but I've never been good at talking to her. What does one say to a little girl? But you've helped me with her. I've learned. And I very much want children. Your children. It would make—make everything complete. I'm sorry, I'm not good at expressing what I feel."

Margaret smiled, her whole face glowing. "No. You said it perfectly."

"I think the more pertinent question is whether *you* want children."

"Oh, yes!" She looked shocked at the idea that there would be any question about it. "More than anything. I've always wanted children, but now..." She floundered, realizing how impossible it was to express the glory she felt at the thought of having *his* children, of carrying the fruit of their love beneath her heart. "Well, it—it would be wonderful."

His gaze turned thoughtful. "Are you trying delicately to tell me something? Are you already—"

Margaret giggled. "No. Oh, no. I wish I could say I were in the family way, but I'm not. It's just something I think of often. Something I want. And I wondered if you did, too.''

''Yes. It would make me very happy.'' He bent and kissed her gently on the mouth. ''You already make me very happy.''

''I'm glad.'' She beamed and linked her arm through his, snuggling up against his side and leaning her head upon his arm. They rode thus all the rest of the way into town.

The Elihu Barton house was a tall, imposing brick mansion, as befitted a banker, and it was ablaze with lights when they pulled up in front of it. A servant rushed to take their horse's head when they stopped, and another threw open the door for them with a bow and a smile.

As Margaret handed over her cloak to a maid, she glanced around her. She had always thought the Barton mansion the grandest house in the world, but she realized now that it was actually smaller than Andrew's home—*her* home. It seemed odd and funny. Once just stepping into the Bartons' foyer had immediately cowed her, and she had been amazed at Emma's ability to act the same here as she did anywhere. Did living in a mansion of one's own make that much difference? She thought not; it was more that she had had no confidence in herself then. She realized, with some surprise, that she was no longer the timid girl she had been. Somewhere, somehow, she had changed in the last few months. She glanced up at Andrew and smiled. It was he who had given her confidence: his admiration and desire for her, his acceptance—nay, even preference—for her as she was. It no longer mattered much whether other people liked her; Andrew did, and that was enough.

"Why, Margaret!" Mrs. Barton, a stately, well-endowed matron firmly stuffed into a corset, came toward her with a wide, false smile, her hands extended to clasp both of Margaret's. "But, no, I should say Mrs. Stone now, shouldn't I?"

"Since you've known me since I was a child, I shouldn't think my married state would require such formality, would you?" Margaret replied calmly.

"My, my, how grand you look."

"Thank you." Margaret knew she looked as grand as she could possibly make herself. Though normally she went uncorseted, as Andrew preferred her, tonight she had cinched herself in tightly to fit into the elegant velvet-and-lace gown she'd had made especially for this occasion. The neckline was low and sweetly heart-shaped, but the expanse of creamy soft breast it displayed was more wickedly stunning than sweet, and the rich, dark green material did wonderful things to her eyes. She and Annie had struggled for hours to twist her hair into the soft arrangement of curls that cascaded down and over one shoulder onto the bare skin of her chest. Around the smooth white column of her throat she wore an ivory cameo that Andrew had given her. She looked, she thought, not only well-cared-for and happy, her primary aim, but also quite pretty.

Mrs. Barton blinked, somewhat taken aback by Margaret's poise, and cast about for something else to say.

Smoothly Margaret interposed, "Mrs. Barton, do you know my husband, Andrew Stone?"

The older woman turned stiffly toward Andrew and gave him a brief nod. "Mr. Stone."

"Mrs. Barton." Andrew stretched out his hand, and she could do little but offer hers in greeting. He bowed over it formally. "I'm afraid I have not had the pleasure of meeting you, but I am well acquainted with your husband.''

''Of course.'' She withdrew her hand, her smile more a grimace than an expression of pleasure. She turned, passing them along to her husband.

Elihu, who knew the exact amount of money Andrew Stone carried in his bank, was more cordial. He seemed a little uncomfortable to be conversing with Stone outside his office, but he jovially patted Margaret's hand and told her how pretty she was, suggesting with a sly wink that marriage must be agreeing with her.

''Yes.'' Margaret smiled back at him. ''I suspect that it would be a rare woman indeed who wouldn't find marriage to Mr. Stone agreeable.''

Drew suppressed a grin at the slightly shocked look on Elihu Barton's face and led his wife away. He leaned down to whisper in her ear, ''It's rather pleasant to find out that I am such a paragon. I'll have to remind you of that next time we quarrel.''

''We don't quarrel.''

''Don't we? Ah. I see. My mistake.''

Margaret cast an impish look up at him. ''There are simply times when it takes you a while to realize that you are wrong.''

He burst out laughing and his arm slid reflexively around her waist. He wanted to bend down and kiss the sassy little grin right off her mouth, but he retained enough sense of where he was not to do so. He only smiled into her eyes. Then he lifted his head and glanced around the room—and right into the furious, pale blue eyes of Damaris Murdock.

Andrew stiffened. Margaret glanced up to see what had brought about such a reaction in him and she, too, saw Damaris. Her heart began to hammer inside her chest.

"How could she?" Margaret asked in a low voice, cold with fury. "How could she have had the gall, the insensitivity to invite the Murdocks to the same party as us!"

"It wasn't insensitivity, my dear. It was a desire to see a little entertainment—no doubt something like what the Romans felt when they set two gladiators in the arena."

"Well, she won't get any satisfaction from me." Margaret's chin came up in a gesture that Andrew was beginning to know—and love. She glanced calmly around the room, not even acknowledging Damaris's presence. "Oh, look, there's Emma. Thank Heavens. Let's go talk to her, shall we?"

They crossed the floor to where Emma stood, surrounded by her usual gaggle of admirers. Emma quickly reached out a hand, a smile of breathtaking loveliness spreading across her face, and pulled Margaret to her side. "There she is. I declare, Cousin Margaret, I haven't seen you in a month of Sundays. And Colonel Stone. My, how handsome you do look tonight." She glanced around at her suitors, a smile dimpling her face. "Now, boys, you will excuse us, won't you? My cousin and I just have to have a little girl-to-girl chat to catch each other up on all the news."

The men looked disgruntled, but there was little they could do except take her very broad hint and leave. Andrew smiled, casting a glance after the departing men. "Well, before I'm done in by those young men's murderous glances, I suppose I better leave you young ladies myself. Shall I bring you a cup of punch?"

"You needn't leave," Margaret said quickly, casting a glance around the room.

"It's all right, my dear," Andrew said, his tone amused. "I don't need protection, I promise you. I will manage to survive for a few minutes on my own."

Margaret looked abashed. "I'm sorry. I must sound silly."

"No," he assured her warmly, bringing her hand up to place a kiss on its back. "You sound utterly delightful. A cup of punch?"

"Yes, please."

"Miss Winstock?"

"No. Frankly, I've had so many men bring me punch tonight, I've had to slip the last two cups in the nearest plant."

Andrew left them and the two young women turned toward each other. "Did you see her?" was Emma's first terse, low-toned question.

"Yes. Almost as soon as we came in."

"That's just like the old battle-ax Miriam Barton, to invite the both of you. She's hoping to have a little fireworks for her party tonight."

Margaret's fine eyes flashed. "I just might provide some with Mrs. Barton herself!"

"Well, steer clear of Damaris Murdock. If looks could kill, you'd have been dead when you came in. Methinks the lady is displeased by the obviously happy state of your marriage."

"I don't know why she should care! She never loved him, anyway."

"Maybe not, but she had *his* love. Even when he hung around, bitterly not remarrying—that's another form of holding on to his heart. She knew she'd ruined him for other women. But now... well, it doesn't take a genius to see that our resident Yankee is very much in love with his new wife. He looks ten years younger—and you! Why, you look positively blooming. It'd be enough to make any woman jealous, let alone the man's former wife."

"It's not jealousy. It's pure meanness. Oh, Emma, if you only knew what that woman is really like! It breaks my heart the way everyone in this town has blamed Andrew all these years for their divorce, the way they've painted him black when all the time it was really her!"

Emma's eyebrows rose. "Really? This sounds rich. What's the whole story?"

Margaret hesitated. She normally wasn't one to gossip, but it would be wonderful to be able to set the town straight about Andrew Stone after all these years. She knew that if she told Emma, it would soon be in the gossip mill of Huxley and would assume a life of its own. People would realize that Andrew wasn't the ogre Damaris Murdock had painted him. Perhaps they would even feel sympathy for him for having been married to an unfaithful, unfeeling woman like Damaris. The problem was that any besmirching of Damaris would perforce besmirch her daughter in the future. When Laura was growing up, the old biddies would watch her, always saying to each other, "Well, you know what her mother was. Blood tells." For Laura's sake, she must keep mum about Damaris's sins.

"No." Margaret sighed a little regretfully and shook her head. "I can't talk about it. It wouldn't be right."

Emma pouted prettily. "There you go, spoiling all my fun. Well, I'll tell you what, I've always suspected that Mrs. Murdock wasn't as lily-white as everybody paints her."

"Really?" Margaret glanced at her, surprised. "I can't say the same. She played me for a fool the time she talked to me. I thought she was sweet and concerned—when it turned out she was trying to persuade me not to marry Andrew, or to make us both miserable if I did. Why did you distrust her?"

"She's too sweet acting. Nobody's as beautiful as that woman without being at least a little spoiled, vain and self-centered. At least I'll admit I'm more than I should be of those things, and I'm not nearly as stunning as Damaris. Maybe it was simply jealousy because she came back to Huxley when I was the reigning belle and she eclipsed me easily. I had a suitor that I was especially fond of and whom I thought was quite enamored of me, but he stopped calling on me rather abruptly. I was hurt, both in my pride and in my heart, I'm afraid, though I think I made a good show of not caring."

"You certainly hid it from us. Who was it? When?"

Emma shook her head and smiled a little lopsidedly. "It's not important. It's long over now. I haven't exactly been wearing the willow over him, have I? But at the time, when the pain was still raw, Mrs. Murdock learned of the situation and she made a point of rubbing my nose in it. Every time I saw her, she would ask very sweetly if he'd called on me lately, and I could see in her eyes that she knew quite well that he hadn't and that it hurt and humiliated me to have to answer her. So I've always put my not liking her down to my own bitterness and envy—not the sort of things one likes to admit to."

"Well, it wasn't jealousy." Margaret squeezed Emma's arm sympathetically. "You were right to distrust her. She's a cruel, heartless woman. She doesn't even care for her own daughter. Andrew says she's never shown a spark of interest in Laura. And she's a dear little girl, really, though she is too quiet and, well, inward looking." Margaret smiled. "But I think Zach and Annie are doing a good job of pulling her out of that."

Emma laughed. "No doubt. Tell me about them. How are Zach and Annie?"

They delved happily into the subject of the younger boy and girl and their doings, leaving behind more distressing topics.

Andrew brought his bride a cup of punch, then left her again, for she was engrossed in talking to her vivacious cousin. He strolled around the room, nodding to the people he knew, returning a greeting now and then. He could feel everyone's eyes on him and hear the abrupt stoppage of their conversation if he drew near, a sure sign that they had been gossiping about him. It was a bizarre situation and he didn't enjoy it. He would much rather be back at the ranch with his family. But Margaret had been insistent on it, and no doubt she was right that it was the best way to clear the path for his daughter into the local society. God knows, he would far rather endure this uncomfortable situation than leave it to Laura to go through.

He stopped at one end of the room and glanced around. The first person who caught his eye was Damaris. She was standing across the room, watching him, and when their eyes met, she started forward. Andrew realized with a start that she was walking straight toward him. Was she actually coming over to speak to him? The last thing in the world he wanted was a confrontation with Damaris in the middle of Margaret's first foray into the social world as his wife! It would spoil all Meg's fun in the evening.

There was an open door in the wall behind him and he quickly set down his cup of punch and slipped through it. He found himself in a parlor, where several of the older women were sitting and talking. They glanced up at him curiously and he nodded to them, forcing a polite smile, then strode through the room and out into the hall beyond. There must be a study or some other room where the men gathered to smoke a cigar or to imbibe in something stronger than punch. That would be a refuge against Damaris.

He turned to his right and strode quickly down the hall, glancing into the rooms on either side. He couldn't understand why Damaris would want to create a scene at one of her friends' parties; he would have thought it would be as embarrassing to her as it would be to him. But, then, he never had been able to understand Damaris. Any kind of drama seemed to be food for her soul. The one thing she couldn't stand was not being the center of attention. No doubt that was why she had decided to approach him; too much attention had been focused upon Margaret tonight. It was he and Margaret who were on everyone's tongues at the party, and Damaris's presence was only noted because people wondered how it would affect Margaret.

Whatever room the men were congregating in, it didn't appear to be down this hall, but he did come upon a dimly lit, uninhabited library, silent and faraway from the party. He stepped into the room, smiling, and shut the door behind him. This was the perfect place to avoid Damaris, as well as while away this interminable party. He lit the oil lamp and carried it over to the bookshelves. He had just settled on a book and was pulling it from a shelf when he heard the sound of the doorknob turning. Damn! He should have locked the door!

He turned. Damaris was standing in the doorway. Her presence startled him. She had never been one to play her scenes without an audience.

"Damaris." His voice was even, his face calm and cool. Once just the sight of her had made him shake with longing. Even after he'd learned her true nature, there had still been a hunger for her inside him. He had been unable to see her without desire—and the consequent shame—twisting his gut. But now, looking at her, he felt nothing, not even the thick disgust that had been his companion since the day he came home from the War and found her in bed with another man. There was only a faint annoyance in him now.

It wasn't because her looks had faded with age. She was as beautiful as ever. If anything, she was more beautiful at thirty-one than the eighteen-year-old girl he had married. She had ripened into the full maturity of her looks. There were no frown lines from worry or laugh lines from humor to mar her pearly skin; no work had roughened her hands. After Laura, she had made certain that there were no more babies to alter the hourglass perfection of her figure. She was vivid in a royal-blue dress sewn with dangling black jets. Her waist was cinched in tightly, and creamy white shoulders and bosom swelled up out of the low-cut neckline.

"Hello, Andrew." Her red mouth pouted deliciously. "You haven't even said hello to me this evening."

Once that pout, that look up at him from under her lashes, would have set his heart pounding and his palms sweating. Now he thought only that it looked terribly contrived and unconvincing. Had he actually been fooled by her pretenses?

Andrew raised one eyebrow. "Really, Damaris, I would think there's little for either of us to say to each other."

Irritation flashed across her face for an instant before she pulled it back under control. "Oh?" Her smile was beckoning, sultry. She started across the room toward him, her hips moving in a subtly provocative way. "I would have said that there were many things left unsaid between us." She stopped in front of him, so close he could smell the heady fragrance of her perfume. "One can cut a feeling off, but it's hard to bury it completely." She swayed closer, turning her face up to him and focusing the full force of her velvety eyes on him. "I still think of you, Drew. Late at night, alone in my bed. An old man is no replacement for your arms."

He chuckled. He couldn't help it. Her words had been so ludicrous. "My Lord, Damaris, what are you playing at? You and I both know you never wanted me in your bed when you had me. Why should you think of me there now? I would think an old man is exactly suited to your needs." He stepped away from her. "Go back to your husband."

Damaris's eyes flashed and her nostrils flared with anger. "How can you speak like that to me? As if you were indifferent! As if you didn't still want me!"

He glanced back at her. "I don't." He had never thought he would say it and mean it, but it was the truth. When he looked at her, he didn't yearn for her. He thought only that her looks were rather overripe and too vivid. They couldn't compare to the pale beauty of flaxen hair and a lissome figure and a grave, sweet face that lit up like the stars whenever she smiled. Now that he had tasted true love and desire with Margaret, the false coin Damaris offered held no value for him.

Damaris's mouth curled with contempt. "Don't take me for a fool. You still want me. Even when you saw me lying naked in bed with another man, your body was hot and randy for me. I've seen you in town. I've seen you look at me and turn away. I've seen the hatred in your eyes, and I know that the fire of that emotion is only the other side of the heat of your desire."

He gazed at her flatly. "If you continue in this vein, you will only humiliate yourself, Damaris."

Damaris went to stand directly in front of him again. "Do you really think that you can resist me? That if I offered myself to you, you wouldn't come running back to me?" She smiled seductively and her hands went to the buttons of her dress. Quickly she unfastened the top three and squirmed the top of her bodice downward. The material scraped slowly across her breast, revealing even more of their luscious tops until finally the nipples popped into view. She tugged the dress lower, exposing the two heavy globes, centered by large, rosy nipples. "You always said I had the loveliest breasts in the world. Remember how you used to want to kiss them? How you would suckle at them and groan because it only made you want more? Can you tell me that you don't want to kiss them now? Take them into your hands?"

Andrew and Damaris stared at each other, both so riveted by their personal drama that neither of them noticed the scrape of a heel at the door or turned to see Margaret stop at the doorway.

She had finished chatting with her cousin and had turned to join her husband, but she hadn't been able to find him anywhere. She had wandered through the house, looking for him and at last, she had thought she heard the rumble of his voice in this room and had come to see. She froze in the doorway, unable to move or even look away. Her worst nightmare had sprung to life before her.

Andrew had never said that he loved her, but she was secure in his desire for her and she was sure that if she was patient and loving enough, someday he would come to love her back. But she knew how fierce his love for Damaris had been; she had seen it in his pain when he talked of her betrayal. Damaris had had the power almost to destroy him, and Margaret knew, though she would not allow herself to dwell on it, that Andrew's passion and love for his first wife was much stronger than what he felt for her. The one thing she feared, deep down inside, was that Damaris might realize what a mistake she had made and try to tempt Andrew back someday. Now, looking at the scene in front of her, she saw that her worst fear had come true.

She waited breathlessly, in an agony of fear, watching the two in the library.

"Touch me and tell me you don't still desire me," Damaris challenged Andrew huskily. She took his hand in hers and raised it to her breast, clamping it against the soft orb. "Feel it? Remember how it was? Don't you want to strip me and take me again? Right here, right now." Her voice throbbed with passion. "I want to feel you inside me again, sweetheart." She stretched up, offering her lips to him. "Kiss me, Drew. Please, kiss me."

"For God's sake, Damaris, stop it!" Andrew's mouth twisted, and he jerked his hand from her grasp. "Button your dress. You look like a two-bit whore."

Damaris's mouth dropped open and she stared at him in complete amazement. "Andrew! You can't mean it!"

"I do." His voice was stony and cold. There wasn't even the fire of anger in it, only a faint disgust. "You don't want me—you never did. We both know it. But there's a difference now. I don't want you. My love for you died long ago, and even that obsessive, insane lust you once aroused in me is gone. I don't desire you, Damaris. I don't want to tumble you on the floor of the Bartons' study or anywhere else. I have a wife, and she is the only woman I want. She pleases me, in bed and out, and she takes pleasure in my touch. I don't know what I felt for you, but it wasn't love and it wasn't any sort of honest, clean desire. Because I've found out what those things feel like. I love Margaret and I would never think of betraying her. It's finished."

They both heard the sudden sob of delight that Margaret couldn't suppress, and Damaris and Andrew whirled toward the doorway. Andrew looked astonished, then stricken. "Margaret!" He took a step toward her, his hand going out to her. "My love, please, it's not what you think."

"Oh, it's exactly what I think," Margaret retorted, and Andrew realized with amazement that her face was glowing with happiness, not anger or hurt. A giggle bubbled out of her and she hurried across the room, her arms stretched out to him. "She tried to seduce you and she failed." Margaret flung her arms around Andrew's neck and went up on tiptoe to kiss him. "Oh, I'm so happy! You love me! You love me!"

"Of course, I love you!" He smiled back down at her. "By God, what a woman you are. There's never been another one like you." He squeezed her close to him.

There was a strangled noise behind them, and they glanced over at Damaris. She stood frozen, her face stamped with horror and disbelief. Her gown was still askew, her breasts exposed. She glanced down and was swept with humiliation. She jerked the dress up and buttoned it with trembling fingers; her face flamed bright red. She looked up then at Andrew and Margaret, and her face was twisted and vicious. All beauty had fled from it, leaving only hatred and vengeance. Her lips thinned, showing her teeth, and she almost snarled.

Margaret thought she would rage at them, letting loose all the fury that blazed in her contorted face, but Damaris's anger and humiliation were too deep, too strong for mere words to express. She let out a strange, almost animal shriek and ran out of the room, leaving Margaret and Andrew staring after her.

"I think she's on the edge of losing her mind," Margaret said, shaken. "Did you see how she looked? I've never seen such—such—"

"Hatred," Andrew finished for her. "Perhaps she is a bit mad. Sometimes I think she's not a woman at all, but some sort of demon." He sighed and shook his head. "But I don't want to talk about her—or anything else." He smiled down at Margaret. "I just want to be with you."

She smiled back, shaking off the shivery feeling Damaris's actions had brought out in her. "That's what I want, too." She stretched up and kissed him, and their lips clung. When she went back down flat on her feet, she was a little breathless and her face a trifle flushed. "Let's go home, darling."

Chapter Fourteen

Damaris rushed down the hall, wildly searching for a door to the outside. When she found it, she pushed open the heavy door and stumbled out. It was dark and cold, but she hardly felt the coldness on her fevered skin. Her blood thundered through her veins, making it hard for her to think, indeed, even to see. Where was he? She needed him now! Where the devil was he? He must be around somewhere, waiting for her. She had told him she would sneak away from the party tonight and meet him.

She glanced around, seeing little in the darkness, then started toward the back of the yard, stumbling over the uneven ground in her haste. He would see her. He would find her. Where was he?

Then she saw the glow of light from the stables. Of course. That was where he would be. She veered to the left, almost running, staggering and falling heavily to her knees once in her haste. But she picked herself up and hurried on until she rushed through the stable doors.

A lantern burned softly, hung on a hook near the back of the stables. A man unfolded himself from the shadows where he had been sitting, smoothly sliding the pistol he had drawn back into its holster. He walked toward her, boots crunching over the straw and dirt. He was not a big man, but he gave the impression of power and danger. He was dressed in rough clothes of denim, flannel and leather; his hair was too long and shaggy; his face was rough, marked by years of deadly experience. He wore the tied-down holster of a gunman.

The man stopped in front of Damaris and his odd, yellowish eyes took in her agitated state. "What's up?"

"I want you to kill them! Both. I want them dead now." She punctuated her last few words with fierce slams of her fist against her leg. "Do you understand me? They must die! Immediately!"

"You're hysterical." He said it without inflection, merely an observation. He didn't care whether she was rational or not. In fact, he rather liked her this way, out of control, desperate. Usually that was the way she ended up, clawing frantically at his back, begging him. He wondered what she would be like when she started out in that condition. It started a throbbing deep inside him, the intense, painful lust that this woman always brought to him.

"Whitman! Will you do it or not?"

"'Course I will. That's always the way we figured it."

"But no more waiting. Now."

He shrugged. "All right. I'll fix it so nobody'll look to us. Your old man will go after him."

"Not unprovoked. Tom's 'sense of honor' won't let him attack a man without good reason." She spit out the words scornfully. "You have to give him a reason. Then I'll work on him so he'll see that the only thing he can do is go after Stone himself."

"And I'll be there to make sure neither of them lives to tell about it."

"And the girl." Damaris's eyes narrowed and her lips thinned. "I want the girl dead, too."

"Mrs. Stone?"

"Yes." The word was a hiss. "*Mrs.* Stone. The little slut."

"Slut?" He gave a bark of laughter. "You're a fine one to be slinging that word around."

She tossed her head back, giving him her haughtiest look. "You dare to imply that I—"

He grinned. He didn't mind that look of contempt—her "lady look," he called it. It was fun wiping that look off her face. He'd never had a lady before her, nor a woman half as beautiful as she was, either. Every time she came to him, it was exciting, dangerous.

"I'm not implying anything," he said, still smirking.

Damaris hated that smirk; every time she saw it she wanted to slap it off his face. She'd tried that before, and he'd taken care of her quickly. She bit her underlip, her eyes darkening a little at the memory.

"I'm saying it straight out," he went on. "You're a whore. Only difference is, you ain't cheap."

Already Damaris's nipples were hardening at his words, and her breath quickened. "You're a peasant." Her eyes flickered down over his chest and lower still to the bulge in his trousers, to the heavy pistol strapped around his thigh. Once he'd taken out that gun and trailed it over her body, caressing her with its cool metal. It had scared her senseless, but she'd also been rocked with explosion after explosion deep inside her. Her tongue stole out and moistened her lips.

"I know. That's why I do your dirty work for you." Whitman paused, watching her. She was already in his sexual thrall and he hadn't even touched her yet. The thought made his blood pound harder. He reached out and took her chin roughly between his fingers, tilting her head back so that she had to stare up into his face. "But I don't work unless I get paid. You know that."

She nodded, swallowing. He plunged a rough hand down the front of her dress and found her breast. He rolled the nipple between his fingers and pinched it so hard she jumped. Her breath caught and her eyes glazed over.

"What are you going to do for me this time?" he asked.

"Whatever you say."

"I didn't hear you."

"Whatever you say."

"Whatever you say, *who*?"

"Sir."

"That's good. Shooting two people—and one of them a woman—that'll require a lot of payment."

Damaris put her hands on his hips and slid them down his thighs, even moving caressingly over the leather holster. "Make it painful," she panted. "I don't want them to die quickly."

"I'll make sure of that." His voice was thick. Her hand moved to the notch of his legs and cupped him through the rough denim. "I know just how to get old Tom on the warpath, too."

"How?" She was working on his belt buckle now.

"Shooting sonny boy."

"Cade?" She stopped.

"Yeah. Cade. That'll send the old fool after Stone. Why? Is there something you don't like about that?" He'd long thought she had some kind of feeling for Cade, though she'd never admitted to it. He'd heard gossip that she had been servicing both the younger and older Murdock.

But she smiled. "You're right. That would do it. And Cade deserves it, too."

Whitman grinned. So the kid had rejected her. Well, somebody that dumb deserved to die, anyway. He reached down and unbuttoned his trousers so that his swelling member sprang free. "There you go, sugar. Make it worth my while."

She smiled up at him, her eyes avid, mouth slack with the hunger that only this man could arouse in her. "Yes, sir."

For a week Margaret's life was peaceful and blissfully happy. Andrew loved her; he no longer had any feelings for Damaris. Oh, at times when he looked at her, she could see the faint doubts lingering in his eyes, and she would know that he still didn't completely trust her, that he wondered sometimes if she really loved him. But that was all right; she was certain that, with time, she would be able to erase that cloud of doubt. The important thing was that Andrew loved her. The bad times were over, she thought a trifle smugly.

Then Cade Murdock got shot in Bannister's Saloon.

Margaret and Andrew were sitting cozily by the fire, her head on his shoulder, talking in a lazy, intimate murmur when they were startled by the sound of horses riding up the road and to the corral. Andrew glanced at her, surprised. "Surely the boys aren't coming back this early on a Saturday night."

He rose and crossed the room to push aside the drapes and look out. "But that's what it is." He turned back, his face worried. "I better go see what happened."

Margaret rose, her stomach beginning to dance with unease. "What's the matter?"

"I'm not sure. Probably nothing. But why would the men come back by ten o'clock unless there was something wrong?"

He strode out of the room and down the hall to the front door, with Margaret trailing worriedly behind him. Just as he reached the front door, there was a loud banging on it.

He jerked the door open and String McAlister, one hand braced against the door, nearly fell inside. He straightened quickly, and his eyes went to his boss in what seemed to Margaret an apprehensive way. Her stomach tightened a notch.

"What is it? What happened?" Andrew waited for his answer, face set. Margaret thought she wouldn't want to be the one who had to tell him whatever was wrong.

"There was a fight in town."

"Our men and Murdock's?"

"Yes, sir."

"Come in and tell me about it." Andrew sighed and stepped aside to let the older man enter. String pulled off his hat and stood fiddling with it, waiting for Andrew's questions.

"Who started it?"

"I don't know exactly. I wasn't there. I was up at the bar, getting a drink. But George Pinckley and Whitman and couple of the other men sat down at a table that wasn't four feet from where Cade Murdock and some of his boys were sitting, playing poker. When I turned around and saw them, they'd already exchanged words. I started over to try to keep 'em separated, like you'd told me. But people was already gathering around, watching, and men kept joining 'em on either side. Well, I started pushing my way through, but before I could get there, I heard a shot. Then all hell broke loose. Begging your pardon, ma'am."

"Damn! I knew this was going to happen! Didn't you tell the men to steer clear of Murdock's bunch? I told you to watch them, to make sure nothing got started."

"I know, sir." String kept his eyes on his tortured hat, his hands still twisting it unmercifully. "I didn't do it. I know I let you down, sir. I told the men what you said and

I was keeping an eye on them, but this argument blew up so fast. I hadn't been gone five minutes, getting a drink.''

Andrew sighed. ''I know. I'm sure you did your best. All right. What was the damage? Was anybody seriously hurt?''

String swallowed, still studiously avoiding Andrew's eyes. ''Pinckley was killed, Colonel, and one of their men, too. And—Cade Murdock was wounded.''

''Cade Murdock!'' Andrew stared. ''Good God. What a disaster. Cade Murdock!'' He turned away despairingly, plunging his hand through his hair. ''Murdock'll be out for blood now.''

''Oh, no!'' Margaret breathed, her hands clenching in her skirts. She moved closer to the men. ''How badly is he hurt?''

String shook his head. ''I don't know. He got shot somewhere in the chest. I saw him lying on the floor, and later, after the sheriff came and quieted everything down, I heard 'em say he was still alive. They sent for the doc. We cleared out.''

''How awful.'' Margaret felt sick. She knew Cade Murdock. Not well, of course. But several years back he had been one of the many boys who had hung around Emma. She had seen him at dances, and he'd come calling on Emma. He had been a laughing, handsome boy with mischievous eyes. It seemed horrible that he could have been wounded, might even be dying, all because of some senseless feud.

Andrew turned to her and saw her white face. ''Meg? Are you all right?'' His hand went out to support her.

''Yes. I'm fine. It's just—it's so insane, so terrible.'' She looked up at him entreatingly. ''How long is this going to go on between you and Tom Murdock?''

"I don't know." His voice was angry. "It's not anything I wanted. Now—I don't see how Murdock'll ever stop. If Cade dies..."

"He sets a lot of store by that boy," String put in.

"His brother, Daniel, was killed in the War. I think Tom Murdock put all his love and hopes onto Cade," Margaret explained.

"All we can do is sit tight and hope Murdock doesn't go off half cocked," Andrew said.

"And pray that Cade doesn't die."

"And that. String, tell the men not to ride alone and for the next few days, stay away from the outlying parts of the ranch. Margaret, I don't want you going to church tomorrow or the children to school Monday."

"Surely Tom Murdock wouldn't attack women and children, even in retaliation for his son!"

"I hope not. I think he's a more honorable man than that. But, even so, that doesn't mean the same goes for all his men, any one of whom might be out for revenge. It's something I can't risk. Not when your life or the children's are at stake."

Margaret nodded. "All right."

He turned from her toward String. "Did you bring George's body home?" String nodded. "Good. We'll bury him up on the rise. Tell Jenks to make him a marker. I'll go down and talk to the men now."

"Good. There was lots of talk of revenge on the way home. Perkins kept saying we'd been set up. And that Whitman—well, he's a killer. He don't care who he shoots or why." String had never approved of Andrew's hiring the gunman.

"Is he the one who started the shooting?"

String shrugged. "I don't know. Like I said, I didn't see it. The men claimed that Murdock's man shot first."

"Naturally."

"Mack Owens says he shot Murdock's man, but nobody's claimed Cade yet."

"I doubt they will. Well, come on, String." Andrew turned toward Margaret. "You'll be all right?"

"Of course." She smiled. Andrew's face softened and he almost smiled back at her. Then he turned and left. Margaret trailed after them to the front door and looked out the glass side panel. She watched Andrew all the way to the bunkhouse, then turned away with a sigh. God only knew what would happen now.

For the next two days everyone at the ranch was tense. Little was said about the incident and the routine chores were done, but there was always a sense of foreboding hanging over everything. Nothing happened and gradually, the overall mood began to ease. Zach, freed from school, spent most of his time with the men, working around the barn or corral. Margaret kept the girls occupied with cleaning out the attic.

On Tuesday morning they were in the attic working when Margaret heard the distinct sound of several shots. She straightened, her heart pounding, and ran over to the small, low window. Scrubbing away the dust with her apron, she peered out. The men were appearing from all over the yard—barn, corral, bunkhouse—alert and ready. A moment later, a rider appeared in the distance, riding hell-for-leather straight toward the house.

Margaret ran across the room and scrambled down the steep attic stairs, with Laura and Annie on her heels. She hurried downstairs and out the front door. The rider had reached the corral and stopped, and the men were crowded around him. Margaret shaded her eyes and watched, but Laura and Annie streaked toward the crowd. Moments later, the men broke up, most of them heading back to the bunkhouse or to the barn. Laura and Annie came back to the porch, their faces alive with excitement.

"The three men that went down toward Briller Creek this morning got attacked!" Annie exclaimed, panting. "They said it was Murdock's men, and Ned Jackson got away and came back for help."

"Daddy's sending a bunch of the men down to help," Laura added, her pale blue eyes wide. "String's going to lead them. At first everybody was going, but Daddy said no, we'd better not leave the house and barn unprotected. He and that Whitman man and Broussard are staying."

"Yeah. Whitman said it might just be a diversion. So Broussard said he'd climb on top of the barn and keep a lookout in case they come for the house, too."

"I think he just wants to look busy," Laura added astutely. "He's embarrassed cause he won't get to fight."

"Zach's not going, is he?" Margaret exclaimed, her hand flying up to her throat.

Annie laughed. "No. He wanted to, but Andrew wouldn't let him. He said you'd have his hide if something happened to Zach, and the men laughed. Zach was maa-aad. You should have seen his face. He looked like thunder."

"Andrew is exactly right not to let him go. He has no business being involved with that kind of thing."

"Yeah, but he's a good shot," Annie said, unable to resist putting in a good word for her brother. "A couple of weeks ago, they were lining things up and shooting them for targets, you know, over behind the smokehouse, and Zach was almost as good a shot as any of the men. Whitman said he had a good eye."

"Yeah. Zach said Whitman's teaching him to—"

"Hush about Whitman—and about Zach shooting. He may have a good aim, but he's only thirteen, and don't either of you dare encourage him with this nonsense. I don't like him hanging around with that Whitman, anyway."

They watched as the men brought out their guns and saddled their horses, then rode off pell-mell, with Ned leading the way. Andrew walked back to the house, his hand on Zach's shoulder. Zach looked thoroughly glum and didn't say a word to anyone, just walked into the house. Andrew turned and looked back toward the cloud of dust that marked the route his men were taking.

"You're worried, aren't you?" Margaret asked him.

He shrugged. "Nothing I can put my finger on. But it doesn't seem right. I tend to agree with Whitman. There's something up."

"Why do you think that?"

"I don't know. But how did Murdock know where to find my men today? You wouldn't send your men wandering all over a ranch on the chance they'd find somebody. They weren't even close to the boundaries of the ranch. Ned was panicky. I couldn't get a reliable estimate from him of how many men there were. He acted as if it was a huge force—but the man's never been under fire before. It's strange. I figured Murdock's men might be out sniping around our borders or might even attack the main house. But this . . ." He trailed off. "I can't help thinking there's a trick. But I couldn't refuse to send a rescue party for the men, especially if the force really is as big as Ned thought. If it is, I'll be sorry I didn't lead it myself."

"Do you think they might attack here, too?"

"It's possible. What if the other thing was a diversion and the main body of men are riding for the house?" He looked at Margaret, his eyes intense. "I can't leave you unprotected."

They turned and went inside the house. None of them could take to any task, and they sat and stood and walked from one place to another, unable to settle down. Suddenly there was a cry from across the yard and they all rushed to the front door. Zach reached it first, with Andrew right behind him.

Broussard had climbed down from the barn, and he ran toward them, waving his arms. "Men! Lots of them! Coming from the river."

Margaret's stomach flip-flopped and she turned toward Andrew. He looked grim. "Girls, get back inside," Andrew said. "Zach, get out the guns and start loading them. There's a gun rack in my study and another one upstairs in the bedroom."

"Yes, sir."

"Annie, you go help him," Margaret added. She turned toward her husband. "Annie and I can both fire a gun. Daddy taught us years ago. Annie's probably better than I, but we can both do it."

Andrew admired her poise. "All right." It was the only way to protect her, after all, as few men as were there. "We need to hold them off until the men discover the other raid was a ruse and return."

Across the way, Whitman came out of the bunkhouse carrying several rifles, a shotgun, two revolvers and boxes of ammunition. "Broussard and I'll take the barn!" he shouted. "We'll catch them in a cross fire."

Andrew nodded. He didn't like splitting up his forces that way, but it made sense. With rifle fire coming at them from more than one place, Murdock's men might mistake them for a larger number. After all, Murdock couldn't know how many men he'd sent to face the other raid.

"Let's get ready, ladies," Andrew said. "I'll close the downstairs shutters. You lock and barricade the outside doors. Leave me a window open to get back in."

Margaret nodded and ran inside to do his bidding. With Rosa's and Carmela's help, they hurried around the house, locking and barricading the outside doors with heavy furniture. From the window panel beside the front door, Margaret could now see the riders bearing down upon the yard. They seemed heart-stoppingly close. And Andrew was still outside!

She ran to the parlor, one of the front rooms of the house, and flung open both the windows. Behind her she heard Zach rattle into the room with guns and ammunition. Andrew came around the corner of the house on the run and vaulted over the porch railing.

The riders had reached the barn. One of them in front opened fire, and a bullet smacked into a porch column. Zach flung himself down at a window, aimed and began to shoot. Andrew ducked through the other window just as a hail of bullets hit the porch. Everyone instinctively dived for the floor.

Andrew grabbed a rifle and began to shoot back. "Girls—upstairs and start shooting. Grab some guns and ammo."

Margaret nodded, crawling on hands and knees to the guns and pulling out two rifles for herself and Annie. "Rosa? Carmela? Can you shoot?"

"Not well," Rosa admitted, "but I can load. I'll stay here and load for the men. Mama can shoot. She'll go with you." She turned to her mother and spat out a few words in Spanish. Carmela nodded, grabbed a shotgun, then picked up a pistol for each of them.

"Laura, you come load for us," Margaret said. "Can you do that?"

"Yes, and shoot." Laura's voice was small and her face was as white as paper, but her words were calm.

"Good. Come on, then." They ran, crouching over, out of the parlor and up the stairs.

"We'll set up in the bedrooms on the right of the stairs," Margaret told them. "That'll make something of a cross fire with them downstairs."

She ran into Andrew's bedroom while Annie took the bedroom that had been Margaret's. Margaret shoved up the window and rested her rifle on the windowsill. The attackers had scattered across the yard, taking refuge from Zach's and Andrew's bullets behind an overturned wagon and the bunkhouse. Margaret allowed herself a small smile. Evidently Murdock wasn't finding it quite as easy as he had thought. Well, she and Annie would make it harder. She aimed and squeezed off a shot. The recoil slammed the rifle stock into her shoulder. Her aim was off; her bullet hadn't hit the man behind the water trough. She thought she was pulling high. She adjusted and fired again.

Down the hall Annie was squeezing off quick and increasingly accurate shots as she adjusted to the rifle. Carmela planted herself at the window beside Margaret and let fly with the shotgun. It wasn't nearly as effective a weapon, of course, but the scattered shot certainly helped to keep the men outside lying low and added to the pretense that there were a number of men shooting. Margaret wondered if they had any idea how many of their enemy were women. They might; women out here had long been a hardy breed.

It seemed as if they fired for hours. Margaret quickly used up both rifles and resorted to the Colt revolver, but by that time Laura had loaded her guns again. Laura rushed back and forth between Annie and Margaret, keeping their guns loaded.

Some time later, much to Margaret's astonishment, a large man's handkerchief went up from behind the wagon, tied to a stick. It waved back and forth slowly, and gradually the firing stopped on both sides. The silence was eerie after the continuous thunder of rifle fire. Smoke drifted on the air and the smell of gunpowder was everywhere.

For a moment everyone waited silently. Then Murdock's voice roared out, "Stone! Andrew Stone! You're a murdering thief and I'll see you dead! But I don't hold with hurting women and children. I'll give safe escort to your wife and her brother and sister and your daughter. They won't be harmed, I promise. Will you send them out?"

Downstairs, where Andrew lay, there was only silence for a time. Finally, he called, "All right. I believe you'll keep your word. I'll send them out."

"Oh, no, you won't!" Annie called from next door, followed by the crack of her rifle. The stick holding the handkerchief neatly split, the white cloth tumbling to the ground, and the hand that held it jerked back down. From the next bedroom issued Annie's clear, silvery laughter.

Trust Annie, Margaret thought, tempted to giggle herself despite the gravity of the situation. Annie had expressed her own opinion exactly.

"No, wait!" she heard Andrew roar below. "Wait, don't fire."

Margaret was sure Andrew was coming upstairs to talk her into leaving. Murdock would suspect that, too. Was his offer merely a ruse to distract Andrew and leave them vulnerable to attack? She kept her eyes on Murdock, leaning against the wall to minimize the amount of her that was visible through the window and also to give her support. The rifle was heavy, and even though she was a strong young woman used to hard work, it was a strain to hold the heavy rifle still and fire it repeatedly. She was certain her shoulder would be black-and-blue tomorrow from the recoil of the rifle butt.

Andrew burst into the room and Margaret glanced at him. He looked ready to explode. "What the hell was that about?"

Margaret eased her gun down, saying to Carmela, "Keep a close eye on them, will you? They may be playing a game."

"Sí, Señora."

Margaret edged away from the window and, once out of view, walked to where Andrew stood. "That was my sister. She tends toward drama. You may have noticed it before."

He grimaced. "This isn't a joking matter. She could have ruined the whole deal with Murdock. But he hasn't fired again, so I think he'll stand firm on it, despite Annie's grand gesture. I want all of you to come down now. I trust Murdock to keep his word to give you safe conduct."

"I'm not as assured by a man's sense of honor as you are," Margaret retorted crisply. "But that's hardly to the point. I'm not leaving, and neither is Annie. If you'd like to take a poll on it, I'm sure Zach would refuse, also. It might be good to send Laura out with Rosa and Carmela. I can't imagine that even Tom Murdock would be so low as to murder his own wife's daughter."

"I'm not going, either," Laura announced from the bed where she was sitting, stuffing bullets into a revolver. She had seized the opportunity of the momentary cease-fire to fill every gun she could in some degree of comfort. She looked up from her work, fixing her serious gaze on Andrew. "I'm not leaving you, Daddy."

"If you go, she will go," Andrew told Margaret. "I want you all to leave. I will not allow you to be killed because some lust-besotted old fool hates me."

"If the women and children leave this house, you will be here alone to fight off Murdock and his men. How long do you think you would last without our reloading and our four extra hands shooting? You wouldn't have a prayer. If I left, I'd be signing your death warrant."

"Better that than that *all* of us die!"

She shook her head. "We may not. As long as all of us are shooting, we may have a chance of holding them off until the others return. Maybe they'll even see the futility of it and retreat." She didn't hold strong hopes for either opportunity. They were already beginning to run low on ammunition. There were guns aplenty, but they would do little good without bullets. "And if we are to die, I prefer that we die together. I don't want to live knowing that my safety cost your life. I don't want to live if you are dead."

Andrew looked at her. She was thwarting him, disobeying him, refusing to do what was the best and safest thing for her. Yet his crazy heart sang within him. Margaret loved him. There could be no other proof as great, as final, as this. If she left, she would live and would be the heir to his fortune. If she had been lying to him, pretending to love him for some nefarious purpose of her own, she would only have to leave right now to gain whatever she wanted without the bother of keeping up the pretense of loving him. He couldn't deny it, couldn't suspect her any longer. His heart had been right this time. Margaret Carlisle—Margaret Stone—was a good, kind, passionate, caring woman, and she loved him.

Andrew sighed and bent down to kiss her lightly on the lips. "I love you."

"I love you, too."

"I pray to God you haven't sealed your death." He turned and strode from the room.

Margaret scurried back to her place at the window, taking up the rifle again so she would be ready when Andrew turned down Murdock's offer. But no word came from downstairs. The silence dragged on. Margaret suspected that Andrew was delaying his reply as long as possible to give his men time to return. It was sensible, but the silence was nerve-racking.

Finally, below them in the yard, Murdock bellowed, "Well, Stone? What's your answer?"

"I fear that my wife is a stubborn woman, sir. She refused to leave."

Murdock's face contorted with rage. "Damn it, man, send them out. I will not be a party to killing women and children."

"Then return home, Murdock. Stop this vendetta."

"I cannot! You are responsible for shooting my son. Because of you, he was only inches away from death! I'll not rest until you're in your grave!"

Margaret watched the scene below, waiting. But inside, her mind was churning, stirring up some thought that had teased at her mind earlier but had eluded her in the heat of the battle. There was something odd, now that she had the time and quiet to reflect on it. Something odd. But what was it?

There was a glint of metal in the sun by the barn and it caught Margaret's eye. The barn door was open a fraction, and Whitman, the gunfighter, was edging out of it, cautiously glancing around him.

That was it!

The thing she had noticed unconsciously struck her full force now. Whitman and Broussard had stayed in the barn to create a cross fire. But since the battle started, she had seen no sign of shots coming from the barn. Murdock's men all faced toward the house behind their various pieces of protection. None had turned to barricade themselves against shots from the barn. Whitman and Broussard had obviously not been shooting. But why?

"Let it be on your head!" Murdock bellowed.

Margaret tensed, expecting the immediate opening of fire. But, instead, there was an uncertain stretch of silence. After the long moments without shooting, Murdock's men seemed reluctant to begin again. Perhaps they had cooled down by now; perhaps they were thinking about the fact that they were firing upon innocent women and children inside the house. These were ranch hands, after all, not hardened gunfighters.

Then, just when it seemed the silence could stretch on no further without something snapping, there was the sound of a weak voice calling, "Father! Father!"

Startled, Margaret looked beyond Murdock's men. There, riding into the yard, was a young man. He was swaying in his saddle and he held the reins loosely in his hands. His head sagged forward and he had to pull it back up with an effort. It was Cade Murdock!

Margaret drew in her breath with a gasp.

Everyone in Murdock's group swiveled around, staring with equal astonishment at the sight. Tom Murdock rose to his feet, not even thinking of the guns trained on him from the house. "Cade! Cade, my God, what are you doing here?"

Cade drew up even with them. "Trying to stop you. What do you think?" His voice was weak and Margaret had to strain to hear his words. "You have to stop. You can't do this."

"What in the hell are you doing? You shouldn't even be out of bed, let alone riding all this way. Look, you've re-opened your wound." His father was right. Margaret could see the red spreading across the front of Cade's shirt. He looked like death warmed over.

"I couldn't let you kill Stone or anybody else in my name. It's crazy, Father. It's insane. You've let her drive you to this—to murdering a man and his family!"

"They shot you!"

"Not Andrew Stone nor his wife nor his child. It was a man in a saloon. I don't even know who. You come over here seeking revenge, next they'll come after you. And over what? Nothing! Nothing but the jealousies of a vain, wicked woman. Damaris has driven you to this. It's not what you would do." Cade stopped, panting. Even as far away as she was, Margaret could see that he was very ill looking. She thought he might faint at any moment. "You're a man of honor. A good man. Please, Father, stop this now. Don't become something I can't respect."

Cade swayed precariously, and Murdock jumped over to brace him. Another of his men sprang to help him, and they eased Cade down off the horse and onto his feet. He could not stand without support and he leaned weakly against his father. He spoke again, but so faintly Margaret hadn't a chance of hearing what he said.

From below her, Andrew's voice came. "He needs to lie down. And he needs a doctor. Bring him inside, Murdock, and he can rest."

Andrew went to the front door and pulled aside the couch Carmela and Margaret had shoved in front of it as a barricade. He opened the door. In the parlor, Zach waited nervously, sighting down the rifle, his finger on the trigger, afraid that this was somehow a trap. Across the yard, Murdock hesitated, looking at Andrew. Then his shoulders sagged, as if something had gone out of him.

"All right. I'm bringing him in."

Murdock and the other man started slowly across the yard, supporting Cade between them. Margaret, like Zach, waited tensely, her gun at the ready, for some trick, some danger to Andrew, who was so carelessly exposing himself.

Andrew opened the door wider. Murdock was almost to the steps and Andrew went out onto the porch to give them a hand with their burden.

Suddenly Margaret caught a movement out of the corner of her eye, and there was the explosive sound of a gun going off in the silence. She whipped around automatically and fired at the man who had just shot at Andrew. Below her, at the same instant, Zach fired, also. Both bullets caught Whitman, one in the chest and one in the stomach, knocking him backward into the dust.

Margaret jumped to her feet with a cry, dropping her rifle and ran downstairs. "Andrew! Andrew!"

Because of the porch roof she had been unable to see Andrew when Whitman shot at him, and she envisioned her husband lying lifeless and bleeding on the porch. Instead, when she arrived breathlessly at the front door, she found him standing on the steps with the two Murdocks and their hired hand. All of the men were staring at Whitman's lifeless form.

"Andrew, you're alive!" Margaret launched herself at him and he caught her. She wrapped her arms around him and kissed him over and over. "Oh, thank God, he missed you."

"I saw the flash of his gun just before he fired, and I ducked. It was instinctive. I didn't even realize it was him."

"But—but I don't understand," Murdock said, looking bewildered. "I thought—wasn't he your man? Why would he try to kill you?"

Now Murdock's men were coming out from their hiding places, holstering their guns as they drew closer to the Murdocks and Andrew. Andrew shook his head, as surprised as Murdock.

"I tried to tell you," Cade said weakly. The sweat stood out on his pale face. "It wasn't Stone. It was her, always her—and him. The one they just killed."

"Her?" Murdock's face froze. "Her?"

Cade nodded. "Damaris. Your wife. She didn't—love you. She just hated him." He nodded toward Andrew. "I saw her with the gunfighter. They were lovers."

"No!"

"Yes! I didn't tell you because I knew it would hurt you. But I know now what she wanted. He was going to kill Stone—the gunslinger was. Probably you, too. She talked you into coming here to kill Stone. She was making you a killer. Father, I—" Cade gasped for breath and his face went even paler. He fainted, sagging in his father's arms.

The next evening, Margaret stepped out onto the porch. Her husband stood at the steps, his hand on one of the porch columns, staring out across the land. He glanced back at the sound of the door closing and saw Margaret. He smiled tiredly and held out one hand to her. "Meg. My love."

He took her hand and pulled her close to him, then raised it to his mouth and kissed it. He returned his hand to his side, but continued to hold hers. They stood for a moment, looking out in silence. "It's so peaceful now."

No one would have thought, looking across the yard, that yesterday a battle had been fought here, with one man killed and two others wounded. Inside the house, as well, everything was straightened up and apparently back to normal—if one didn't look at the tears in the curtains and the pockmarks of bullet holes that had peppered the front porch. There were quite a few slugs still in the parlor walls, as well, though at least the broken glass had been swept away.

"Such a tragedy, such waste," Andrew murmured.

"Yes, but at least Cade is all right. He will live."

Andrew glanced at her. "Yes, but I dread telling him."

Yesterday, after hearing from the doctor that Cade would be all right, Tom Murdock had ridden home. The housekeeper had heard sounds of his arguing with his wife, and of Damaris's hysterical crying. There had been the sound of two shots, and the housekeeper had rushed upstairs to find that Murdock had shot his faithless wife, then turned the gun upon himself.

"I don't think it will come as much surprise to him. He knew how much his father loved Damaris. He said he hadn't told him about Damaris and Whitman because of what it would do to him."

Andrew sighed. "That woman. She wrecked so many lives."

"But not all." Margaret gazed up at him. "Not us."

He smiled at her. "You're right. She didn't ruin us. Out of all this, there's one thing I've learned—and that is that I love you. I love you more than anything else on earth."

"You've learned one other thing."

"And what is that?"

"That I love you, too."

"You're right, as always." He enfolded her in his arms and held her tightly against him. "Ah, Margaret, I will love you to the end of my days."

"And after, too. That's how long I'll love you."

He bent and kissed her gently. "Yes, if that is possible, I'll love you even after death. For all eternity."

*   *   *   *   *

Six exciting series for you every month... from Harlequin

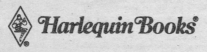